MW00790554

THE HENCHMAN TRAINING ACADEMY 1: EVOLUTION

L.K. URBAN

The Henchman Training Academy 1: Evolution

Copyright © 2022 by L.K. Urban

EBook ISBN: 978-1-7364582-4-2
Trade Paperback ISBN: 978-1-7364582-5-9

Edited by Kailey Urbaniak
Cover design by Angela Stevens
Cover artwork images by

Published by WIP Publications LLC
Colorado Springs, CO 80907
Kailey Urbaniak, Publisher

WIP Publications eBook Edition 2022
WIP Publications Trade Paperback Edition 2022
Printed in the USA

Get your writing in progress: wippublications.com

To the four brightest lights in my life, Nicholas James, Christopher Tyler, Jennifer Taylor, and Kailey Rose. Without you in my life, the world would be so dark. Thank you for your support and love. Xoxo

CONTENTS

CHAPTER 1
A DAY JUST LIKE ANY OTHER

MATT HIT the glass door of Tailgaters Insurance harder than he meant to as he left for the day. The fact was, he almost punched the door rather than giving it the gentle nudge it needed to open. Most days, he tried to convince himself that spending days selling insurance was not the way to a slow painful death, but today he wasn't so sure. Taking a long breath and feeling what was left of the day's sun on his face gave him hope that tomorrow may not be as empty. *Eight hours locked in cubical hell is over for today!*

His life had turned into routine and monotony at the ripe old age of twenty-three. Matt wasn't sure how much longer he could stand the incredible weight of dullness that surrounded him every day. Taking this job as an insurance sales agent after college had almost been an act of desperation. Matt had thought his world after college would be filled with friends, money, parties, and loads of free time. Little did he know it was nearly impossible to get a job upon graduation. He had never had to work so hard with so little return and so much rejection. Interview after interview, thanks but no thanks. Matt had a predictable life, growing up with good fortune and not much drama. It blindsided him to see the absolute lack of interest in him when it came to finding a job, let alone a good job.

What was a good job anyway? No job that involved stuffing his long legs under a too-small desk sounded enjoyable to him.

Thank fucking God I am out of there, Matt thought as he walked—almost ran—to his old gray Dodge Ram truck. He really wondered how people worked jobs like that their whole lives. Most of his co-workers were nice enough people, but just so goddamn boring. The comments were pretty much the same thing, week after week, especially during football season. "Hey big guy, how was your weekend? Did you have a good night? Did you see the game last night?" Did they really think all he did was watch football and relive his glory years? They would be shocked to know that he spent his time outside the office playing video games in a bar. He learned to prepare himself to answer the slew of meaningless questions with the nod and smile technique that he had perfected over the last year at Tailgaters.

Despite being entirely too bored for someone his age, his nights at The Basement were what made life tolerable. The first time Matt drove past, he remembered noticing a rather large, brightly lit sign across the length of the building that flashed *The Basement* in bold purple letters. Smaller neon signs hanging in the window indicated that the place had something to do with gaming. The signs read, *Play by the Hour, All Nerds Welcome.* He was intrigued. Quickly, The Basement became where Matt spent weeknights and a lot of his weekends.

He needed The Basement like a person needed a drink, it was a place he could shut out the harsh reality of his Monday-through-Friday, eight-to-five gig. The Basement was his Mother Ship, a safe place to have connection and community, however nerdy it was; it felt like home when he was there. Going there each night added to more monotony, but right now, it was a lifesaver.

He hadn't realized that he was a few minutes behind his usual arrival time at The Basement until he got a text from his gaming buddy, Jonesy. Matt gazed down to read the text, *"Dude, WTF? Where are you? And do you want food tonight?"*

At a red light, just as he was about to respond to Jonesy, he saw started to hear yelling and horns honking. Matt glanced up to see a black GMC Suburban a few cars ahead of him had stopped abruptly at the diagonal. Two men in suits jumped out of the vehicle and started shouting at a motorcyclist sitting at the traffic light. The motorcyclist turned and, without a thought, immediately pounced on one of the two men in suits.

Matt had never seen an all-out brawl in the middle of an intersection before, and he couldn't help but stare. The biker was much smaller physically but scrappy, jumping on the man in the suit from behind, attempting to put him in a headlock. The guy in the headlock was spinning around in circles, almost as if he was trying to reach the jumper. The more he spun, the tighter the biker's grip around his head became. The spinning was making it difficult for the second guy to grab the biker off the back of his friend.

Road rage at its finest. That biker really has no chance against those massive dudes. Oh, shit! That's what I thought would happen . . . As soon as the one man in a suit stopped spinning, the second man in a suit got a hold of the biker's waist and pulled until the biker was forced to let go. The force of the final pull catapulted the biker several feet across the road. He hit the pavement hard and didn't move upon impact. Watching to see what move the men in suits would make next, he realized the Suburban was similar to the ones that routinely parked out front of The Basement. The Suits!

A few months ago, guys always wearing nice suits who

drove similar black Suburbans had started renting out the back room at The Basement. Matt and his friends always called these fellas Suits, as their attire stood out from the usual Basement crowd that donned t-shirts and sweatpants on the regular, maybe a pair of jeans on a nice day. It always scared him and his friends shitless when these guys walked in.

Matt quickly grabbed his phone to text Jonesy. *"Dude! You aren't going to believe what I am watching go down in the middle of the fucking street! Too much to text, but I'll give a hint: the Suits have fucking insane road rage. Be there soon."* No cars had moved since the brawl began with the Suburban blocking the road.

The Suits gathered their wits and swiftly walked to the dazed biker. Matt knew this was about to get ugly, two against one were never good odds. The Suits began to kick the biker, sparing him no mercy. *Jesus, they're going to kill him! What the fuck can I do about it?*

Being intelligent enough to know he was not going to be able to rescue the biker single-handedly, but not wanting to witness a murder, he began to press on the horn on his truck. It seemed he wasn't the only person wanting the assault to cease, because several of the other blocked cars also began to honk their horns. The noise startled the Suits into submission. The kicking and stomping came to an abrupt end. Without a glance back, the two Suits walked back to their Suburban, flipped everyone off, and unceremoniously drove off, leaving the biker on the side of the road crumpled in a heap. Several of the stranded motorists rushed to his side while on their phones, presumably calling 911. *No need for me to stop, poor bastard...*

Tonight, Matt had wanted to tell his friends at The Basement the story of how he had finally asked the cute girl at the office, Catherine, out, but this story would no doubt top that. He had rehearsed in his head how he had wanted to tell them about asking Catherine out in front of the entire office, wanting to get the best reaction out of his friends, who he didn't think had ever actually asked a girl out. He knew they were going to want to hear the little details, to live vicariously through him.

As the Suits drove off, traffic began to flow once again. Thinking it best to not actually follow them to The Basement, assuming they were the same guys he always saw there, he turned and took a different route. He had a feeling he might have been beaten like that biker if they had noticed him following them. Taking his time to arrive at The Basement, he parked his truck ten minutes past his usual arrival time and noticed that most of his friends were already there, but that there were no black Suburbans. *Good*, he thought, *I can tell them both stories at once without having to look over my shoulder.* Matt crossed the parking lot with a focused, intentional pace, eyes wide and on alert, he was still feeling the effects of watching the road rage play out. Opening the front door, he felt as though he was safe and secure, enveloped by familiar sounds, smells, and faces.

"Hey, hey, hey, look who's here! What's up, buddy?" shouted Danny when Matt came through the door.

"Hey, Boss," Matt called back. He called both Danny and his brother Paul "Boss" as they were the owners of The Basement. Danny ran the bar side of the business and Paul was the sole member of the IT department and kept the network up and running. Matt didn't know they were twins until almost a year after he started coming in. In Matt's defense, Danny stood about 5'4" and had a full head of red curly hair, while Paul was almost as tall as Matt with thinning dark brown hair. When Matt found out, he thought it was a joke.

"What can I get you tonight, the usual?" Danny asked while stacking clean glasses back on the shelves of the tiny but sufficient bar.

"That would be great, except make it a double tonight," Matt replied with a smile.

Danny raised his eyebrows before grabbing a bottle of gin. "Sure thing, what's the occasion?" Danny finished pouring the drink, sliding it along the counter to Matt.

"I'll tell you, but I want a couple of the other guys to come over here too. I think they'll want to hear it too."

"Oh shit, this sounds good. Hey Paul, come here and grab Mikey and Jonesy. Matt has a story to tell," Danny called across the bar.

As the crew gathered around, Matt began the story of how he asked Catherine out, deciding he would wait to tell the story of the road rage until after he finished with explaining his bravado with Catherine.

"Wait, wait, wait. You just walked up to her?" Mike asked. Jonesy sat beside him with his mouth agape.

"Of course he did, you numb-nuts. You think he just shouted across the entire office asking her out?" Paul snorted.

"I might as well have," Matt said. "You could hear a pin drop the moment I got to her desk."

Danny chuckled. "So, what'd the lucky girl say?"

"You really think I'd tell you guys if she said no?" Matt laughed.

The guys cheered and smiled, and Paul reached out to fist bump Matt. Before Matt was bombarded with the inevitable questions about the specifics, the group of them were distracted when a black Suburban pulled up. Two men in suits got out of the Suburban and headed to the back corner of The Basement. The guys paused their conversation to watch them walk in.

"What the fuck is going on with the Suits lately?" Paul whispered, looking at Danny.

"Dude, I don't fucking know, and I don't really care. All I care about is the fact that they pay a hefty monthly rent to have access to the VIP room. If no one gets hurt, then I don't give a shit," Danny replied.

"Remember the first time they came in? Jesus, if looks could kill. They scared the shit out of me," Paul said. Matt remembered months ago when the Suits first came in. It was as if time stood still while they made their way to the back of the gaming den. All eyes followed them in a casual, nonchalant way. The gamers were close to terrified to make proper eye contact because the vibe the guys in suits threw off could melt you in your tracks. They were the guys that gave off a vibe that made your hair stand up on the back of your neck. From that day on, their presence raised Matt's curiosity.

Paul continued, "That big fucker that came up to the bar, remember? He paid to reserve the VIP room a full six months in advance, with cash. I asked him for a name to put the reservation under. I was so nervous. I didn't really need a name; I didn't know what else to say. He just looked at me like I was a complete asshole for asking. I just wrote in the calendar, 'Suits.'"

Matt laughed. "Oh, is that where you came up with the nickname? I was wondering about that." The nickname fit, and there was never a question of who when someone referred to them as such. They all knew who the Suits were; no one else there had a suit on.

"Hey, speaking of Suits, you didn't finish telling me about what you saw on the way here," Jonesy said.

As Jonesy spoke, Matt looked up as another group of men in suits came through the door. He quickly recognized them as the guys from the road-rage incident. "Well shit, now I can't tell you. See those two that just walked into the VIP room?" Matt said through a clenched jaw.

"Yeah, so, what did they do? Come by Tailgaters to buy a policy?" laughed Paul.

"Seriously, not until they leave. It was fucked up what they did, almost killed a guy. I don't want them knowing I watched the whole thing," Matt said.

When the Suits finally made their way to glassed-in VIP room in the far back corner of The Basement, Matt launched into his second story of the night, detailing the beating he'd seen in the middle of the intersection.

"Jesus," Paul said when Matt finished. "Do you know why they fought that guy?"

"I literally think it was just road rage. Maybe the biker cut off the Suburban or something, but either way, it was totally uncalled for violence," Matt said.

"If I ever see a black Suburban on the road I'm turning around," Jonesy said.

Danny shook his head, glancing back at the VIP room. "I just want to just stare at them the whole time and try to figure out what they are talking about. It's like when you know you shouldn't look at something, but you're drawn to it. But I feel like if they catch me staring, I won't make it to my car one night, you know?"

"Right. I stop myself from staring at them too. They're intriguing to me though, almost like they're characters from a movie or something. From what I can tell, they aren't doing anything illegal. I mean, I've never seen them exchange things for money or anything, have you?" Matt asked.

"Nope, I sure haven't. I'm glad too, because can you imagine me going up to them and saying, 'Hey fellas, looks like I am going to have to ask you to leave and take your drugs and guns with you.' I guess in that sense, they're being fairly respectful, as far as gangsters go," Danny said.

They all laughed at the thought of any one of them having an actual conversation with the Suits, much less asking them to leave.

"Whatever it is they do, they all dress really well. Believe me, I know a suit that fits that size of a guy is not anything you would buy off the rack. Those are custom," Matt said, starting to tune out the guys as he eyed the first group of Suits settling into chairs.

Matt had been paying close attention to the men in suits who were often holed up in the VIP room. The Suits always arrived in pairs, two ominous-looking men, and headed straight back to the VIP room. Most of them looked like they were hitmen or real gangsters. Matt noticed that no matter the weather, they always had a suit on like it was a required uniform. Most of the time, he pretended to not notice or pay them any attention, and it seemed he was the only one who made a mental note of what he observed during visits by the Suits.

The Suits were going about their business as they usually did, talking, having a few drinks, but Matt could tell they were waiting to start the meeting.

As Matt was drowning out the other guys talking about *Call of Duty*, a group of men who were not the ordinary Suits entered the building. These three new guys reminded Matt of a cross between Tony Soprano and Sonny Corleone. The three men walked in an intentional formation, with the two exceptionally large guys on either side of a man much smaller in stature with salt-and-pepper-colored hair. There had not been anyone other than the muscle coming in until that day. Matt deduced that the older gentleman was the one in charge, or the boss. He looked to be in his early 60s and like he had seen a thing or two. Matt saw that the boss walked with confidence, like he knew what came next. The two men who flanked him looked like they had balls of steel and the word 'flinch' was not in their vocabulary. Matt was careful to only watch them through the mirror on the back wall of the bar.

Direct eye contact was more than likely forbidden with this group.

"Matt, you there?" Danny shouted, waving a hand in front of his face, and bringing him back to the conversation at the bar.

"Sorry, what? I was zoning out," Matt said.

Paul rolled his eyes. "You stare at those Suits too much."

"Don't look directly into their eyes, you may turn to stone," giggled Jonesy.

Matt ignored the banter, watching the two large men guard the door as Salt and Pepper took a seat in the VIP room. "Jesus, who are these guys?" Matt asked under his breath. "They look like they mean business, and not the good kind. Where do people like that come from?"

"I literally think my fight or flight response kicked in when they walked behind us. I'm going to just pretend I didn't see any of it. Like I said, rent is paid, that is all I'm concerned about," Danny said. "Let's just all get back to our evening. You guys shake it off, drinks on me tonight for having the shit scared out of you in my place."

After sharing his heroic story of asking Catherine out with the guys, Matt didn't think the night would get any better. "Thanks Danny. Is this going to be a regular thing? When scary guys come in here, you give us free drinks?" Matt laughed before he downed his first drink to make room for another.

"Don't get used to it," Danny said with a wink.

CHAPTER 2
VIP ROOM GONE WRONG

THE GUYS each went to their pods just like any other night, except with a free drink in hand and an urgent sense to disconnect from whatever was going on in the VIP room. Matt was the only one who was hesitant to throw on his headset and begin a new game, but he did anyway. For him, it was like watching a car wreck about to happen. *Why didn't anyone else want to watch the car wreck about to take place?*

He wasn't exactly staring into the VIP room, but his attention was more focused on what was going on there than anything else. There was certainly nothing this exciting going on in the Tailgaters Insurance cubicles. By now, the other gamers had their eyes trained on their screens. Instead, Matt had one eye on the screen in front of him and one eye on the VIP room. Matt was half listening to the chatter coming through on the headset, his teammates asking him to engage, otherwise he would be killed.

"Dude, what the fuck are you doing?" screamed Jonesy. "Get with it, or get out, you're going to get us all killed."

Still distracted, Matt answered back while quickly engaging in the game, "Ok, I'm here now, I have that guy on the left, I got him, now go, go, go!"

Still noticing what was going on in the VIP room, Matt could see the conversation was getting intense and tempers were flaring. The salt and pepper boss was now standing and obviously shouting, finger pointed at the men across the table. His face was getting red as he spoke aggressively, with saliva spewing as he told them all to fuck off. His two bodyguards also stood and entered the VIP room, while inching closer to the other side of the table. Most gamers could have a bomb go off and never even blink. However, Matt was not a gamer from the start, just a jock turned gamer out of boredom.

"Matt! What the hell? You just got us all killed, what are you doing?" Matt heard Jonesy yell through the headset.

"Are you guys paying attention to what is going on with the Suits? It looks like shit is about to get real in there," Matt said to the others in the game.

"Oh, damn, I did glance over there. The old guy looks like he is going to blow a gasket. They usually don't get that pissed off in there," Jonesy said.

"Who cares about them, dude! Get in the game, that's what you're here for, not to fantasize about what the gangsters are doing back there," Mike snapped.

Matt didn't have time to respond to Mike. As the two bodyguards made their way to the other side of the table, the three men on the other side of the table all stood up, shouting back, arms flailing, chests puffed out. To get closer, the two bodyguards threw chairs out of the way, one hitting the glass wall, cracking it from top to bottom. Matt peeked around The Basement. None of the guys in pods even noticed the commotion. Danny and Paul must be in the back, Matt didn't see them anywhere.

As soon as the first chair hit the glass, all five men except the salt and pepper boss reached inside their suits and pulled weapons out. Matt's heart thumped harder at the sight of the guns. *Is this really fucking happening?*

There were no shots fired in the first moments of all brandishing their impressive arsenal, only waving them about as if to say, 'no fuck you, you leave' until one of the two on the other side of the table opened fire on the two bodyguards and the salt and pepper boss. Matt heard the shots and saw blood, all before he could even duck and take cover.

Matt gasped. "Guns . . . shots fired!" he spluttered into his headset.

"That's the spirit, Matty," Mike cheered.

"No, actual shots, man! The Suits are shooting up the place! Get down!" Matt shouted.

Matt took off his headset to get his friends' screaming out of his ears. As he hit the ground, Matt quickly crawled underneath the pod where he had been playing. He spun himself around so that he could still see what was going on. They had shot out all the glass walls of the VIP room. There were three men laying presumably dead on the table in the VIP room.

Matt's warning seemed to have sprung all the gamers into action. Headsets went flying as people went rushing toward the front door. He could hear Paul instructing everyone to evacuate immediately.

What the fuck is happening here? He desperately wanted to look around and see if his friends were ok. For him to be able to do that, he just needed to see past his pod out in front of him. As he peeked his head around the side of the pod, he heard more shots coming from the back corner of The Basement. The sounds of gunfire quickly pulled Matt back in underneath the pod. *Christ, why did I have to be in the last pod in the aisle?* With the angle of the pod, all he could see safely were the remnants of the VIP room. *Guess at least one of the Suits isn't dead yet.* There was no way of knowing if any of them were friend or foe. Would he be a moving target, or were they just after revenge on each other?

Matt scanned the other pods, and they were empty. Were they empty because of dead bodies lying where he couldn't see them, or empty because they got out safely? Movement in the parking lot grabbed his attention. He saw Jonesy and Mike had already made it out to the parking lot. Their screens were eerily left mid-game, headphones thrown to the ground in their haste to make it out. The men in the parking lot ran behind a parked car. There, laying sprawled out across the hood of the car was Paul. He had been hurt in the mayhem and was bleeding from his midsection. Jonesy and Mike quickly and forcefully slid him off the car, pulling him to safety. A large SUV pulled next to the men that blocked Matt's view. Within seconds, the SUV sped off, and the men were gone.

Matt could hear one of the bodyguards yelling, "Where are you? I may be bloody fucking mess, but I'm not done with you, old man."

The gunshots and yelling continued for what seemed to be an eternity. It was as if the lone bodyguard was aimlessly wandering around shooting at the debris trying to find whomever he was looking for. "Come out, come out, wherever you are," the bodyguard sneered.

Matt's mind was racing with thoughts of how he could get out alive. He had the floor plan of The Basement memorized. Matt knew that either trying to make a run for it out the front or back door was about the same distance. He quickly ruled out the back door, thinking that he didn't know who or what would be back there since he would have to go through the hallway that led to the offices, through the office, and then out the back door. He figured that the front door would be better because he could see his path better. Plus, he could get in his truck and leave quicker, which was priority one. The downside to that was there was no place to use as cover. If he ran out the front door, he would just have to run and hope that he wouldn't be shot in the back on his way out. It seemed like waiting for the police to arrive would be too late, and this would all be over by the time they got there. He reasoned that whoever had made it out alive would already be gone and the Suits would have more than likely killed anyone who was there that could be a potential witness.

There was a lull in the gunshots when Matt heard footsteps coming to his pod from the front, where his vision was impeded. Not knowing who was standing over him, he braced for the unexpected.

"Matt, dude, let's go! Why are you still here? Let's go! We're the last two here, come on now!" screamed Danny.

With more rustling coming from the back of The Basement, Matt crouched even further into the space under his pod, wishing he could become invisible. Even though his brain told him to move, he was frozen. His fight, flight, or freeze response was not what he expected it to be. He was scared, yes, but he could not get the flight response to engage.

"Oh shit, I gotta get outta here, Matt, please hurry man!" shouted Danny as he turned and ran out the front door.

Willing his flight response to engage, he began making his way out of the row he had been sitting in. Did he hear someone near him? Didn't everyone leave? Trying to focus on making a quick exit, he could not shake the sense there was someone near him. Just then, he heard the pitiful sound of someone gasping and wheezing, fighting to keep alive. Out of the corner of his eye, Matt quickly looked over and saw the salt-and-pepper haired Suit who Matt had figured was the boss, sprawled out on the floor, eyes fluttering to stay open and aware. Matt gasped when he saw he was holding a weapon in right hand. He was clearly injured and bleeding heavily from his upper body and cuts on his face. He looked wretched, and his face was twisted in pure agony.

Shit! Matt took a quick glance around; he was already almost halfway to the door. Matt crawled a few more feet towards the door, not having seen another person. Matt was so close to the door that he could see his truck in the parking lot. He was going to make it out alive.

Matt instinctively looked back to Salt and Pepper and thought, *Christ, this is real! There is a man dying right in front of me, and I'm going to just run out and leave him? I already did that once today!*

As panicked as he was to leave this massive crime scene, Matt could not look a dying man in the eyes and walk, or in this case, crawl, away. He quickly crawled back to Salt and Pepper, to see if he even was worth trying to save. Salt and Pepper's shirt was drenched with blood, still warm when Matt touched his chest. Matt quickly determined Salt and Pepper was clinging to life, so he moved on to Plan B. *How could I grab him and go, there's no way I could crawl with him on my back,* Matt thought. He decided that the best way to grab him was to get him to a semi-upright position, throw him over his shoulders, and make a run for it.

As Matt was on his knees trying to get Salt and Pepper in a position to be moved, he saw movement from what was left of the VIP room. With a quick glance back to the VIP room, Matt saw two men lying motionless. The Suit walking towards him looked like a real-life zombie, bloody, riddled with gunshot wounds scattered across his body. The sight of him startled Matt.

"There you are, old man, I knew you couldn't have gotten too far," spewed the gravely injured Suit.

How the man was still standing was a question that will never be answered. Before Matt could make any sort of move, the last remaining Suit was standing over him with his gun drawn pointed right at him. As if he was a professional, Matt reached for the gun in Salt and Pepper's bloody hand and fired. Boom. Done. Matt just killed someone, or at least severely injured that man. There was no time to think about it, or how the hell he was that good of a shot. Matt instinctively tucked the gun in the backside of his waistband, directing his attention to Salt and Pepper. The sensation of shooting someone on a screen was something he had done thousands of times. This scene was no video game. Seeing blood, smelling blood, and watching people take their last breaths of life was not anything he imagined being part of in real life.

Matt turned back to Salt and Pepper, who was lying on his back, grabbed him around the waist, sat him up, and threw him over his left shoulder. Getting to a standing position and steadying himself, Matt ran like hell right out the front door. Fumbling to keep the injured man from sliding off his shoulder, Matt reached into his pocket and grabbed his keys. With keys in his right hand, he pushed the key fob to unlock the doors to his truck. Matt's goal was just making it to the truck safely, knowing that if he could do that, he could get his passenger to the closest hospital ER. Matt saw the lights on his truck light up, showing that the doors were unlocked, and headed straight to the passenger side of the old Dodge Ram. He paused for a moment to look and see if anyone had followed him. All he saw were the dim lights of The Basement glowing out into the parking lot. There was an eerie silence.

Opening the passenger door, he gently lifted Salt and Pepper into the seat. Salt and Pepper winced as he landed softly on the seat, his head flopped back; he was barely conscious now. Matt could see that he was in terrible shape, his breathing had become shallow, and he wasn't able to keep his eyes open. Matt ran to the driver's side of the truck and took his seat. Although he hadn't heard any sirens in the distance, logically, he knew that something like this would alert someone to make a call to 911. He sat back and said a silent prayer of relief to himself that they were coming and took a deep breath to settle his nerves. Salt and Pepper was still bleeding, gripping his right shoulder. Matt reached back to the backseat of his truck and grabbed an old sweatshirt.

"Here, put this on your wound, it will help stop the bleeding," Matt instructed Salt and Pepper. Quickly realizing there was no way this guy was going to hold the sweatshirt, Matt shifted in his seat so he could apply pressure to the wound. "The cops will be here, and they will get you to the ER quicker than me. You'll be good."

"Get the fuck outta here," the Boss muttered.

It startled Matt hearing him speak. He fumbled over his words and said, "But the cops will be here, and we can get you some help."

Again, the Boss responded, "Get the fuck outta here!"

Matt looked up with the sound of a vehicle pulling into the parking lot. *The police are here, how do I explain all this?* Instead, another black Suburban, driving too fast for the small parking lot, flew up to The Basement, barely stopping before it would have driven right through what was left of the glass front. Matt silently watched as two more Suits raced out of the vehicle, running into the shambles with their guns drawn. They quickly exited, standing out front shouting at each other and frantically pacing.

"What the fuck went on here! Where is he?" shouted the stockier of the two.

"Fuck! We should have been with him. Do you think he left? But how, the Suburban is still here. Christ, did you see Rodgers and Adams splattered all over the fucking place?

18

When I find the little fucker who did this . . . " the second Suit shouted.

"Dude we have to go now! They're almost here, get in. We don't need to get stuck here. Let the CUC do their work. I'm glad you called them before we got here," the stocky Suit said.

Then, two large black windowless vans pulled up. *Who are these guys?* Matt wondered. The Suburban with the two late-arrival Suits sped off, and Matt took this as his cue to leave as well.

Matt checked in with his survival instincts, which yelled for him to get the fuck outta there. He put the truck in gear and sped off from the scene of several murders, one which he may have committed. He was trying to remember how many bodies he saw. At least four. Matt gulped, thinking, how was this not going to turn out terrible for him? Leaving the scene of multiple homicides, including one he committed.

"Thanks, kid, I owe you one," Salt and Pepper mumbled.

Matt was so focused on not throwing up, running the truck into a tree, or passing out, he simply gave him a nod and said, "You need a hospital, I need to get you there."

In a barely audible voice, Matt heard Salt and Pepper attempt to yell in what came out as an aggressive whisper, "Take me to 3475 Oakwood Drive, they will know what to do and get me taken care of. No fucking hospital, you hear me?"

What? Take him where? Matt's old truck did not have a GPS and his phone had been left in the carnage at The Basement. *Great.* He didn't have time to think about that now. First on his to-do list was to get this guy to some address that he had no clue how to find. Matt tried to think about where in the hell this could be. Matt wondered, *What did people used to do before they had Google Maps on their smartphones telling them how to get places?*

Matt asked Salt and Pepper, "Can you give me a hint what part of town that address is in?"

Salt and Pepper wheezed, and Matt felt bad for asking him to speak. His voice had become so quiet that Matt had to put his ear to Salt and Pepper's lips to hear. "It's in the fucking ghetto—just go."

Instincts, again, kicked in. Matt turned his truck around and drove in the general direction of the 'ghetto' area of town. Once he was in the general vicinity, he did what you did when you didn't have a GPS. Matt went inside a convenience store and looked for a map. The cashier was looking at him with a bit of horror, a bit of suspicion, and a look of, 'Do I need to call the police?' Matt wondered what the deal was, why this reaction? Then, he looked up and saw himself in the security camera video screen. Matt was covered in blood, covered. *Well, no shit this guy is going to look at me like that,* Matt thought.

Screw finding a map, Matt didn't even think they sold maps anymore. Matt asked the bewildered cashier, "Hey dude, it's been a really fucked up day, can you help a brother out and tell me where Oakwood Drive is?"

Maybe it was because of the neighborhood they were in, Matt was not sure, but the cashier did not ask questions. The cashier said to Matt, "My friend, you look like you have seen better days. I don't know that address. Say it again."

The cashier was holding his smartphone, perhaps he was going to call the police, but he listened intently to Matt giving him the address a second time. He had pulled up Google Maps on his phone.

"Ah, I see now. My friend, you were very close to this place." The cashier handed Matt his smartphone for him to see the driving direction on the map, taking the phone back, the cashier quickly pulled a piece of the register tape off the 1980s era cash register to write the several steps of driving directions to 3475 Oakwood Drive.

"Dude, thank you. I really appreciate you doing this. Not that it matters, but just so you know, you probably saved a guy's life," Matt said as he turned and walked out.

"Good luck to you, my friend, be safe," said the cashier as the glass door swung shut.

Matt was glad it was dark out when he ran back to his truck. It would not be easy to explain away the blood all over him, and the half-dead guy in his truck. Luckily, the cashier had been helpful with the directions. Within a few minutes' drive from the convenience store, Matt found 3475 Oakwood Drive.

CHAPTER 3
THE HOUSE

FROM WHAT MATT COULD SEE, 3475 Oakwood Drive was a complete shit hole. Had he heard the wrong address? Oakwood Drive did not have any working streetlights, and since it was dark, it was hard for Matt to see anything behind the enormous, twelve-foot, black iron gates that surrounded the large, but not-so-elegant house. As Matt got closer to the drive, several bright motion sensor flood lights shone on his truck. The gates that surrounded the house looked to cost more than the house itself. Matt slowly drove his truck up to the speaker that was attached to the black iron gate that surrounded the crap house as if it were a fortress.

With unsteady hands, he pushed the 'talk' button on the speaker attached to the iron gates. Before he could say a word, the voice from the speaker simply said, "Drive up."

Matt thought about his choices here. Option one: As soon as the gates opened, roll Salt and Pepper onto the front lawn and take off. Option two: Forget this nightmare and take him to a hospital and basically do the same thing. Or option three: Finish what he started and lug Salt and Pepper's dying, bloody ass up to the front door and see what happens from there.

Matt wasn't sure what sort of organization Salt and Pepper

ran but, based on the events that just took place at The Basement, he knew entering the gate had the risk of potential violence. Looking to his right and seeing the now unconscious Boss, for some strange reason, Matt found himself trusting Salt and Pepper. At the very least, Matt figured he was saving the Boss of the Suits, that should keep him from being killed. Right?

With a leap of faith, Matt cautiously drove up the driveway, stopping the truck as it came parallel with the front door.

Matt could feel his heart beating out of his chest as he climbed out of the truck. He had absolutely no idea what he would find behind the door. As Matt was walking around to the passenger side of his truck, the sound of the iron gates startled him, slamming shut behind him. Going with option three, Matt threw Salt and Pepper over his shoulder to carry him towards the decrepit-looking house. He hoped no one would drive by and see this. How could he explain? Matt lugged Salt and Pepper's limp body up to the front door and rang a video doorbell. As he stood there, Matt took a few deep breaths of what he feared could be his last breaths on this earth.

Matt heard the door open, and he braced for what was next. Anything was possible after this crazy, fucked up day. One of the largest men Matt had ever seen off the football field answered the oversized dark oak door. Even Matt had to glance up to look him in the eye. *What is it with all the Suits looking the same? All fucking huge and tall?* Matt thought. If he did not know better, he would say the guy answering the door looked just like the guy he just shot at The Basement.

"Dude, what took you so fucking long to get here?"

Not the greeting he expected, but at least Matt knew he was in the right place. Just inside the door, three more Suits rushed forward and lifted Salt and Pepper off Matt's shoulders, rushing him into a nearby room, and slamming the door behind them. Thinking his work was finished, Matt turned to leave.

"Where do you think you're going, dude?" the Suit who answered the door hissed. The Suit grabbed Matt before he could react, pulling him into the house and spinning him around, pushing him up against the wall.

With a resounding thud, Matt found himself pinned on the wall, one arm pressed across his shoulders and neck, the other sifting through his pockets, and feeling up and down his pant legs. Matt had forgotten about Salt and Pepper's gun that he had stowed in the waistband. What was going to happen when they found that during the pat down?

"Ok, asshole, what's this? Who do you think you are?" shouted the Suit as he pulled the gun from Matt's waistband.

"Well, that's a gun, but it's not what you think," Matt said, wide eyed.

"And what do you think I think it is? Because to me it looks like a fucking gun, and we don't let strangers in here, period, and strangers with guns, well, that's an absolute fucking no," the Suit replied, pressing his elbow against Matt's neck. "I should snap your fucking neck right now!"

"Hey! Hold up a minute! I got that from the guy I brought in here, that's all! You can go ask him, I used it to shoot someone, to protect him!" Matt choked.

"How do I know that? You could be one of them, coming here pretending to be one of us!" the Suit seethed in a scary, quiet voice.

Matt's airways were nearly closed with the pressure of the Suit's elbow. "Look, man, I don't even know what 'us' means or who you are. I don't have any ulterior motive here, I just brought the guy here because he asked me to, and now I want to go home. I don't know what you are even talking about. I just happened to be at The Basement when this shit went down," Matt gasped.

An unknown voice called out, "Snoop, let him go. He's cool; we know who he is. Let him go, now."

Matt wanted to turn to see who was there, who had literally saved his windpipe from being crushed, but his head was pinned to the wall in the opposite direction.

The elbow didn't release from Matt's neck. "You sure, Franco? I'm just trying to do my job, you told me not to let anyone in. I know tonight was different, but I thought I did the right thing," Snoop said, suddenly in a more childlike tone.

"Snoop, yes, I'm sure. He's ok, for now. He helped bring Fowler back here tonight. Now let him down. Hand me the gun, Snoop, I'll take care of it from here," Franco commanded in a gentler tone.

Matt slid down the wall in the same position he was in while being pinned. His neck needed to slowly be moved back to a normal position.

"Don't leave this room," Franco ordered. Franco had moved on before Matt could get his head turned back around. *Shit, I wanted to see who that was! I wanted to thank him!* Matt thought.

Getting the kink out of his neck, Matt continued to observe the house. The contrast between what the house looked like on the outside and what it looked like inside was hard to explain. Shithole on the outside, million-dollar mansion on the inside.

He noticed it was a beautifully decorated house with awfully expensive furnishing. At least, Matt assumed they were. What did he know, really? He had gone from living in college housing with a bunch of jocks to his own small sparsely furnished condo, so expensive furnishing was only a guess, but the shit in the house looked expensive to him. The house reminded Matt of Mary Poppins's bag. It was gigantic inside, almost an optical illusion. So much space, so many rooms, so many people.

Matt was sitting in the entryway that seemed to connect to the whole house. There were men rushing around into different hallways and rooms, most wearing suit coats, and those who didn't were armed with shoulder holsters. The men rushing about were swearing as they strode by.

"That fucking asshole, I can't believe he pulled this shit. I can't wait to get my fucking hands on him, that fucking little prick," was the bulk of the conversations that Matt had been privy to hear.

No one seemed to pay any attention to Matt, which at this point, he was grateful for. The smell of fresh brewed coffee permeated the air, and Matt thought a kitchen must be nearby. Coffee was not the drink Matt would have preferred if anyone would have bothered to ask. A couple of whiskey shots was more like it. His nerves were still on hyper-drive, but he thought it was odd that no one spoke to him after his run-in with the door guard, Snoop. From what he could surmise, he had done them a favor by bringing Salt and Pepper back to the house, theoretically saving his life. An acknowledgement of that would have been a nice response instead of the unwelcome violent episode at the door.

More Suits, each one looking more or less as big and intimidating as the next, continued bustling around.

Standing there awkwardly with his hands in his pockets, swaying back and forth from his heels to his toes, Matt was not sure if he could leave now, or if he was just going to be shot dead right there. It was a hard vibe to read at this point. It was a mix of energy all around. Matt prided himself on being able to intuitively read places and people, but this time, he was a little out of it. He wasn't sure if it was him, or if the fact that this was a scene from another world he wasn't part of, that made it a hard read. It almost seemed routine. Grab the guy who's hurt, take him to the room, go about your business, and trust that whatever happens behind those closed doors is out of your hands.

Matt was not sure if he should ask to leave, or if he should just sneak out nonchalantly. Looking around, the nonchalant part did not seem like a viable option, as there was not a lot of nonchalant stuff going on here. Just as he was about to attempt the great escape, a woman about Matt's age came out of nowhere.

She was calm and very serene amongst the structured chaos. She was as beautiful as any model, tall, fit, with the most incredible green eyes he had ever seen that stood out exceptionally against her caramel skin. The color of her eyes was a green that could mesmerize you with their special magical powers. She wore jeans and a blazer that accentuated her almost six-foot frame. Matt observed that none of this whole scene seemed to distress her. Her face showed no signs of panic.

Once she noticed Matt, she looked him up and down, and then with a perplexed look on her face, said, "So, you're the guy, huh? Not what I expected."

Matt smiled because he was not sure what else to do. Was that a compliment, or a cut? He put his hand out and said, "Hi, I guess I'm the guy. I'm Matt."

She just looked at his hand, which was covered in dried, caked blood, and said, "Maybe another time with the handshake, Sport. My name is Liz."

Matt looked down at his hands and saw the cuts and dried blood. Only then did it hit him what had happened the last ninety minutes. Matt gasped and felt like he was going to pass out. Liz grabbed his arm and guided him to one of the expensive brown leather couches, the ones that no one ever sits on, more for show. Liz gently sat him down and instructed him to put his head between his legs and to breathe.

"Hey, take some slow deep breaths through your nose, it will help center you and keep you from passing out," she said.

Matt did as she instructed, staring down at the striped pattern of the rug beneath his feet. It was a mix of earth tones, browns, creams, and ivory, with a splash of red. He thought, *ok, time to wake up, asshole. This nightmare is over, get up! Wake up and let's go home.*

Matt sat up, determined to shake off the panic, nausea, and dread that had hit him, wondering if he could just pretend this day never happened. He took a deep breath and looked at Liz, who had a bit of a smirk on her face, and said, "Well, it's been real, I think I'm going to head out." Matt almost said it like it was a question, rather than a statement.

"Not so fast, Sport, I think my dad or Jimmie is going to want to speak to you before you go. Well, I don't think so, I *know* they are going to want to talk to you before you head out."

Ok, so it was a question, and now he was sure; he could not just leave. "Oh, that was your dad?" he asked Liz.

With a tilt of her head, Liz replied, "Yes, that's him, dear old dad."

Matt wondered where they had taken Salt and Pepper, Liz's dad. What was behind those closed doors? Did they have a surgeon on standby or something?

In a quiet and timid voice, Matt said, "Your dad seems like a nice guy, I guess. I hope they're taking care of him. He was in pretty awful shape."

"We have it covered. We've all seen worse than this," Liz replied.

After seeing the events of today, Matt figured he would take her at her word.

Liz stood up, tilting her head in the room's direction with

the closed doors and said, "Hang here a minute while I see what's going on in there, don't go anywhere, Sport."

He watched Liz walk away and wondered if, at the very least, he could get to a bathroom to wash the shit off his hands. Matt took another look around and saw what he thought was a bathroom. *I'll see how far I get. Will someone stop me, or shoot me? Deep breaths, deep breaths.*

Matt stood up, only a little wobbly this time, and headed to the bathroom. No one stopped him.

He gently closed the door behind him, turning on the light. The face looking back at him was not the face that he had seen this morning when he was shaving and brushing his teeth. He wondered if it was possible to age ten years in ten hours. Trauma and stress have a funny way of settling quickly into your genetic code. Again, he took more deep breaths. He felt a small sense of relief in this small, closed space, but to say he felt an overwhelming sense of confusion would be an under-statement.

Matt quickly washed his filthy, blood-stained hands. He had never experienced such pleasure in his entire life as he did when he watched the dried blood wash off his hands and flow down the drain. He splashed water on his face, bent over the marble pedestal sink, and took some deep breaths.

Grabbing the white hand towel off the nearby rack, he stood up, looked himself in the eye, and silently said, "You got this bro; you got this," just like he had as an athlete before a game, or before a fourth-down play when he knew the quarter-back was going to run. Thank God he had developed a keen sense of intuition, that was about all he could count on right now. With that, he could get through the rest of this day, and perhaps his life.

"Feel better now?" Liz was standing next to the door he

emerged from, arms crossed, and Matt swore she was tapping her foot with impatience.

"Yes, I do. That was some crazy shit that went down. I'm still not sure what all happened, or if my friends are ok. I am pretty sure my friend Paul was shot. Can you find out about him specifically?" Matt said. He shuddered thinking of Paul lying there, with Mike and Jonsey dragging his limp body away.

Liz motioned for them to walk back to the fancy couches, "It was fucked up, I agree with that. We aren't sure about anyone else right now. When I hear the details, I will let you know. From what I could piece together, you and my dad were the last ones out," Liz said.

"Yeah, I'm not sure who was where when it all went down, it happened so fast. I would appreciate you passing any information on to me if you hear anything about my friends. I don't have my phone. It must be in the rubble that used to be The Basement." Matt sighed.

"Sure thing, Sport. When I know, you will know," Liz said, half-smiling. She paused before looking Matt up and down again. "You know, when I heard some guy from The Basement was the one who brought my father home, well, let's just say, you're not what I pictured you to look like. You're definitely not a typical gaming nerd. Football player, yeah?"

With a puffed chest, Matt replied, "Yeah, I was a football player in college."

"Thought so, defensive line, I'll bet, not O-line, you aren't a big fat guy like those O-line guys are, just a big guy," Liz said.

Hey, this chick knows football, that's kind of cool, Matt thought.

Just as soon as he let his guard down, Matt noticed Snoop coming toward Liz and him. He noticed Liz looked annoyed, and her foot started tapping again.

Snoop narrowed his eyes at Matt, then turned to Liz. Liz

nodded to him with approval. Snoop looked back at Matt and said, "I see you got cleaned up. Jimmie would like to see you now."

Matt looked at Liz, back to Snoop, and took another deep breath, making a mental note to himself that this deep breathing bullshit really did work and had saved him from having a stage five panic attack twice already.

"Who's Jimmie?" Matt asked. Just as he asked, a man magically appeared out of the dark corner of a hallway. The intensity in energy shifted as he approached. Matt noticed this guy was not as big physically as the others he had seen, but he also threw off a vibe of being silent but deadly. Someone you wouldn't want to anger. Jimmie was just about as tall as Matt and seemed to be close to the same age as Salt and Pepper but looked extremely lean and fit. Matt's first thought was that he looked like he was a yogi or marathon runner. Jimmie was the only one who didn't either have a suit on or shoulder holster, rather, he had a long string of thick black beads with a tassel hanging from his neck and was dressed casually in jeans and a black polo shirt, which accentuated his long, sinewy, muscular arms.

"Liz, how are you doing?" Jimmie asked in a gentle tone.

"I'm doing ok. This isn't the first or last time, I'm sure, I've had to deal with this shit. He's still a lucky guy though," Liz said.

"Indeed, he is. I will go check in with the medical suite in a few. So, this is him?" Jimmie said, turning toward Matt.

"Yes, this is Matt. Matt, this is Jimmie," Liz said.

"Nice to meet you," Matt answered, offering his hand out.

Meeting Matt's hand in a firm embrace, Jimmie said, "It is good to meet you, Matt. We—Mr. Fowler, the man you brought back here, and I—appreciate what you did tonight. I can only imagine the confusion you must be going through right now.

We can explain more later, but for now, Liz, I need you to take Matt back to his place so he can collect some of his things," Jimmie said, looking towards Liz.

"Collect my things?" Matt asked.

"Matt, you will be staying with us for the time being," Jimmie said in a firm tone that implied staying at the house was not up for discussion.

Matt felt the panic begin to rise in his chest again and his breathing became quicker. "Staying here? But why? I just want to go home, I don't understand," Matt stammered. He didn't know these people; he didn't know what 'staying here' meant. Was a prisoner or a guest?

"Sport, it would just be better, safer, for you to be here. There is a lot of shit to explain that just can't be done right now. I know my dad will want to talk and express his appreciation, personally, for what you did," Liz interjected, shooting him a reassuring smile.

"If you can, Matt, please look at this as a good thing, not bad. Maybe look at it as a way for us to pay you back for your actions," Jimmie added.

Matt was not fully on board, but he was in no condition emotionally, physically, or mentally to argue his way out of this. The adrenaline was wearing off, and he was close to hitting total exhaustion. What he could weigh out in his mind was that they seemed grateful for his act of bravery, and they did appear to want to keep him safe. Maybe staying in the house surrounded by iron gates wouldn't be so bad.

"I guess that would be ok," Matt said. "Just for tonight then?"

"We can talk about the length of your stay here tomorrow when things have calmed down a bit," Liz said.

Matt frowned but before he could respond, Jimmie said, "Matt, I'm not sure if Liz had the chance to talk to you about a small request that we have for all of our unexpected guests."

"I don't think so," Matt replied.

"I didn't have a chance yet, but I went to grab one when I was in his office," Liz stated, pulling a sheet of paper from a folder she'd been holding.

"Ok, perfect, I wanted to make sure we got that taken care of before things went much further," Jimmie said with a smile. "Matt, we will need you to sign an NDA, a Non-Disclosure Agreement, before you head out. It is something that ensures our privacy. It has been a long night, so it is my recommendation that you just sign it. All it covers in a nutshell is that you will not speak to anyone outside of DMF about any of the events of tonight, the location of the house, and any names you may have heard. Things like that," Jimmie said sternly.

"Look, I'm too tired to negotiate or put up too much of an argument over signing this. Believe me when I say I want to forget everything about this night." Matt sighed. "But I don't know what DMF means, and I already did tell someone where I was going."

Liz and Jimmie's looks turned to concern. "You told someone where you were bringing my dad? I thought you just drove straight here, and you didn't have a phone?" Liz asked.

Matt felt the energy of the moment shift from a casual business interaction to possible violence. "Well, yes. I had to stop and get directions to this place. Your dad was in no shape to tell me anything except the address."

"It is important that you tell us where you stopped, and who you spoke to. We will need to follow up with that individual," Jimmie said with a deadpanned look that Matt couldn't decipher.

Matt explained to them where he stopped, and that it was close to the house, but he was not able to remember the exact location, or the name of the helpful cashier. "I'm sure he will cooperate with whatever you ask of him. He seemed like a nice guy."

"I'm sure he was a nice guy, but we will need to pay him a visit just the same," Jimmie replied. "And to answer your question about what DMF is, it stands for Dominic and Marlene Fowler, DMF Enterprises, the company which you stumbled into this evening."

Liz handed him the document and instructed him where to sign and initial. Matt acknowledged the terms of the agreement with slight nods of his head. He wasn't really reading it, only pretending to show interest. He just wanted to get out of there and move forward with his life.

"Looks good to me, can I get a copy of that?" Matt asked.

Jimmie and Liz looked at each other and smiled. "Sure thing, Sport." Liz said.

"I think now would be a good time for you two to get going, Liz, you good?" Jimmie asked with his eyebrows raised.

Liz nodded and turned to Matt. "Let's get going."

CHAPTER 4
HOME SWEET HOME

Liz turned and walked down the long, elegant hallway toward the back of the house. Matt obediently followed her. As they neared the back of the house, the smell of coffee became stronger, and the kitchen Matt had imagined came into focus. There were at least a dozen more Suits gathered here and there in the spacious kitchen. Matt felt like they were all talking about him, noticing the glares and stares in his direction. Matt awkwardly kept his gaze downward, thinking that not drawing extra attention was best, as he wasn't sure how he fit into all this yet.

He noticed the Suits were standing in a circle, all with drinks in their hands. Walking a little slower, Matt wanted to see what they were doing. It looked cultish, all the same type of clothing, in a circle. What was going on? They all had shot glasses, that was what he could use right about now too.

One man signaled Liz to slow her pace. Liz and Matt paused by the doorway and the man said, "You all know that we lost two of our own tonight. It's a horrible thing, but as we all know, part of our jobs. Here today, gone tomorrow, right? How many times have we all said that?" The surrounding men all nodded in agreement. The voice sounded familiar to Matt, *where would he have heard him?* Matt realized that it was the voice of the man who had rescued him from the crazed door-man, Snoop. Franco's bleached blonde hair made him stand out in the crowd of oversized men and he had a naturally down-turned mouth and narrowed eyes that gave him a serious RBF—resting bitch face.

Jimmie appeared behind Liz and Matt, the sound of his voice causing Matt to jump. "Thank you, Franco, for your kind words. Let us raise our glasses in memory of our two fallen comrades, Rodgers and Adams, both good men who served DMF well over the years," Jimmie said.

All the men said in unison, "Here, here." Then, they downed their shots, slammed the glasses on the table, and walked away. *Was that their version of a funeral?* Matt thought, *what kind of place is this?*

Liz continued on through the kitchen and grabbed a set of keys from the long rack that had places for nearly a dozen sets of keys to hang, and they headed to the garage. The size of the garage and parking lot did not disappoint. Just as the house was an optical illusion, the garage was the same. Matt counted four cars inside and another half dozen in the adjoining driveway. She clicked the key fob and the Mercedes 450SL sedan lit up. *Not a bad way to get to my place*, Matt thought. But where was his truck? Last time he saw it, it would have been blocking the driveway. Barely able to focus on explaining to Liz where he lived, he decided that apparently there was no need for anyone behind the iron gates to steal his truck, and he would investigate its whereabouts in the morning.

After settling in, without asking, Liz calmly put Matt's home address into her car's GPS.

"Uh, how do you know where I live?" Matt asked.

Liz turned, paused, and said, "Your name is Matt Clemmons, you played football at the University of Northern

Colorado and until today, you were employed at Tailgaters Insurance, I like the name of that place by the way, and you live at 556 Chestnut Street, unit 101B."

"Wait a fucking second, how did you know that?" Matt asked, his voice rising slightly. He was getting more and more suspicious of this DMF organization. *Note to self*, Matt thought, *nothing here can be kept a secret*.

"Calm down, Sport, relax. People in our organization can run people's background. With you, we ran your license plate number through the DMV, got your name, and we went from there. I know it sounds creepy, but we didn't know who you were or who you may have worked for. We didn't know if you could be trusted," Liz said.

"Are you fucking kidding me? You didn't know if I could be trusted? I could say the same for you. I don't know anything about you or DMF and I'm just supposed to trust you? I was almost killed tonight. I'm not even sure why, but I listened to a total stranger telling me to bypass law enforcement and a trip to the ER to bring him to a place I didn't know where it was. That's fucking nerve if you ask me," Matt fumed.

"I get what you're saying. Will you do me a favor?" Liz asked.

"Are you kidding?" Matt sighed, then said, "Yeah, I guess so."

"Chill the fuck out. Please, just fucking chill. I know you have no reason to trust me, or what I'm asking, but please, it would just be better if you did," Liz said.

With Matt's energy level almost tapped out, he agreed to chill, as best as he could, at least until he had a sit-down conversation with Jimmie and whoever Salt and Pepper, *Mr. Fowler*, turned out to be. He did, however, feel like he deserved at least a little information to help process the events of the evening.

Once they were on their way, Matt took a deep breath and

shifted his thoughts to begin the interrogation. Liz also took a deep breath, and beating him to the punch, said, "I'm sure you have a lot of questions. I can only answer some, so instead of you asking, I'm going to tell you what you need to know."

Matt would take whatever he could get.

"Matt, you aren't a dumb guy, I can tell. I'm sure you've noticed my father has a, well, *special* life, and a special type of company. In this business, he is an enormously powerful man with many connections. Some of his connections are with people you probably don't even know exist in this world. It's probably best to just leave it at that. My father is an expert of sorts in moving things financially. Someone needs something moved. They ask my father to do that. You follow? And no, it's not drugs. You're not in any real danger, as long as you stick with us anyway. Part of what my Team does is protect, keep people safe. Tonight was an anomaly. That shit is rare. I think it is fair for you to know that your life, the life that you had when you woke up this morning, has unfortunately come to an abrupt end. I hope that you at some point can see the positives in this. I know it's a lot to take in."

Matt never thought much about having out-of-body experiences, but it certainly felt like he was having one at that moment, like he was just watching these events take place to some character in a movie. Liz's words were floating around in his head, not landing anywhere in particular. *Life as I knew it is over? What does she mean? Danger? What is real danger to these people? What if I don't want my life to change?*

Matt noticed the time on the clock in the car. It was nearly 3:00 a.m. He would be waking up for work in three hours if this were a regular Tuesday morning.

Matt felt a mixture of relief and nostalgia thinking about his insurance job. While it had not been a dream job for Matt, it had been nice, stable income. The job was easy enough, the main reason he chose it was because he never knew what he really wanted to do as far as a career. Matt had been one of those kids that when asked what they wanted to be when they grew up, it was always the same answer, "I'm going to be a football player and play in the NFL." At one point, Matt had a chance to do that, had an agent all lined up and was headed in that direction, until the fourth, or was it fifth, concussion basically stopped him in his tracks. The last one was scary. It really fucked Matt up and made him look and say, *they cannot replace my brain*. So, it was off to the dazzling world of insurance sales.

Liz pulled up in the driveway of the small condo Matt bought after his first actual job out of college.

Matt walked up to unlock the front door of the two-story brick condo. It seemed like Matt had not been there in days. It was an odd sensation, like he was walking into someone else's world. Liz was standing right behind him, tapping her foot while Matt struggled with the lock. Matt thought, *I'm glad that I had cleaned the place just the other day*. His home was modest compared to what Liz had grown up in, he was certain.

"Grab a bag with enough clothes for a couple of days, I think that should do it," Liz huffed.

Matt wondered if she ever was happy, or if she was always irritated and serious. Liz slumped over onto his dark grey sectional couch as Matt climbed the stairs to get his bag packed. Liz shouted up the stairs that she thought he had a nice couch, giving him full points on comfort.

Matt half smiled at her comment and his stress level went down just a touch. As Matt dug his bag out of the closet, he paused, not knowing what exactly he was supposed to pack. The majority of the guys he saw tonight were wearing suits, or dress shirts and pants. Should he pack the only suit he had stuffed in the back of his closet? He had only worn it once for a friend's wedding a few years back. That Jimmie guy was casually dressed, maybe he would just grab the suit just in case, and some jeans. Absent-mindedly, he grabbed his toothbrush and razor and shoved them into his duffle.

He glanced around his bedroom, feeling an odd sense of nostalgia for the room he had slept in only the night before. He gave it one final look before turning to walk back downstairs, but as he turned the corner, he paused at a loud sound, as though the front door had been kicked in, with wood shattering and glass breaking. His fight, flight, or freeze instincts kicked in yet again, in what seemed like the longest day of his life. Matt could hear men's deep voices, yelling.

"Where is he? I want his ass now!"

Matt heard Liz's reply. She sounded way too calm. "Who the fuck are you talking about? I'm the only one here, why don't you get the fuck out? What do you want here, anyway?"

A man shouted, "We saw you come in with him. We know he is here. You better come down here, you little prick, or we will find you!"

Matt gasped and instinctively put his hand over his mouth. *Oh shit, this is why they said I couldn't come home . . . Why didn't they send some Suits with me? Why just Liz?*

Matt wasn't sure what his next move should be. *Do I jump out my window, shimmy down the drainpipe, and escape? Do I go downstairs and see who is in my house, what do I do?*

Before he could make a decision, from the living room, Matt heard gunshots, but with some type of silencer. It was like in the movies, an easily identified but very muffled gunshot noise, the high pitched, *whoop whoop.* With that, there was silence, no more voices.

Matt was more than hesitant to go downstairs. God only knew what he would find. It was anyone's guess who shot who.

Matt started to slowly make his way down the stairs, a tiptoe, slow-motion version of what a normal trip down the stairs would be. He was about halfway down the stairs when he was startled by Liz's voice. Matt let out a sigh of relief knowing that Liz was ok.

"Are you just about done up there? I would really like to leave now," snapped Liz.

Matt landed on the last step of the stairs and could not process what he was looking at. He stood there with his bag in hand and looked at the sectional couch. *What. The. Fuck.* There were two very dead men laying across it, both with a single shot bleeding slightly from the middle of their foreheads. Both with large guns laying near their lifeless bodies. Matt must have looked like he did earlier today when he was about to pass out.

Liz rather forcefully grabbed Matt's shoulders and looked him dead in the eye. "Matt, look at me, you need to breathe, you need to breathe, can you do that? We need to go. Now!"

Matt did not speak; he only could nod his head to answer yes to her question. Having been a basically law-abiding citizen most of his life, it was not Matt's first instinct to leave the scene of a crime. This was a unique set of circumstances, though. Plus, he had never been part of a murder-for-hire plot before either. His morals and values needed to be upgraded and adjusted to the current situation. Just like earlier in the day when he thought it best to wait for the police to arrive at The Basement, he learned to just leave, and leave quickly. Matt pondered for a moment, *How does this all get 'fixed?'*

Liz grabbed Matt and his bag and headed out the door, gun held out in front. The decision was clearly hers to make, not Matt's. He was just along for the ride on this one. He followed her out the door and turned to take one last look at his first home, his first little two-story brick condo, then turned his back and continued to the 450SL.

Once Liz and Matt were on the road, he looked at her and

41

it hit him; she just killed two men. She calmly, quietly, and instinctively killed two men. Matt never heard her flinch or show that she was intimidated or even surprised at the situation. How does a person get like that? Do they go through training, or electroshock therapy to be immune to danger and the impending trauma? Had she seen so much that this was not a big deal? Could this actually be a way of life for people?

"Please tell me what happened, who were those guys, why were they in my house, and what the fuck is going on?"

Liz, with her eyes focused on the road ahead, took a long deep breath, tilted her head down slightly, and sighed. She pulled the car over to the side of the road and put it in park. Matt wondered if he would be the next person she killed that night.

"I suppose we need to talk," Liz said. She was still not looking at Matt and was tapping the steering wheel in a gentle, rhythmic fashion. She took another deep breath in before letting out a long exhale. The tapping stopped, and she gripped the steering wheel tightly with both hands, twisting it nervously. She put her head down, slowly shaking it from side to side. Matt could tell she was not angry, but conflicted.

"I will tell you what you need to know for now. It really is not my call to have full disclosure with you. But yes, I killed those pieces of shit back there at your house. No, it is not the first time I have killed someone. Yes, they were going to kill you. Yes, I expected them to show up. And yes, you're safe now. Please don't look at me like that."

"Wait a second here. You said I *would* be safe! Why would you lie to me and tell me my life wasn't in danger?" Matt shouted.

"Your life wasn't in danger, Matt. You very clearly saw that I took care of things. As I mentioned earlier, if you're with us, my Team, you will be ok. Honestly, I didn't want you to come back here tonight. I was going to go alone. But I thought it would be good for you to see your place and grab your own things. It would have been too difficult to explain. And please, give me fucking break. I know you have had a long day, but so have I. We have *never* had to deal with a situation like this before."

"Situation like what?" Matt demanded, pounding his fist into the dashboard. "I deserve to know. My life got turned up-fucking-side down tonight, saving *your* dad!"

Liz glared at him with a side eye. "Again, chill the fuck out, dude. Situation meaning, someone from the outside coming into our very private world, plus losing two guys from the Team. None of us knew exactly the right way to handle you. I, we, all of us are doing the best we know how."

Liz put the 450SL in drive, punched the gas pedal and continued down the road. "It's a Beautiful Day" by U2 was playing on the radio as they drove. As Bono was belting the upbeat tune, Matt shook his head and vowed that he would never hear a U2 song again without thinking of this moment and this day, the day that life as he knew it ended and began again, all without him asking it to. *My mom always said, "be careful what you wish for,"* Matt thought. He woke up bored with his mundane life wanting some excitement. Boy, did he get what he asked for.

CHAPTER 5
NOW WHAT?

Matt woke the next morning in an unfamiliar bed, in an unfamiliar room, in a semi-familiar house. Liz got them back to the House, and that was about all he could remember from the day before upon waking.

Matt had slept late into the next day. The extended slumber he was certain was partly because of exhaustion, but part was also not wanting to wake up to the reality of what had taken place. Perhaps a little unconscious avoidance.

He wasn't even sure if it was only a day ago or was it a lifetime ago that he hopped into his truck to go play a few hours of games and to brag to the boys about his date with Catherine.

Catherine. Oh shit. He had almost forgotten about their date this weekend. There was no way he would be allowed to go out, would he? He had to at least text her that he couldn't make it, it would be rude to completely stand her up. *I miss my phone!* Matt's intentions had been good and honorable when he asked her out, he could have never predicted that he would become wrapped up in some strange Henchman-like house. He hoped one day he would be able to explain why he stood her up for the date they were to go on.

Matt stayed in bed a few extra minutes after he woke,

trying to decide if he should shower and go downstairs, or just shower and stay there until someone came looking for him. It was difficult to make any sort of decisions, except for one. He needed a shower, big time.

Upon returning from the incident at his condo, he had been too tired to pay much attention to his surroundings, but now that he was awake, he looked around the room they gave him. The room was larger than any he had ever had, with three large windows that faced east, making the room light and bright first thing in the mornings. The king-sized bed fit Matt's gigantic frame, which only led to his comfort to settle in for a deep slumber. His room was as beautiful as the rest of the house, everything in the room was first class. He didn't even know there were sheets that felt this incredible, pillows this soft, but firm.

Matt's bag had made it up here with him and was sitting on an oversized dark brown leather chair. The bag looked like it was just sitting there waiting for him to open it up, like he would find his life back inside of it. As Matt sat up, his head throbbed, a familiar feeling from when he would wake with a concussion after a football game or practice back in the day, or from a terrible hangover; *this has to be stress related.*

Matt stumbled up to his feet with only a few sways back and forth. Deep breathing, once again, was his only way to feel somewhat grounded. He gathered his bag and opened the door to the bathroom. It was ultra-sleek and modern with marble everything, and glass where there wasn't marble. Matt looked at his face in the crystal cut mirror and was pleasantly surprised. He looked better than he felt. That was a good sign.

Matt said a prayer silently to himself. Thank God when he packed, he was alert enough to have grabbed his toothbrush and a razor. Matt turned the water on in the black, brown, and beige speckled marble walk-in shower, and it was an amazing feeling. A long hot shower can make you feel like a new person, he felt like he was washing the trauma off his soul.

He heard Liz in a softer voice than he had heard before saying from behind the bathroom door, "It's about time you get your lazy ass out of bed. When you're done there, come downstairs to the office."

"The office?" Matt shouted over the sound of the water.

"Just get downstairs, Sport. I'll leave a map on your bed, so you know your way around," Liz said, shutting the door behind her.

Matt quickly finished in the shower, dried off with the most expensive plush towels he had ever touched, got dressed, and mentally tried to prepare for whatever the meeting was to be about, and whoever it may be with. He was pleased with his choice of clothes he grabbed last night. Jeans and a t-shirt felt comfortable to him right now, and he needed to feel something familiar to him. He looked on the bed for a map, until he realized, *Oh, she was fucking with me* . . .

Matt walked out into the bright, sun-kissed hall. Windows along the hallway guided him down the stairs. The oak staircase creaked slightly as he wandered down to the office as Liz had instructed. The creaks must have alerted Liz he was on the way. She stood up from the couch and gave him the once over.

"A shower and a shave did you well." She tilted her head and motioned for Matt to head into the office.

Finally, Matt got to see what was behind door number one. He was right, they did have a surgical suite in the house and a doctor, a nurse, and a bunch of medical equipment. Matt sort of ducked his head as he went in with some trepidation and saw the patient, who he now knew was Mr. Fowler, not just Salt and Pepper. He looked a hell of a lot better than when Matt had lugged him up to the front door. He was lying flat with oxygen tubes and hooked up to quite a few monitors with some IVs in his left arm.

Salt and Pepper's eyes were slightly open, but Matt knew he saw him, or sensed him. There were a couple of other people in the office-turned-fully-operational-hospital-room. He wondered if they were on staff full-time, or on call as needed. He was leaning towards having them as being full time since it seemed from his short amount of time in the house, they would benefit from having an immediate medical response team available 24/7.

"Hey, kid, come over here," Matt heard in that familiar raspy whisper from the night in his truck.

Taking slow steps towards Mr. Fowler, he kept his eyes to the floor, unsure of the etiquette of direct eye contact within this 'family.' He heard Jonesy in his head telling him not to make eye contact or he'll turn to stone. Matt got within a foot or so from Mr. Fowler. He could see that The Boss was close in age to his parents. Matt noticed he looked tired, a kind of tired like he had worked hard his whole life, whatever kind of work that may be. Mr. Fowler had the most intense, piercing green eyes, similar to Liz's shade of green. They looked right through Matt down to his soul. *Here I go again with those deep breaths,* Matt reminded himself.

"Mr. Fowler, nice to see you again, I'm glad to see you looking like you are on the mend. My name is M—"

Mr. Fowler held up a hand to silence him. "I know who you are, Matt Clemmons. You grew up around here, played football at the University of Northern Colorado, four-year starter until you got your head smashed up one too many times."

Matt took a step back and shook his head, remembering that Liz explained how the Suits could find out details of his life.

"Are you impressed that we know who you are, Matt? I

know Liz gave you a quick rundown of things we need to do with new folks, you understand," Fowler said. "Most folks don't realize that their license plate can lead to so many things, if you know the right places to look." Fowler paused to clear his throat. "I wanted to thank you for what you did there, in that place. Shit was not supposed to go down like that, and I would not be here if it were not for you. I cannot explain what that means to me, and how indebted I am. I have seen some crazy shit go down, but never in my life would I have expected to be, well, rescued I guess is the right word, by a gamer. But then again, you really do not look like a gamer, and you certainly did not respond like a gamer. Where did you get such a cool head and learn to shoot like that?"

Things were looking up as far as Matt getting out alive. Indebted, that was a good thing, right?

"You're welcome for getting you out of The Basement and back here. I gotta tell you, never in my life would I have expected to have anything like this play out. I don't know how else to explain it, but I work a lot from instinct, and that is just what kicked in when everything went down." Matt looked up, to see if his answer was sufficient and thought, hopefully, they would let him go home now.

Just as Matt was eager to get his leave approved, the doctor in the room made his way to the edge of the bed. The conversation between Matt and Fowler ended abruptly.

"Mr. Fowler, you know the drill, no more visitors, you need to rest."

"Yeah, yeah, yeah, I know, shut the fuck up, Doc. Matt, you and I are going to have to have a longer chat when Doc over here says it's okay. And because I know you probably want to know, I can't have you head home permanently until we have a debrief, I am sure you understand. Liz, you got this?"

"You know I do, Pops, rest up. No worries on this end," she

said. Matt hadn't realized that Liz was in the room. Her answer startled him. How many times in a day can they startle a guy before it becomes a serious problem, Matt wondered. She turned to him. "Matt, let's get outta here."

What in the fuck is going on? Where did the indebted stuff go? What the hell is happening here? Do they think I'm going to talk to someone or call the police? Matt was confused and not really digging where this was going. *I just want to go home and forget these characters. Deep breaths.*

Liz headed straight for the kitchen, walked right past, and grabbed a set of keys off the rack.

"Let's go, slowpoke, what are you doing back there? We already missed breakfast here, I thought you may like to grab some food," Liz said without expecting an answer, not turning around to see if Matt agreed.

"You read my mind. I didn't realize how hungry I was until we walked by the kitchen. I could use a big shot of caffeine too," Matt replied, trying to keep up with Liz's pace.

Hopping back in the same black 450SL they rode in the night before, Liz flipped her sunglasses off the top of her head onto her face and pushed the engine into start. Despite the unsettling feeling of not knowing what was going on in the House, the purr of the Mercedes's engine made Matt smile. There was something about driving in a $100,000 car that can change the way you see the world.

The black iron gates opened ahead of them. As was customary, Liz waited on the other side of the gates, making sure they were fully closed before proceeding on.

"That's something we need to do here, Sport. Make sure the gates close before you go, an unspoken rule, okay?" Liz said, looking at Matt over the top of her gold-rimmed aviator Ray-Bans.

Matt nodded in agreement. "Got it, and I won't ask why."

"You're learning quick." Liz smirked, speeding off down the street.

Matt was looking forward to a nice sit-down meal, one where his coffee cup was never empty. He thought this would be an opportunity to get to know Liz a little better. The freedom he felt driving in the most amazing car he had ever been in was in sharp contrast to the visions that kept reappearing in his mind from the night at The Basement.

Liz pulled into the drive-thru of McDonald's. The good vibes Matt was feeling all but disappeared. "Drive-thru McDonald's? Seriously?" Matt groaned.

"What's wrong with McDonald's? We come here all the time, what did you expect?" Liz shot back.

"I don't know, I was thinking of a nice sit-down breakfast, leisurely taking our time, not rushing back to anything in particular," Matt said.

"Well shit, sorry for disappointing you, Sport. We don't do leisure here, and we don't have sit downs, *anywhere.* More to come on the reasons for that," Liz said, pulling up to the drive-thru speaker.

"Anything on here sound good?" Liz asked. Matt was still pouting from disappointment when the drive-thru speaker asked what she could get started for them. With no reply from Matt, Liz ordered, "Can I get four of the bacon, egg, and cheese biscuits, two orders of hash browns, and two large coffees, some cream and sugar on the side?" She turned to Matt. "I hope that will fill you up, Sport."

Matt got out of his pouty mood about a block after leaving McDonald's. The smell of the food was just too much for him to ignore.

"Thank you for breakfast, I'm just not used to how you do things," Matt said, taking a bite of the biscuit. "Are these all for me by the way?"

"All I need is coffee," Liz said.

———

Getting breakfast proved to be the most exciting part of the day.

The next few days passed without drama or meeting any new people. Matt spent his time sleeping, more than usual, he was feeling like he was in a constant state of jet lag. Liz gave him the space to begin to acclimate to the House, only checking on him at mealtime when she would bring him much-needed sustenance. She also gave him the Netflix log in, explaining that it would be best for him to relax for a few days. Matt was in no mood to disagree, as they made it clear he would not be leaving soon. He was curious and looking forward to his next meeting with Fowler. This whole place was getting more interesting by the day. He wasn't too sure on what the house 'rules' were, and what parts, if any, were off limits to him. Getting out of his room was a priority while he was in limbo waiting for next steps. Sitting on the familiar couch across from Fowler's office seemed like a safe bet for a change of scenery. Matt brought a copy of Popular Mechanics magazine from days gone by that was left in his room and stretched out his long legs on the couch.

"Hey asshole, what are you doing down here? Trying to spy on the boss?" shouted Snoop.

"Are you talking to me?" Matt asked.

"Are you trying to be a smart guy now? Who else would I be talking to! I think Boss is going to be interested to know you are sitting outside his office trying to hear private meetings. I have proof that you can't be trusted," Snoop said in an eerie tone.

"Hold on, Snoop. I'm not eavesdropping on anyone. I just came down here to get out of my room for a change. Why would I not be trusted? I brought your boss back here, I saved his life. Did they not tell you that?"

"Don't talk to me like I'm stupid! Yes, they told me that, but there is always a chance you aren't who you say you are. Like why would a guy that looks like you hang out in a place like The Basement? You aren't the nerd type," Snoop said, walking closer to Matt.

"Sorry to disappoint you, but I am a gaming nerd. And for your information, I would rather not be here. If I could go back home, I would. One of my friends was hurt that night, and I don't even know if he is okay. It sucks being here," Matt said, standing up to face Snoop.

"Boys, boys, boys, let's take it down a notch," Liz said.

"Liz, I was doing what you asked me to do, keeping an eye on anyone who looks like they are up to no good. He was just sitting here listening in to Fowler's meetings. That can't be good right? I wasn't sure if he passed our security checks yet," Snoop said.

Matt sighed. "Security checks? I don't believe this."

"Sport, relax. Snoop, you did what I asked, yes. Thank you for that. But if you noticed, Fowler's door is closed, he is not doing business now. He is still recovering. If it wasn't for Matt, he would be dead, so we do owe him a bit of gratitude for what he did. His checks came back clear. I can take it from here," Liz said.

"Okay, if you're sure. I just want to do the right thing," Snoop said as he walked back down the hall.

"Fuck this. I can't leave my room now, and I'm being vetted to see if I am some sort of plant that is plotting a takeover," Matt said.

"Sport, chill the fuck out. In case you haven't already noticed, Snoop is a little slow. Dedicated to DMF, but very slow. We give him dumb little jobs to make him feel important.

You can sit wherever you want to sit, and of course we checked you. You already knew that when we ran your plates, so calm down." She looked down at a new message on her phone. "I'll catch you later, *gater*," she said with a smile.

"Oh, I get it, a reference to where I *used* to work, Tailgaters, very funny. I think I will stay out of Snoop's way, probably best to stay clear," Matt said. Liz gave Matt a thumbs up and a wink.

She paused and spun around to face him again. "And for your information, your friend Paul is fine. The bullet only grazed him. He's embracing all the attention he is getting from being shot in a mob shootout." Matt sighed with relief.

———

On the third day, Matt's predictable stomach complained and told him it needed to be fed. He had no way of contacting Liz and was not entirely sure about how meals worked here. She had been prompt with the meals up until this point. His energy was back, and he was getting restless to leave his room. Pondering the dilemma, Matt decided he would go exploring and see if he could navigate his way to the kitchen and grab some dinner.

Finding his shoes, Matt sat on the edge of the bed, bending over to tie them. He never heard her come in the room, all he saw were her black Converse stepping to eye level. *How did she know I was getting ready to leave the room?*

Looking up to see Liz standing by his bed with her hands on her hips, Matt said, "It's like you read my mind. Want to join me to grab some food?" Matt stood and straightened his shirt, pulling it from the bottom.

"My dad is ready to see you now, come with me," Liz said flatly, spinning to leave the room.

CHAPTER 6
THE OFFER

MATT IMMEDIATELY FORGOT about his growling stomach as he followed Liz back downstairs.

The doors to the office were closed, and Liz gave him an approving nod to knock. *Deep breath, deep exhale,* Matt reminded himself as he knocked gently on the closed door.

"Come in," a voice replied.

Matt opened the door. There, behind an enormous mahogany desk, was the man he rescued just a couple of days earlier, with bandages visible from under his white button up. Matt thought he must be a tough SOB to even be sitting upright and back to work so soon after he was injured. However, it looked as though he was pacing himself since the hospital bed was just on the other side of the large office for when he needed to rest.

His eyes were looking at Matt over the rims of the small silver spectacles. "Well, I see you are still in one piece even after your trip with Liz the other night. That was quite the first few hours here. If all that hasn't broken you, I think you will do just fine here," he stated, removing reading glasses.

Matt knew he had met briefly with him since the event at his condo but figured it best to forgo explaining that. "Yes sir, quite an unnerving situation for me. I'm glad to see you are doing so well already."

Mr. Fowler took the glasses off and set them gently on the table. He smirked. "You ain't seen nothing yet, kid. Have a seat, would you like something to drink? Have you eaten dinner yet?"

"I haven't eaten dinner, no sir. I would love to have something to drink too, that would be great. My stomach started talking to me a while ago," Matt stammered.

It startled Matt when he noticed movement from the back corner of the room. He hadn't even noticed there was someone else in the room.

"Jimmie, grab Matt and me a couple of beers, okay? And whatever is left in the kitchen as far as food," Fowler commanded.

He turned to Matt, "I have to say, I am fairly impressed with how you handled yourself during, let me say, some pretty intense and fucked up situations. I can imagine you may have a few questions. For now, I have to make sure you understand the current state of your well-being, so to say," Fowler said.

Matt remembered what his mom used to say when he was nervous, "Don't fidget when you are anxious or nervous Matty. Keep your cool and you can get through any situation." Matt's attention drifted, not hearing the first few minutes of what Fowler was talking about. Anxiety about the future of this conversation had begun to take over, so many *what if* scenarios. He had zoned out, with way too many thoughts running through his head. Matt literally felt like he had fallen headfirst into a movie or a TV series.

The people he had met so far were real-life characters. His keen observation skills were on overload. He was compartmentalizing all the events and attaching some of the characteristics of each person he encountered to a version of a character in a movie or TV show. Fowler, a Harrison Ford-type guy, rugged, smart, and brave. Jimmie, a Samuel L. Jackson chameleon, able to fit in whether it be calm leadership or being a complete bass ass that was called for, he could deliver. Liz, Matt had deduced, was not like any woman he had ever met, although he knew that Liz would make a kick ass part of the *Charlie's Angels* crew.

"Look, I'll just tell you straight, I think that being as transparent as possible is the best way to handle this. I'm not the best at having, shall I say, *delicate* conversations. Let me jump right in and say that the life you had days ago is over, it is gone, it will never come back, you can never go back. It is an extremely dangerous place to go back to. I am not a guy who minces words, I do not fuck around, you know? Do you get what I am saying?" With a slight pause, Fowler continued, "Just know one thing here: you will be well taken care of and compensated for what you did. I am a well-connected guy."

Matt had mentally checked out while he was talking. Fowler patiently waited for Matt to come back to the present moment, leaning back in his chair, hands folded on his lap. As the blank stare on Matt's face disappeared, with his eyes coming more into focus, Matt shook his head as if to clear it out and make room for him to focus.

"You back in the room now, kid? I routinely deal with this blank stare shit from people in my business. I call myself an expert at reading the moment when it's time to speak again."

Blinking several times before he answered, Matt replied, "Yes, sorry. I drifted off in my thoughts. I guess the last few days, events, people, houses, and all that is a lot to take in."

Matt nearly jumped out of his seat again when Jimmie came back to the office with the beers and some dinner. *I never used to be that jumpy, must be from the trauma and killings I witnessed. Of course, now, when I don't need it, my flight response is in good working order.*

After setting the bamboo tray in front of Matt, Jimmie immediately left the room. The food that Jimmie brought in smelled just like a place Matt used to go when he was younger with his family. When he was a kid, they didn't go out to eat much since it was expensive to take four kids out to eat at a sit-down restaurant. Every so often, the five of them, Matt, his brother, twin sisters, and mom, would go to a diner that had the biggest menu he had ever seen. Despite the many pages of the menu, he always got the same thing: chicken pot pie. He began to feel homesick.

Matt was trying to process what Fowler just said. He guessed that he really knew on some level that there was no going back, and strangely, Matt thought he was okay with that. Selling insurance was not exactly a career he wanted to excel in any way. "I figured as much after . . . " he stammered, "Well, after Liz uh—"

"After she took care of business at your place?"

"Yes, after that," Matt replied.

Matt didn't realize how your sense of smell can trigger memories and emotions. The plate of meatloaf, gravy, and heaps of mashed potatoes and rolls, were the same comfort foods that they served at the diner he and his family frequented. He inhaled the plate of food set in front of him, guzzling the beer as Fowler looked on.

"That was impressive, kid. I have seen hungry guys eat before, but you destroyed that plate. Do you need more? Jesus," Fowler said, amused.

Matt's face flushed from the comment. He hadn't realized how quickly he had finished the plate of food. "No, I think I had enough. I didn't know I was that hungry."

Fowler continued on, "Here's the deal, kid. I have an

incredibly successful global business. My competitors are ruthless, violent, and, mostly, greedy pieces of shit. I do not do things by the book, the one that the rest of society follows. I wrote the book I follow."

"What kind of business do you run, sir?" Matt asked. He instantly felt like he spoke out of turn, but Fowler didn't seem bothered.

"Here at DMF, we do business as a mix of electronic banking mixed with cyber security. It takes a lot of muscle, security, and oversight."

Electronic banking and cyber security didn't sound like a dangerous profession that required muscle. Oversight, sure, security, yes, but why were guns drawn at The Basement if it was just a simple business meeting? Matt knew there was more to this business than Fowler was letting on. Based on all that had happened in the past few days, whatever they did here was more secretive, dangerous, and profitable than they let on. Matt wondered if it had something to do with hacking.

"DMF? That's the name of the business. I sort of remember asking about that the first night I was here."

"Yes, DMF Enterprises to be exact. That is the name of the company I run, with many subsidiaries under it. Dominic and Marlene Fowler, my parents. I don't want to bore you with details," Fowler said.

Hoping to get more clues about the business and who it was that tried to have him killed, Matt pressed, "Don't worry about boring me. The more details the better."

"Kid, there are many facets to my business structure. When the time is right, perhaps we can have a more thorough, in-depth discussion about that," Fowler said firmly. Matt sensed not to ask more questions. "Since it was my business that got you into your current state of events, I feel responsible for you. I am not typically known for being a softy, but, really, I would be dead if you hadn't stepped in," Fowler said.

Matt audibly took a sharp breath in. He wasn't sure how to respond. "Um, well, I guess that's true. I'm sure we can work something out. I'm cool with just getting back to normal. I was just glad to help. We can leave it at that."

Fowler smirked and gazed at Matt and said, "We have some sort of connection, and I want to repay you by helping you stay alive and transition to a whole new life. Of course, whether or not you decide to stay with DMF, that will be up to you. What I can do is try to impress upon you the alternative world you woke up to because of selflessly saving mine."

"I have a choice?" That was the first time Matt had heard that. "I thought you said the life I had was over?"

"Yes, Matt, you have a choice, you're not a prisoner. There is always a choice. Absolutely, you can go back out into your world, but after what happened, it won't ever be the same world you left. I don't imagine you could just waltz back into Tailgaters like nothing changed for you, and shit, The Basement is offline as well. That was a bit of a joke, get it, offline, gaming bar, yeah, never mind. You get the point."

Matt was at a loss for words. Fowler continued on, "I would like to make you an offer, an offer of employment at DMF. It would be an entry level position for now. You can be the one who decides what level you end up taking it to. You have impressed me with your heads-up thinking and your ability to go with the flow. Like I said, a part of me feels responsible for the sudden and abrupt upheaval of your world. I would like to offer you a job as part of my security Team. Have you heard the term Henchman?"

Matt pushed the empty plate away so he could put his hands on the table to steady himself to stand. He stood up and started pacing around the room, hands on his waist, and muttered aloud. Matt thought he must have looked a little schizophrenic, pacing and muttering to himself. *Did he really just say Henchman? What in the absolute fuck is this guy talking about? Are you kidding me? A Henchman? I thought so but . . . What happened to my life?*

Matt started to piece it all together. They did in fact work for a criminal organization, protecting a boss, Fowler. Plus, most of them didn't seem like the brightest bulbs on the tree. Their jobs were to be muscle and to intimidate. *Well, they had that part down, my neck can testify to that.*

Matt remembered watching movies with Henchman in them, and he always wondered how and where the bad guys always found these unwaveringly loyal, dedicated men, all of whom would literally lay their lives on the line for, most times, complete assholes. These guys were intimidating yes, dumb as a bag of rocks, yes, but they deserved all the credit in the world for being absolute champs at taking orders.

Jesus, Matt thought, *what have I gotten myself into?*

"I don't think I heard you correctly, Mr. Fowler, did you say you wanted me to be a Henchman? Like the guys in the movies that kill people, that are assassins. The big stupid guys who lay their lives on the line for bosses who are always the evil, undesirable characters? When I think of Henchmen, I think of comic books, Marvel movies, that sort of thing. Those guys? I don't even know how to shoot a gun. The other day there was a fluke! I haven't even gotten a speeding ticket; I don't want to go to jail, and it seems to be a real possibility if I were to work here. I think I'm going to have to pass on this job."

Matt wasn't sure if he would actually shoot him dead right there. Fowler didn't seem like he got told 'no' very often. Instead, once Matt stopped rambling, instead being killed or beaten on the spot, Matt glanced up to see Mr. Fowler, who was actually laughing, not at all pissed off, but actually laughing out loud.

Wiping the tears from the corners of his eyes, Mr. Fowler spoke in a muffled voice, clearing his throat, "Matt, I have to say that was a little entertaining for me, thank you for that. I don't get to laugh like that very often. Sit back down, take a couple of breaths, and calm yourself. Jesus, I sound like Jimmie, what in the fuck . . . "

Matt walked over to one window and stood there for a moment. It was a beautiful park-like setting, the view helped to ground him. The scene reminded him of his old, predictable life. There were birds and trees and flowers, but his head was spinning, and for a minute, he thought he was going to get sick. What was going on in this room was not real. Matt put his hands on the wall to brace himself and took some deep breaths but wasn't ready to sit down just yet. He closed his eyes and only felt the sun on his face, which was helping to bring him back to reality.

Matt sighed heavily, then turned and walked to the chair in front of Fowler's desk. As he sat down, he sighed again with his eyes locked on the floor. In a split second, he thought about the options. He took a long and slow inhale, looked up, and said, "Mr. Fowler, I'm getting the feeling that I'm kind of being put into some kind of witness protection program. What exactly is my choice here? All this talk of my life is over as I know it. What does that mean? Do I have to change my name? What about my family, can I see them, are they safe? Same question about my friends? Mr. Fowler, please tell me what I need to know about this position at your company."

Mr. Fowler sat back behind his desk, looking amused. "Matt, it is not as complex as being in the Witness Protection Program. We here at DMF have our own little WPP. What, or who, I should say, you took out the other day was the mouthpiece for a guy who, for lack of a better way to describe him, is a 'wanna-be.' He's an up-and-coming wanna-be successful cyber security entrepreneur, not unlike myself back in the day, but he's infringing on what is mine. There has been some back and forth about the proprietary rights to a very successful business plan that I created many years ago."

Took out? Is that what they call killing someone?

"Thanks for the reminder, Christ, I think I blocked that out, that I killed someone," Matt mumbled.

"Yes, you sure did Matt. It's good for me you did, otherwise there is a very high possibility that neither of us would be here having this conversation right now." Fowler said this like it was a routine part of his day. No urgency, no, "I know it is hard to deal with," no compassionate words of wisdom. It was as if Matt had just made an insurance sale, the same amount of pat-on-the-back he would normally get from his boss. Fowler's attitude had a very, 'you will get over it,' 'it's not that big of a deal,' 'don't be such a pussy,' feel to it. Matt felt his stomach tighten, and he started to get lightheaded.

Fowler continued, "This fucking guy. He likes to play these silly little games. Apparently, he has been trying to come work at DMF and we somehow *wronged* him. He keeps sending these little encrypted threatening emails. 'Let me come work for you or else' kind of bullshit. He says he wants to fix what's broken. Nobody seems to know what's broken, so we have just ignored him. We all just call him the OT, the Outside Threat, nobody even knows his name. But I will tell you what, he is fucking pissed at what went down with you and me at The Basement."

"Pissed at me? Is this OT guy the one who is after me? But why?" Matt asked.

"Why, because you 'got a job here,' we took you in. He wants in, and we have ignored him. Typically, with this sort of shit, there is talk of retribution, revenge, you know, that type of shit. But not with this asshole, he is unpredictable, which you saw firsthand the other night. Therefore, you need to stay here and begin your new life, at least for now. At least that is how I see it. You have a choice, to leave, but that would be ill advised. This guy knows where you live now, and he knows how to find you. You're not safe out there. You can stay here as long as you need to, but I ask that you follow our house rules and confer with Jimmie or me before making any big decisions. This asshole has been a challenge for us to take care of. He never comes to any of our scheduled business meetings. That is just not how anyone should conduct business. The little prick sends different guys to speak for him every time. Because of that, we get nothing accomplished. It is definitely the oddest way I have ever tried to do business, and it becomes a waste of my time."

Matt wondered then, who did he shoot? The guy seemed like a boss to him.

"Excuse me, Mr. Fowler, but I'm a little confused at the sequence of events at The Basement. I saw you there, in the VIP room, with guys in suits. Who were all of them?" Matt asked.

"I didn't want to get in to all the details right here, right now, but what the fuck, I may as well. Are you ready for this? This is your first debrief, here we go," Fowler said as he grinned.

"I'm ready, I think it would help me to have a better understanding of what direction my 'new life' will be headed in." Matt sat back like he used to do in college when an interesting lecture was about to begin.

"So, this asshole, from the intel we have been able to gather, we know he is a hard-core hacker, a cyber genius. He has eluded us and has been able to infiltrate high-level data and processes. We have had to come up with innovative ways to defend our property. To say he has been a nightmare, well, that is an understatement. Let me tell you, back in the day none of this work was faceless, I mean none of it," Fowler said as he moved around to the front of his desk. He sat on the edge of the desk, arms bracing himself as he looked up at the ceiling, breathing stressfully through his nose, teeth clenched.

Matt shifted in his seat, and his mind wandered to movies and TV shows, the types with the classic good versus evil struggles. The confusing part was, it sounded like to Matt that there was not a clear good or evil facet in this genre. They both were bad, one trying to outdo the other. Matt just continued to listen and gather as much information as he could.

"We have been trying to assess whether this guy is absolutely brilliant or just one of those fucking millennials trying to make a name for himself. No offense, I know you are a millennial too. Anyway, the reason we were at The Basement was that we had picked up on some chatter that he used to go there to play. Is that what you call it? I'm not sure."

"Yes, we play, or hop on, but ok, got it, I think. But I still don't know who the guy was I shot?" Matt questioned.

"Oh, yeah, I got off topic there for a second. Like I said, this asshole never shows up like a real man would. He hires Henchman to be his mouthpiece. Who does that? Whatever, so the guy you took out was a hired Henchman."

Matt laughed out loud and waited for the punchline to the joke Fowler just told, but there was none. Fowler sat there, stone faced.

"What is so fucking funny, may I ask?" Fowler looked pissed as he sat back in his chair with his fingers laced behind his head.

"You said Henchman, again, are you serious? I thought you were kidding when you said I would be hired as a Henchman," he gulped, not laughing any longer.

"Well, yes, of course we have Henchmen, who the hell do you think takes care of our security? Who do you think all these guys in suits are? We are old school here, and that is what I refer to them as, Henchman. They are not just in comic books!" Fowler's voice thundered. He didn't yell, but the intensity of his tone shot through Matt like a bullet.

"Oh, man, I apologize, I meant no disrespect. I just never knew that there were such things as modern-day Henchmen," Matt said quickly, trying to redeem himself.

"Well, get over yourself, Matt, it is an actual profession," Fowler snapped. He briefly collected himself and continued in his normal raspy tone.

"Back to this asshole who is now wanting a piece of you. There is some heavy, behind-the-scenes work going on with our objective to keep you, your family, and your friends safe. There is also some work being done to eliminate the source of the problem."

Shit, it hadn't even occurred to him he wasn't the only one in harm's way. "Are you sure that my family and friends are safe? Are you sure I'm safe? How can I know? What are you doing to protect us? If anything ever happened to my mom, or sisters, my brother, I would lose my shit. I seriously could not handle that. How are they being kept safe?"

Fowler looked Matt dead in the eye with those piercing green eyes and said, "I understand your concern. Family is the most important thing in the world. Your mom, sisters, and brother all have 24/7 security around them. We have had people watching your friends too. It seems like you don't have too many outside of the guys from The Basement. I know this sounds surreal but believe me, I know this shit better than most. Jimmie is the fucking expert on all things security. In our experience, it's better to not tell the people being surveilled that they are being watched over. They just don't need to know, as it causes undue stress, and they change their normal routine. Those changes make mistakes happen. I have a team that is very good at what they do. So, when I tell you they are being taken care of, they are."

Matt felt a slight sense of relief, because strangely, he believed Fowler, and even more strangely, he trusted him. "Ok, I appreciate you taking care and making sure they're safe. What are you doing to, as you say, eliminate the problem? I mean, we can't live in danger for the rest of our lives."

Just then, Jimmie walked into the room. "I had a sense that I perhaps needed to be part of this conversation. Ed, am I right?" Jimmie asked.

"Jimmie, as usual, you have impeccable timing. We have gone over the safety plan for Matt's family, and Matt was just inquiring about what we are doing to eliminate the source of the problem."

Jimmie smiled and said, "This is the good part. I love this shit, and I love sharing a well-thought-out plan. Right now, I won't bore you with going over all the details, because there are a lot. But I will tell you that soon, there will not be any more worries or concerns to be had for you, your family, and friends when it comes to safety. I'm sure that Eddie explained we value family above all else. Part of my job is to make sure that everyone in our family is safe and well taken care of. I don't have any of my own biological children. I consider our Team here to be my blood and I will defend that to my end."

Fowler stood up and joined Jimmie. With both of them staring down at Matt, Fowler, said, "Back to my original question, are you in? I could really use a guy like you on my team. This is not the usual way I hire guys for this, but it seems like a good fit."

Before he knew it, Matt was nodding his head, "Yes, I will come and work for you, Mr. Fowler, why the fuck not? You only live once. I appreciate the opportunity." Matt figured there were not that many options for him right now. Was this the best decision he would make, or the worst? Only time could answer that.

Mr. Fowler looked at him with those deep intense eyes, and said, "Welcome to DMF Enterprises, Matt. We need to get you a suit."

CHAPTER 7
THE SUIT

MATT SHOOK Fowler's and Jimmie's hands, turned, and walked to the door. He was feeling a rush of energy that he wasn't able to explain. The moment it took him to reach the door, Matt felt something he had never felt in his life. Sacking the quarterback was always a huge adrenaline rush, but nothing like this. A Henchman, who would have thought? Pretending to go along with the idea of being a Henchman was the only way he knew how to get out of the most bizarre conversation he has ever been part of. Choice? Bullshit he had a choice. The crazy Outside Threat was after him and his family. He saw his only choice was to play along with this charade until he could figure out a way to get free. Although, not ever going back to Tailgaters Insurance sounded really good.

Liz was sitting on the nearby couch as he left Fowler's office. She had not exactly been a fountain of emotions since he met her, but as he approached her, there was a tiny bit of amusement in Liz's eyes.

"He said I needed to get a suit. Is that, like, code for something?" Matt noticed Liz didn't always wear the well-fitted, polished look that the rest of the guys wore. Today she was dressed in athletic wear, leggings and an oversized sweatshirt.

Matt thought she must only wear a jacket when she needs to carry her gun. *This really is a strange world I have come across.*

The slight amusement on Liz's face disappeared when Matt made that comment. "You are totally fucking clueless. It means you need a suit to start your job. It's not a secret code, Jesus."

Matt held his hands up in defense. "Hey, in my short time here, I've learned it's always better to ask than assume. So, when does training start?" Matt asked.

Liz blinked at him, her brow furrowed. "Training?"

He didn't think it was a dumb question to ask but seeing Liz's reaction made him think he shouldn't have said anything. "Yeah, you know, training before I go out to the field? I have no clue what I'm doing, I assumed I would at least get shown how to use a gun," Matt said slowly. Liz was still silent, so Matt asked hopefully, "Maybe some on-the-job training?"

"On-the-job training," Liz repeated, then she chuckled. "Shit, our version of on-the-job training is usually we hire you and the next day you'd be out the door on your first job, with some of the other guys to show the ropes, of course."

Matt's eyes widened at the thought of being sent out on a job tomorrow. He almost forgot how to breathe.

Liz laughed. "Don't worry, Sport, I won't send you to any jobs tomorrow. You can breathe easy. I think you're right, some training for a complete newbie like you wouldn't be such a bad plan. I'll talk to Jimmie to get some sort of training schedule set up."

"I would appreciate that," Matt said, feeling his panic level drop.

She yawned. "I guess I'll be the pseudo-HR department. I'll get you a training schedule and I'll take you to get your suit picked out. Lord knows what you would come back with if we left it for you to do on your own with just the guys. I'll go over how you get paid and some more details of the job later. Since it's late, we'll take our trip to get your suit in the morning."

"Sounds good to me. I have a lot to think about after my talk with your dad. I'll meet you down here in the morning, then. Does nine work?" Matt asked.

Liz nodded. "Nine it is. The boys can get back from the gym by then." She glanced down at her phone. Not looking up, she said, "I saw how you wolfed your food down in there. I'll order a pizza and send it up to your room, so you have a snack later if you want."

Matt smiled sheepishly, knowing he'd be hungry again soon. "Perfect, thank you. See you tomorrow."

The next morning, Matt wanted to be prompt for his first outing with his new co-workers. He was rushing down the stairs only to see Liz making her way up. "I was just coming to get you. I wanted to let you know getting a suit is a tradition here, so this is to be taken seriously. First thing anyone on the Team does is get a suit or two. We are also taking a couple of your new co-workers with us, this is Franco and David H. When we leave the House for the next few days, it is probably best if they tag along."

Franco and David H. appeared from down the long hallway and stood behind Liz, both nodded in a 'what's up' kind of head tilt and they headed out the back door. Matt's eyes widened when recognized these two as the Henchman who had come to rescue Fowler at The Basement. Chills ran down his spine when he flashed back to that night. With the vibe these two threw off, he was relieved that they were there with him, and not against him. Franco, that was who was giving the

70

toast to the two dead Henchman in the kitchen the first night he was in the house.

Both Franco and David H. had suits on, and they looked like guys from a gangster movie. Franco was in the lead, he drove, and no one yelled "shotgun" for the second front seat. It was routine. He drove, and David H. was shotgun. Liz quietly sat in the back and never looked up from her phone. They were both exceptionally large men, the 6 '4', 300 pounds-plus, O-Line size men, but they looked mean and intimidating as hell, like they had zero fucks to give. No one seemed to talk much. Matt thought about mentioning the fact that he had seen them at The Basement that night but wasn't sure how they would react. They were pretty flustered when they were there. He chose to keep his mouth shut for now.

Once they arrived at the tailor, Matt was surprised when he looked up to see that they ended up at a non-descript brick building. The building had some old, like really old, vintage 1970s suits and jackets hanging in the windows. It's not like they would just go to a mall or to Men's Warehouse or something, but these were definitely not the suits Matt had seen the other Henchmen wearing. He wondered if they were playing a prank on him. The old brick building's window had a hand-painted sign reading, *Redd's Suits, All Sizes Welcome.* The door had one of those old fashion Open-Closed signs with a clock with moveable hands on it.

Franco put the Suburban in park, and David H. looked like his head was on a swivel. Up, down, side to side, wait another second or two, and do it again. Matt had his hand on the door to open it and quickly realized that they were not just hopping out. Liz looked up from her phone and glanced at him from over the top of her sunglasses, shook her head no, and put her hand onto Matt's. *What the fuck is going on now? Every time I think I get it, I'm reminded that I really do not know anything about the life of a Henchman.*

"Did you see them?" Franco grunted.

David H. replied, "Fuck yeah, I saw them. What do they think they are fucking doing? I want to go out there right now and fucking blow their goddamn faces off."

Franco sighed and shook his head. "Calm the fuck down, man. They are just fucking with us. I'm sure they're not too happy about what Miss Hot Shot back there did to their pals the other night. They just want us to know they are not letting this go. If they were going to do something, we wouldn't have seen them. They wanted us to see them."

Liz said nothing about his Miss Hot Shot comment except to roll her eyes with an extra 'go fuck yourself' raising of her eyebrow.

Matt looked to see who they were talking about. He scanned the few cars that were parked near them, and then he saw it. A few cars down the block was a black Ford F250, windows tinted, and very ominous looking. It was like they were playing a game of chicken, who could sit here the longest and not move. Matt's heart raced, and he was getting a little anxious. Liz put her hand on Matt's again. This time she did not look at him, just covered his hand. The gesture had a calming effect, and Matt remembered what she had done to these guys' pals the other night. And no doubt Franco and David H. could handle just about anything. The lights of the Ford turned on and the truck came towards them.

Franco and David H. both instinctively reached under their suit jackets and pulled out some very impressive guns. Matt knew nothing about guns except for what he had seen in video games and movies, but he thought these were automatics because they had clips in them. Liz slouched down in the seat, not so much that she couldn't see, but enough to have some protection if needed. Matt followed her lead, and he slouched down, only he slouched all the way down. He did not want to see any of it.

The Ford truck pulled slowly down the street. Matt could hear the engine as it got closer to them. Just like that, the sound was gone, and the guns were stowed. Franco, David H., and Liz all opened the doors and got out. Matt was the last one out of the Suburban. All three of them stood there and looked at him like, 'what the fuck are you doing, dude?' Matt gingerly opened the door of the Suburban and hopped out onto the sidewalk. His first instinct was to run into Redd's, but he would probably never live that down. So instead, he moved quicker than usual into Redd's.

Inside Redd's was like going back in time. The rest of the store looked like the vintage suits in the front window. He still wasn't sure if he was being tricked. There was obviously no one else in the store. It was dirty and dusty and smelled of stale air and cigar smoke.

Liz walked toward the back of the store like she knew something Matt didn't. She got to a particularly awful lime green, wide lapel leisure suit, and pushed it aside. Behind the suit was a well-worn, slightly rusted button the size of a tennis ball on the wall. Liz placed her palm on it and gave it a big push.

With the press of the button, the whole panel door swiveled open. It was a secret door, like in a James Bond movie or something. A secret lair, to be exact. They all stepped inside into a modern, beautiful, and clean tailoring studio. A man about half the size of Franco and David H. appeared. He looked to be in his 70s, white hair, and was a mix of Latino and black, Matt thought. Franco and David H. smiled at Redd as if they were old friends. First Franco, then David H., bent down ever so slightly to give Redd a gentle, big man hug. It surprised

Matt at the tenderness they showed Redd when not less than two minutes ago, they were ready to kill whoever was in the Ford F250. With that, Redd smiled brightly and said, "Who do we have here?"

Liz, who had actually smiled when she got a hug from Redd, explained that Matt was *The Guy*. Redd had a bit of a waddle when he walked over to Matt, probably from years of being on his feet. As Redd walked toward him, Matt could see he had kind and gentle eyes, but looked like he had seen a lot, heard a lot, and kept a lot of secrets. When he got closer, Redd reached out his hand to give Matt a welcome handshake, no hugs for him just yet. By the time Matt and Redd were introducing one another, Franco and David H. positioned themselves by the door, which was kept open to keep a lookout for the Ford F250's possible return. Liz's nose was trained to her phone screen.

Redd grabbed the tape measure that was draped around his neck and said, "Let's get you all taken care of so you can get that new suit, Matt." As he got Matt's measurements, he looked up briefly with those eyes that saw too much and said, "I heard what you did for Mr. Fowler the other day." Then he went back to the job at hand.

"You did? Word gets out quickly around here," Matt said, looking down at Redd while he wrote down some measurements.

Once he finished getting Matt's measurements, Redd instructed Matt to go pick out a fabric for the suit. He pointed Matt towards the racks of fabric bails to pick a couple of his favorites out. Matt quickly glanced at Franco and David H. to see what their suits looked like, color-wise. They were both wearing dark colors. Matt saw the same fabrics in the bails, but he did not want to get the same thing as them. Or did he? Liz must have seen Matt being indecisive, as her foot was tapping, and he could hear her sigh. Matt looked over to her with the 'please help me out here' look.

"I knew it," Liz huffed. "I knew you wouldn't have a fucking clue about what to pick. Have you ever even had a suit?" Matt nodded his head yes, of course he had. Matt had been to prom and a couple of his friends' weddings, but he had never had to pick out the complete kit and caboodle.

Liz moved some bails around until she found a couple options: one dark with a grey undertone, and one dark navy blue. The fabric felt expensive, and Matt was glad he was not paying for it himself.

Matt was appreciating Liz more and more each day. She was a tough read, and Matt had not quite figured out what her place in the organization was. Apparently, she had a wide knowledge base of all things DMF.

Matt could count everything he knew about Liz on one hand: he knew Liz was Fowler's daughter, he knew she would kill with no reaction, he knew she was a cool cat, and last night she told him she was the pseudo-HR department. *One of those things doesn't fit with the other*, Matt thought. There are guys on the Team, the muscle, but what exactly does Liz call herself? What do you call a silent killer and the HR admin, is she a Henchman too? The rest of the Team appeared to have respect for her and treat her like one of the guys, which Matt found interesting because she was a very attractive, fit, bad ass chick. If she wasn't so hard to read and so closed off, or the boss's daughter, Matt thought, one or a few of the guys would certainly be into her.

Like most of the Henchmen, Liz was someone who showed little on the outside, but Matt could sense there was a lot going on inside. Matt sensed she was very isolated, and now that Matt thought of it, he had not seen another woman since he had been at the House.

Matt carried the fabric over to Redd, who nodded approvingly at the choices. Matt smiled nervously at Liz, who returned a slight smile as well. Redd assured Matt that his new hand-tailored, custom suits would be ready by the end of the next week. Matt paused for a second and wondered what his life would be like by the time those two weeks were up. Liz was already giving Redd a goodbye hug when Matt reached out to give Redd a handshake. Franco and David H. had already left the store and were standing on the sidewalk beside the SUV.

Franco and David H. stood outside like secret service agents, both wearing dark shades, with their heads on swivels, almost looking like owls moving their necks side to side. Matt felt presidential for a split second. There was no sign of the F250 as they made their way back to the House.

"How is your wife doing?" Franco asked David H.

"She's big as a house, don't tell her I said that. But damn, I didn't know a body could get that big," David H. said.

"I remember that. Sydney got pretty big too. I had to keep telling her she was beautiful and not fat," Franco said.

"When is she due again? It's coming up soon, right?" Liz chimed.

"Yup, two weeks. But from what we have been told, it could be any day."

He couldn't help but wonder where they came from. So, they do in fact have families? What did they tell their family and friends they did for a living?

It relieved him that the drive back to the House was relatively peaceful, with no guns being drawn. However, Matt was entertained by Franco and David H.'s heated argument about who was the stronger and tougher of the two. Both had stories to tell about themselves and what bad asses they were. Matt knew guys like them who lived in the past and considered all of their notable events as superhuman triumphs, heroisms.

They arrived back at the House right around lunch. There was an incredible spread laid out in the kitchen. A buffet with pasta, salads, sandwiches, and fresh fruits and vegetables. Matt had yet to see who prepared these meals. He had pictured in his head a house-elf, like Dobby from the Harry Potter books, as the person who meal-planned, shopped, and prepared meals like this three times a day, every day. Each meal, it seemed more men came out of nowhere. Matt wondered where they were all day. What were their daily tasks?

CHAPTER 8
ORIENTATION

Schedule/Itinerary for Matt

Tuesday
8:00 a.m. to 11:00 a.m.: *Meeting with Jimmie in his office. His office is down the hall directly across from Fowler's office.*
Meeting intel: Jimmie is my dad's best and oldest friend, and my uncle. He spent 20 years in the Army and was in a special unit that took care of things that kept many people safe without them even knowing. Pretty much an undercover bad ass. Jimmie will give you a rundown of the organization and how you will fit in.

11:00 a.m. to 1:00 p.m.: *Lunch on your own.*
In the kitchen, help yourself.
FYI, cool kids sit at the table closest to the back door.

1:00 p.m. to 3:00 p.m.: *Meet with the DMF legal team, Garrett McCloud, Head Council for DMF.*
Not that scary, just need to go over some paperwork.

Office is on the 2nd floor, the last door on the left, can't miss it.

P.S. You may need more than one of these meetings scheduled, most guys do.

5:00 p.m. to End of Day: *Dinner in the kitchen.*
Grab whatever you want and chill. It has been a long day!

Wednesday

7:30 a.m. to 8:00 a.m.: *Breakfast in the kitchen.*
Did you find the cool kids yet?

8:00 a.m. to 10:00 a.m.: *Field Trip to Pinky's, the DMF gym—not really DMF's gym, but it's where all the guys on the Team go to work out.*
You need to work out again! No more sitting around, Sport.
You will meet Franco and David H. in the garage. Be ready to go hard, they don't play around.

11:00 a.m. to 2:00 p.m.: *Meet with Jimmie to debrief from the meeting yesterday.*
Meet in Jimmie's office like last time.
Ask questions and get clarifications on whatever.

5:00 p.m. to End of Day: *Dinner in the kitchen.*
Whatever else you want, but no leaving alone just yet. If you need to pick up things from a store, just let me know and I can help plan for you to go. You're not a prisoner, if that's what you were thinking.

Liz had set up a schedule for Matt to meet with people so that he could get started with his on-the-job training. Matt's first highly anticipated meeting with Jimmie would be first on the schedule. From what Matt had gathered, Jimmie was high in the ranks and had a close relationship with Fowler. Matt had only seen him a couple of times since his first meeting with him in the hallway. It was actually Jimmie who had helped ease Matt in deciding to stay and not try to make it alone on the outside. Jimmie had wise and soulful eyes that gave off a warm vibe, hypnotizing really.

The meeting with Jimmie was set for 8 a.m. His office was on the main floor, just down the hall from Mr. Fowler's. Before he went, Matt grabbed a quick cup of coffee from the kitchen that was really more like a cafeteria, which made sense considering the size of all the Henchman. These 300-pound guys had to be eating every few hours to keep looking like they did, especially since they were all working out too.

They set the House up like a hotel that served a continental breakfast in the morning. They kept all the cooked food on warmers while the bagels, pastries, and fruit were set on a table, cereal on another, and an awfully expensive coffee bar on another.

Liz had given him a detailed hand out with his scheduled meetings and directions to where the meetings were, who they were with, and what they were going to be about. Matt had a couple of weeks before his suits would be ready for pick up and he would use this time to transition into his new job. It was good to have this transition time to observe, watch, and learn a whole new career and way of life.

Matt had not seen Liz yet this morning. He was hoping he would or that she would at least be around for moral support. The schedule that Matt was given was for a few meetings each day. Liz noted on the schedule that she didn't want him to be more overwhelmed than she thought he already was.

Matt had studied the schedule so much that he memorized it. He was most curious about the meeting with Jimmie, and the most anxious about the meeting with the DMF legal team. Matt followed Liz's directions and headed to Jimmie's office right at 8 a.m. When he approached the door, Matt could hear music coming from the room. It was soft and meditative, no words, just floaty and supernatural. Not what he expected to hear coming from any room in this house. He knocked lightly and heard Jimmie say to enter.

Matt's jaw dropped when he opened the door. After the talk about Jimmie being the security expert, the years in the Army, Matt had a very different vision of what he thought Jimmie's office would look like. He thought there would be a folded American Flag in a frame, medals of honor, strewn about as decorations, and more military swag. Instead, Jimmie's office resembled the spa that Matt's mom and sisters went to.

There was a mini waterfall trickling in the background, an enormous statue of a cross-legged, smiling Buddha, with rocks and crystals scattered around the room. The lighting was dim and almost smoky with a scent of candles. Or was it incense? The oddest thing was a large photograph of two squirrels in a park setting taking up the side wall. *Why squirrels?* Not only was there a photo of squirrels, but there were little squirrel figurines placed throughout the room. Though it was strange and unexpected, Matt felt like he was walking into a Zen Den.

Jimmie's office was in stark contrast to Fowler's. This was like a meditation resort, for fuck's sake. Once again, Matt reminded himself not to have expectations, because this was confusing as hell. At least Matt didn't feel like he was going to pass out or throw up in here like he had in Fowler's office. The scene was too chill for anyone to get anywhere near to feeling enough anxiety or stress to induce a psychotic ramble like he went on the other day. He half expected a masseuse to come around the corner and place cucumbers on his eyes, isn't that what they did at spas? *No wonder my mom and sisters like to go to the spa, I could get used to this.*

Jimmie was sitting on a pillow on the floor, his legs were crossed, and his hands were clasped in the prayer position near his heart. He took one long inhale and exhale, then slowly opened his eyes. With a serene, content expression on his face, Jimmie said, "Welcome home, Matt."

He invited Matt to sit on the extra oversized pillow on the floor. Matt set his coffee on the floor before he attempted to bend and fold into the pillow. He felt awkward drinking coffee, as this was absolutely a more tea-friendly zone.

Jimmie welcomed him to the floor with a heartfelt smile. Strangely, Matt felt especially safe here in this Zen Den. "I wanted to thank you for stopping by to meet with me today. I have been meditating on how to approach you and the most mindful way to explain what your new position here at DMF will look like, at least daily. This is a delicate conversation to have. Before I get started, do you have questions for me?"

Clearing his throat, Matt replied, "I think I would prefer to listen to what you have to say first."

Jimmie smiled tenderly, clearing his throat as he spoke. "Matt, this is a world that most people don't know exists. I have been with Ed, Mr. Fowler, since really, well, the beginning. We grew up together, just a couple of kids coming up on the wrong side of the tracks, you know? He was always the brains of the business, and I was involved in the business's security. We never imagined that it would turn into this; the level, the magnitude, the financial aspects of it. In many circles, we are a global success. With this kind of notoriety, there comes greed, violence, and ruthless, dishonest behavior."

Matt frowned, wondering why it always seemed to come to violence with whatever sort of business DMF was.

Jimmie continued, "The evil of human behavior is what I have studied and have become somewhat of an expert in. Believe me, Matt, I have seen some incredibly horrific and violent scenes play out over the years. If I hadn't learned how to process all of this, I would not have survived. I see you, Matt, as a new version of an ancient business. I bet you have heard the term Henchman, am I correct?"

Matt nodded in agreement with him. *Here we go with that word again.* reaching for his coffee cup, he held onto it like it was one of those stress balls you squeeze when you get anxious, gripped the mug, and took a deep breath of the incense filled air. *Better to squeeze the mug than roll my eyes.*

Jimmie continued on, "When you are the man in charge of an organization with as much power, influence, and wealth as DMF, you become the envy of others with a very large target on your back. What we, myself and the Team, do, is take care of the safety of DMF and Mr. Fowler. Some of our work is not 'above-board.' We skim the line between ethics and law while dealing with things that maybe aren't so ethical and law-abiding. It works for us in a big way. This is where you come in. Well, you, and the Team."

"Um, Jimmie, I have a quick question before you move on," Matt said.

Jimmie smiled with his right-hand palm up extended in Matt's direction, motioning that Matt had the floor to speak.

"The Team? I keep hearing about that the Team. I have only met Franco and David H., and some guy named Snoop, I think. I saw guys in the kitchen, giving a salute to fallen members, but I'm wondering how many there are on the Team?" Matt asked.

"That is a good question, thank you for asking. Right now,

we have sixty on the Team, well, excuse me, I mean fifty-eight. The night at The Basement, we lost two of the Team. That total includes the Henchman who runs errands, and the behind-the-scenes guys," Jimmie noted.

"Behind the scenes? Who and what does that mean?"

"Those are the Team members who aren't expected to be physical in the traditional sense of being a Henchman. It is amusing to look back and know that years ago, there was not a need for someone to monitor the cyber or more technical part of being a Henchman. Now, almost our entire business is run online. We consider ourselves as one Team, but over the years, the guys have come up with some nicknames to help distinguish the two sides. M&M is for the Meat and Muscle side, and CM is for the Cyber Minds side of the Team."

Matt chuckled at the acronyms. "Any new job has a lot of acronyms to learn, thank you for the heads up on that one. So, I did want to ask about that ceremony I saw going on in the kitchen the first night I was here. Is that how a DMF Team member's death is acknowledged? All that happens is there is a toast given? Do they get grief counseling or anything? I assume that could be traumatic?"

"That's it. I have trained my Team to accept life and death as it comes, and not to dwell on either for very long. Living in the present is the best way to keep our minds connected to what we need to do in our jobs."

"Well, that is an interesting take on death. I suppose that mindset is helpful when death is a constant part of your daily routine," Matt said.

"We protect. We anticipate. We target. We collaborate. We serve. We prepare. We fight. These are the laws we as a Team stand behind. I'm just going to say this because I feel a certain level of trust with you, Matt. The other day, you saved the life of my dearest and closest friend. I told you that family is the

84

most important thing in the world. Ed, well, he couldn't be closer to me if he was a biological brother. I consider him my brother through and through, and he feels the same way about me," Jimmie said.

"Sometimes you are in the right place at the right time, I guess. Everything happens for a reason, right?" Matt replied, unsure of what Jimmie wanted him to say.

"That is a wise statement to make Matt, I appreciate your depth. I don't know what your beliefs are as far as spirituality, but I believe that there are no accidents, like you just alluded to. This is the troublesome part to speak about to some. It is a part you have seen with your own eyes." Jimmie sighed. "Here it goes, Matt, we sometimes kill and hurt people that get in our way and try to take what is rightfully ours. I don't mean to be blunt, but that is what we do. I can trust you to tell you this. You were in a situation the other day that gave you a brief glimpse into a day in the life of being on the Team. Are you following me? Do you understand what I am saying to you?"

Matt looked at Jimmie and said, "I'm in, with whatever you need me to do, I'm in."

When he was younger, Matt always had a tribe, a place where he knew he fit in. Ever since Matt stopped playing sports and stopped being an athlete, he had felt lost, and like he was looking for a home other than nights at The Basement. Matt had not felt a connection to his life, and he saw this job as just what he needed to be part of something larger than him again. Except for killing people, Matt was all in. Matt still wanted to know more of what other duties are included as part of being a member of the Team. On a side note, what options did he really have, anyway?

The illegal part? Matt wondered what that would be like. But hell, Matt had already killed someone and not thought twice about it. How was he able to do that? What Matt was more concerned about was where did that killer instinct come from? How was he able to kill another human with no hesitation and no afterthoughts? Matt tried to summon up the inevitable guilt you should have when you take another's life. It wasn't like Matt walked up to a total stranger and blew his brains out. Matt was on the defense when he shot the man. It was a kill-or-be-killed deal. He would have died if he hadn't pulled the trigger that day. That is what they must call a justifiable homicide.

What Matt found most perplexing about this whole new scene was that extraordinarily, Matt not only felt at home, but he felt safe. It did not occur to him to even wonder if he would be in some sort of legal trouble or that law enforcement would come after him. Matt had a deep sense of knowing that if anyone would come investigating either the shooting at The Basement or the two dead bodies in his condo, things would be taken care of, most likely without him even knowing about it.

"Matt, you look like you are deep in thought. I would love to continue the conversation and answer your questions, but I do have another meeting planned and I know Liz has you on a tight schedule. We will have opportunities to meet as needed."

"You're right, I do. I want to wrap my head around what being called a Henchman will be like. Before I go, I do have a question. How are my family and friends getting on?" Matt asked.

"Your family and friends are doing well; we have had no issues or concerns. The OT is so unpredictable, but we are ready for whatever action he takes. They are safe. I think doing some on-the-job training will provide you with a much better picture of what a Henchman does on the Team. I will look into getting that set up for you," Jimmie added.

"I do worry about everyone that was close to me. Thank

you for looking out for them. It is so important to me. Some on-the-job training would do the trick. I'm looking forward to it."

"I am delighted that you have agreed to become part of the DMF Team. I think you will find that this is a wonderful place to call home. I almost forgot: I know your phone was misplaced. I have a replacement for you," Jimmie said, offering him a brand-new iPhone.

"I must sound like a classic millennial, but I hadn't realized how much I missed holding a phone in my hand until just now. Thank you," Matt said.

"You're welcome. Just a few rules that go with the phone, for now anyway. We ask that you limit your calls and texts to just family and friends at a minimum for now. Ease back into the world slowly. No posting on social media. You good with that?" Jimmie asked.

"I sure am, no worries. It is just so great to have a phone again. I got used to not having one, but I also didn't like it much," Matt replied. "Just to be clear, what can I say to people? I am sure they want to know what the hell is going on with me."

"Great question. We've already begun tying up your loose ends, putting your condo on the market, putting your belongings in storage, selling your truck, all that. So no one in your life gets suspicious or worried, you need to let them know that you needed to take some time to yourself after what happened at The Basement. It was traumatizing, and you need some space to reflect on your life, career, and relationships. Leave it at that, plain and simple," Jimmie said.

Matt hadn't really considered what had happened to all his stuff. But it didn't really feel like his stuff anymore anyway, he supposed. That condo, that truck, his old junk, all that belonged to the old Matt. This new Matt had pretty much nothing to his name, and in a way, it was kind of freeing. "Got it. It's not too far from what the actual truth is anyway!"

After the meeting, Matt sat at the bottom of the stairs. Using his new phone, Matt tried to complete his end of 'tying up the loose ends,' as Jimmie had instructed. The first thing he did was let his family and a few close friends know that he needed to reassess his life and make some changes, do some random traveling. He officially sent an email resignation to his job, which made him happier than he expected.

Standing Catherine up had been weighing heavily on him. Texting Jimmie for permission first, he got the go ahead to text her a 'it's me, not you' text with the hopes of mending any animosity he may have created. He was expecting a middle finger, fuck you emoji back from her, instead he got a, "sure whatever you say," reply back.

The last time he saw his friends from The Basement, they had thrown an injured Paul into an SUV. Again, with Jimmie's permission, he texted the guys who had been with him that night.

Danny replied almost immediately. "Paul is fine, but what the fuck happened to you? We have been stressing out about you man!"

Matt smiled at the response, relieved Paul was ok, but missing his old friends. Matt told Danny and the guys the same response he told his family. The reactions from the rest of The Basement guys were varied in response. Mike responded, "Good for you, I wish I could do shit like that, just walk away," while Paul joked, "Who are you running away from?" Jonesy asked, "Did the Suits scare you off?" Matt could hear Jonesy's nasally giggle in his ears reading that. Danny assured him, "You aren't missing much here, we have nowhere to go play now anyway." Matt hoped The Basement wouldn't be out of business for long, for all his friends' sake.

Convincing his mom that nothing was wrong was the more difficult conversation. She knew he wasn't being straight with her, and knew that Matt taking 'me time,' was a load of shit. She believed him when he told her he was safe and that perhaps one day, he could give her more details.

What would life look like after DMF? Matt thought.

CHAPTER 9
LUNCH ON YOUR OWN

Matt needed a minute to himself before he headed to lunch on his own. He was trying to keep to the schedule Liz had given him, but after that meeting, he needed time to think in solitude, without the constant distraction of trying to figure out who was doing what and why. This was a lot to take in, and the changes Matt was being forced to make to his entire life were enormous. Besides, he didn't have much of an appetite.

Too many emotions were racing through his heart and soul for him to focus attention on just one. In a matter of a few days, he had gone from a mild-mannered insurance sales agent and proud owner of a nice little two-story brick condo to a murderer, a fugitive, a more-or-less homeless guy, and a modern-day gangster, or was he part of a mob now? He was still not clear about where a Henchman fits in the continuum of a life of crime. Sitting under house arrest, not being able to make proper goodbyes, and just felt off. Emotionally, there was some resentment, but also, he felt conflicted because there was excitement. How could that be? How many other unknown parts of him were left to discover.

Taking a moment in the backyard, Matt noticed that the front of the house was in stark contrast to the back. The front of the house was left to more or less blend in with the rest of the low-income, inner-city landscape. The backyard mimicked Jimmie's office. It was professionally landscaped with meticulous detail placed on the various flower beds. There were benches to sit or meditate on. The large trees provided shade and a cocoon-like feel. This was an ideal place for Matt to process all the information he had heard, his own actions, and his future. He suddenly felt homesick. He wasn't sure what he was homesick for, but he longed to hop in his car and take off and go to the gym on his own, or to even just go to the drive-through at Taco Bell. *Boy, could I use some Taco Bell.* After some more digestion of his current situation, Matt would give it a shot, try it out for a few months, or at least until they made him aware that they had contained the danger to him and his family. In reality, he really couldn't leave now, but once the threat was removed, he would reassess. That realization made him feel better, and less trapped.

He was feeling revitalized after connecting with a few people from his past and had his appetite back when he saw Liz coming his way. She had a tray with some of those fantastic sandwiches on it. *Damn, that looks good.*

"I guess you haven't found where the cool kids sit yet," she said. Matt gave her a half-smile and she sat beside him.

"No, I haven't even figured out who the cool kids are, much less where they sit. I do know that I'm not anywhere close to making that list," Matt replied.

"I'll give you a hint. The cool ones sit at the tables nearest the hallway. The M&M Team. They are usually the loudest, and most immature. They will be the ones you notice first. The not so cool kids are the ones from the CM Team, the IT nerds. More your speed I would think at this point."

"Thanks, I guess. I haven't seen any of the CM Team yet, I don't think. They must fly under the radar in this place. I'm having flashbacks to high school, the jocks versus the nerds all over again."

Liz laughed. "Let me guess what group you belonged to."

"It wasn't like that, really. I was fairly neutral in high school believe it or not. I was a jock, but I had all sorts of friends. Anyway, I will start to scope out the cool kids and see what happens with that. But for now, this is some pretty intense shit I'm dealing with. I will figure it out, I just needed a minute alone. Thank you for bringing me some food though, I suddenly got hungry."

"What makes you think this is for you?" she asked. Matt cringed at his assumption, but Liz smiled and winked, then she handed Matt the plate of sandwiches.

Matt wondered what in the fuck he would do without Liz.

———

After lunch, Matt pulled the schedule out of the notebook Liz had given him to look at, despite knowing full well that he was to meet with the DMF legal team next. He had never met with an attorney in his life, he had never needed one. Matt decided he would just listen to what the attorney had to say and go from there. Instinctively, he did his well-tuned deep breathing. He hadn't had to use those breathing techniques in the last few days, which was a pleasant change of pace for him.

Garrett McCloud, Attorney at Law, was the name on the schedule. *What kind of character will he end up being? Maybe he will be a guy in a Hawaiian shirt and flip-flops, or maybe a guy in a Dr. Strange cape, who the hell knows?* This was becoming a sort of game for Matt. He wasn't as anxious as before and was learning to not be surprised at the new characters he would meet on his journey to becoming one of the Team at DMF.

Matt found his way to the office on the second floor, the last door on the right. The hall took a slight turn to the right, so the room wasn't visible if you were to look for it at first glance. Near the door in the hallway, there was a small table with a lamp on it beside a chair. The door to the office was closed and like Liz had said, you couldn't miss it. It was a beautiful oak door that looked like it would fit in an old gentleman's club. The clubs in New England that were fashioned around men coming in and socializing with one another, with very high-end furnishings and a lot of old money in the air.

Matt went to sit in the chair, but then wondered if he should knock on the door to alert Mr. McCloud that he was there. Not sure of the right move, Matt decided that the door being shut meant he should wait, and not knock, probably the reason for the random chair in the hallway.

Matt walked back over to the random chair in the hall and took a seat. He would wait until he was called into the office. He fidgeted and bounced his knee up and down with some anxiety. Matt thought it would be nice when he wasn't so new to every single experience, when there was some more routine. Matt checked his phone to see the time and noticed it was 1:00 p.m., and with that, the large oak door opened.

Standing in the doorway was a man who looked like he walked right out of Harvard Law Review. *Impeccable*, was the first thought Matt had. He didn't think he had ever seen a man look that put together. McCloud motioned for Matt to come into the office. Matt stumbled to his feet and walked toward the open door, nodding to his new attorney on the way into the office.

The office mirrored the hallway furnishings. Wood paneling, dark plush rugs over the top of glossy dark hardwood floors, loads of bookshelves with the books you don't read, but are just for show, and another enormous mahogany desk and matching conference table. Matt took in the office and shook his head a bit with the grandeur of it all.

McCloud went straight to his desk and motioned for Matt to sit in one of the leather chairs across from him. He was an interesting looking man, not much older than Matt. He was tall, slim build, which made the perfect frame to wear suits. Matt wondered if he had his suits made at Redd's as well. He could have sworn Garrett's nails were manicured and that he must shave twice a day with the baby soft skin he had. His hair was slicked back, and the smell of expensive aftershave permeated the office. McCloud sat back in his chair, still not having said a word, and just stared at Matt, making him turn around to see if there might be someone else in the room.

Matt nervously smiled and noticed that his knee was bouncing up and down again. He heard his mom's words in his head again, "Don't fidget, Matty."

Matt broke the silence and said, "Good afternoon Mr. McCloud, I'm Matt Clemons, I think Liz set up this meeting." Matt felt a little awkward calling him Mr. as he was so close in age to Matt himself. This guy seemed to command 'Mr.' in front of his name, so Matt went with it.

McCloud smiled at Matt's obvious nerves, then in a frat boy sort of way, he burst out, "Hey Mattster! I have been waiting to meet you, you badass! Did you like the stare down I gave you? I have been practicing my intimidating look! Did it work? Did you feel intimidated, just a little?"

Once again, Matt was completely thrown for a loop. The voice didn't match the body or the office one bit. Matt just laughed.

Before Matt could reply, Garrett continued, "Throw me a bone, man! Do you like my digs? Fucking awesome, am I right? I had Liz research what a fancy, high-end, east coast law office looks like. I think she did a pretty good job! Wow, so cool to meet you."

"Yeah man, this is a sweet office. It certainly gives you the impression that you take your job seriously. First impressions are everything, right?"

"Couldn't agree more, bro," Garrett said, then turning his voice more professional, he continued, "Now, tell me everything about what happened in The Basement."

"I'm assuming there probably isn't much you haven't already heard about The Basement," Matt said.

"Come on dude, yes, of course I heard different versions of how shit went down, but I want to hear it from the source!"

Nervously shifting in his chair Matt said, "I don't know what to say. I just happened to be there when Mr. Fowler needed me, I guess. It was over really quick, and it was just pretty fucked up."

"But you got to shoot some asshole, right? What was that like? I don't get to see action like that with my job here. I bet it was a rush, am I right?"

"A rush, that's not how I would describe it exactly. It was more of a survival instinct kicking in. If I hadn't pulled the trigger, he would have. It has been surreal to think back to that night."

"I bet I would have done the same thing. Act first, and think about it later, good motto to live by in this line of work," Garrett said.

He continued in his frat boy lingo, which included lots of 'dudes,' and 'no fucking ways,' bringing Matt back to his college days and making him feel right at home for the first time in a long time. Matt thought he needed to hear the backstory on this character. *This is the guy DMF entrusted to represent them, to represent me? How is that possible?*

Matt cautiously asked, "So, Garrett, where did you go to

law school, and how long have you been practicing?" Garrett's face dropped back into the imitating scowl he mustered up when they first sat down.

"For your information, Matt, I am a graduate from Baylor Law, and I passed the bar on the first try, I may add. I'm just having some fun here! Law school kicked my ass for sure, just making up for lost time. I am part of the Fowler family. Did cousin Liz tell you that Mr. Fowler is my uncle? Don't look at me like that dude, I worked hard and had to meet certain standards to be hired for this. I take this job and who I represent seriously." The frat boy look disappeared when he spoke of how serious he was about keeping things running smoothly at DMF.

"I'm sorry, I meant no disrespect. Since I got here, I have just met so many new people and had a lot of new experiences. I didn't mean to imply that you were anything less than professional. I'm just putting all of the pieces of the puzzle together. I'm sure you do a great job representing DMF when they need your expertise," Matt said.

With his frat boy persona completely vanished, Garrett began, "Apology accepted, I'm sure you have had a lot to process the last few days. Now, let's get down to business, Matt. I need to make sure you understand a couple of things. First, let's start with the events that took place at The Basement. Things were taken care of there. You probably hear that term, 'things have been taken care of,' a lot. It's a fan favorite here for the guys on the Team. Let me translate that for you, this means, 'ask no more questions, it's all good.' I also needed to double check you didn't tell anyone else the address other than the convenience store clerk, correct?"

"The who?" Matt asked. He had blocked that part of the crazy night out until that moment.

"The clerk who you got directions from the night of The Basement massacre," Garrett repeated back.

"He gave me directions from his Google maps app on his phone. You didn't hurt him or anything, did you?" Matt asked.

"Why would we hurt him? We're not complete savages, Matt, no need to do that. He willingly signed the NDA," Garrett said. "Our address is almost never spoken out loud, and the clerk literally had blood on his hands, thanks to you touching his phone. When things like this happen, thank God it's rare, we need to reach out to the people who were innocently brought into the fringe of DMF. He is fine, not to worry Matt."

"I guess I understand that, and the, you know, killing, that is taken care of?" Matt asked.

Matt must have looked guilty of something as he slid down in his seat and dropped his head. He never thought that he would have a conversation with an attorney about him killing a man. He thought he had come to terms with it, since he would be dead if he hadn't killed the guy first. Who was he anyway, the guy he killed? Did he have a family? After all, Henchmen were real people too.

Garrett looked at Matt like he was speaking a foreign language, "Are you fucking serious? What don't you get about being here? I told you everything has been taken care of, I told you that means everything is all good. Trust me. I think you need to speak with Fowler or Jimmie again. Get a grip, it's fine," Garrett snapped.

"Look, I know you told me that things are taken care of, but I still have questions I think I am owed answers too. There are a couple of things I would like to understand better. The main one being, am I going to jail for any of these things? Have these 'things' been taken care of, as far as me being a fugitive?"

With his attorney face on, Garrett spoke in a calm, slowed

down version of himself, "Matt, as long as you are in good standing with DMF, you will never have to worry about things like that. Well, I should say, never say never, but it's pretty close to never."

"Never have to worry? That is a fairly broad statement to make. Can you tell me what being in good standing looks like? How will I know when I am not in good standing?"

"Do I look like someone you can trust? Does it look like people here are worried about going to jail? I don't think so. As far as knowing you are not in good standing with DMF, well, let's just say it wouldn't take you long to figure that out."

"Ok, I guess you look trustworthy. And I have been here long enough to realize what you mean about falling out of good standing with DMF."

Garrett had moved on to reading notes he had made on his phone. He was silently saying, check, check, check to himself as he read off the list of things to discuss with Matt. "Now onto the scene at your condo. I know it wasn't you who wasted those two, but since it was in your house, you may wonder what is going on with your place. As for the bodies, they have been taken care of." Garrett gave Matt a pointed look that said, 'don't ask questions.' "I see that you already signed some papers to get your condo listed for sale, is that correct?"

"Yes, I did that a few days ago," Matt replied.

"Perfect. Things are getting all tidied up quicker than I thought they would be. I'm sure you are wondering what happens to the proceeds of the sale of the condo."

"I hadn't thought about it, but now that you bring it up, yes. Where will my money end up? I still don't have access to my credit cards or bank."

"And I am sure you understand that for security reasons, there needs to be no way to track you. Plus the fact that you aren't going anywhere anytime soon, are you? DMF will hold all of your earnings until such a time when you can safely have access to your funds."

"Ok, I guess. What choice do I have at this point?"

Nodding in agreement, Garrett finished going down his list and taking notes, set his phone down, and looked Matt in the eye. "You may wonder if there is more to the legal team than just yours truly. Well, that is a 'duh' question. Do you really think that they would let me loose with a company this size with as many complexities as DMF holds? I am what they call the in-house counsel. My office is here in the House, so I can take care of the day-to-day legal needs. Off-site, there is an entire legal team dedicated to DMF. The legal team comprises some seasoned legal minds. They take care of the larger issues and situations, all while keeping yours truly in the loop. I know what I need to know, which ends up being a lot. You catch my drift?"

Matt understood Garrett may be a good guy to get to know better. He could be the one person, other than Liz, who could help Matt navigate this new and unique life.

"So, it sounds like the work that the Team does means that there needs to be legal counsel available regularly? I just want to make sure I understand when I need to let you know that something happened that would be considered a little dicey—in a legal sense, I mean," Matt said.

"Hey look, the deal around here is that I am always, somehow or another, informed when such 'dicey' things come up. It would be cool to tighten up the process of how I hear shit too." With a dramatic eye roll and heavy sigh, he said, "The way I usually find out information is by standing in line waiting for a coffee downstairs in the kitchen."

"So, what is the best way to get this information to you then?" Matt asked. *When my ass is on the line, for whatever reason, I want the guy who I know can 'take care of things' to be in the know.*

Garrett sat back and pondered Matt's question. Garrett opened his mouth to speak a couple of times before anything came out. *It must be a rare occasion that Garrett is at a loss for words.*

"You know what, Matt? You know that no one here has ever asked me a question like that? There is not a formal process for any of the information to be passed to me. When I actually think about that, it is not cool. Don't get me wrong, I love working here for DMF and my uncle, but I have to say something that I hope doesn't get repeated."

"Well, sure, I won't say anything to anyone, it's not like I even know anyone yet to tell secrets to," Matt assured him.

Garrett continued as if Matt had said nothing, "You are an educated man, just like me. None of these people, none of them, have an education past high school. Now, that doesn't make them bad people, just not book-smart people. There are all types of intelligence that people possess. Running a business is not in their wheelhouse. I guess what I'm saying is that we all have strengths, things we are good at. They run this business, this House, and the Team with absolutely no policies or procedures in place. It is all word of mouth, like 'hey did you hear about what Liz did last night' kind of stuff."

Matt listened to Garrett with a heightened interest. Developing business plans was something he learned in college and was good at. He could formulate good, easy-to-implement plans that would have a significant impact on the bottom line of the company. He had done the business plan for Danny and Paul at The Basement to help get their liquor license and eventually get the bar up and running. The original version of The Basement didn't have the bar, just the gaming cubicles. As Matt had predicted, the profits far outweighed the risk in spending the money to get the bar side of The Basement established. The revenue nearly doubled the first few months and continued to bring in more business than they had ever dreamed of. The best thing about him helping out was that Danny and Paul agreed to 'pay' him by offering free online game play for life. If having a formalized business plan could do that much for a small place like The Basement, it would be incredible to see what it would do for a place the size of DMF.

"That is a tough spot to be in. I would love to work with you to get things up to speed here. I'm not that busy right now since I haven't started my job on the Team just yet. I have another meeting with Jimmie tomorrow, maybe I can run it past him to see if I could spend some time setting up policy and procedures for the in-house legal team?"

"Dude, that would be outstanding. I think I know what the answer will be though. Jimmie will not want you to drift away from learning your job within the Team so soon. You're just a Henchman, they won't let you make any changes just yet. I mean, you can ask, but I have known Jimmie a long time, and I know how he sees things. Shit, he wanted me to start with the Team as well! I told him no fucking way, but in a professional sense. Jimmie is a firm believer in working your way to the top."

Matt heard this and was a little disappointed. He was also grateful for the insight on how Jimmie rolled, it's always good to have that sort of knowledge at the beginning. On the bright side, Matt briefly thought about a career here at DMF. As with any new job, it was up to him to look for opportunities for growth and advancement. He started at Tailgaters as an entry level agent, with no other insurance experience, only having just passed the licensing exam. It took a few months for him to get the hang of it, and he ended up being promoted twice in the year there. The second promotion came after he had been able to make changes to efficiency of the claims being processed. It relieved him to know that if he stayed long term, he wouldn't be stuck on the Henchman Team indefinitely.

Garrett looked up from his phone and said, "Well dude, it's been good meeting you, but I'm off to hear some of the latest gossip. This helps me stay in step with the day-to-day shit that goes on here. You know where to find me if you need anything, or if Jimmie gives you the thumbs up to come work with me." With that, Garrett stood up in a very lawyer-ish way, reached out to shake Matt's hand, and offered him the door.

Matt stood in the hallway for a second before making his way down to his room. He pulled out the schedule Liz gave him; perfect, he had nothing going on until tomorrow. The next morning would be his first trip to the gym with David H. and Franco, which was somewhat terrifying. They hadn't exactly made him feel welcome.

CHAPTER 10
DINNER AND LARGE AMOUNTS OF TESTOSTERONE

MATT GOT to his room and shut the door. *Finally, I'm alone.* Much needed time to sit with his thoughts and process the conversations with Jimmie and Garrett. He laid down on his king-sized bed and sat straight up, looking around and noticed that it was made up. Having a maid come in and make your bed, could it get any better? Definitely a huge perk of living in the House. Matt thought he could get used to this . . . He drifted off to sleep almost as soon as his head hit the pillow.

Being able to fall asleep in the middle of the day, Matt knew he was relaxing into his new life and not in flight or fight response one hundred percent of the time.

When he woke from his nap, he wasn't even startled, and knew exactly where he was, which was a positive direction for him to take.

He sat up, scratching his head. He felt as if he had slept for twelve hours straight. Now what? He was hungry again, and it was dinner time, according to Liz's schedule. Matt's insides flipped and flopped a little when he thought of walking into the kitchen alone, the new kid, with no friends and not sure where to sit. His hunger, however, would not let him wimp out and not put some food in his belly. He doubted Garrett ate with the Team in the kitchen, or that he even lived in the House.

Matt went into his bathroom and looked at himself in the mirror. He looked a lot more like himself than the first time he had seen his reflection in the House. He had been a hot mess when he took that first look, with dried, caked-on blood and the look of shock mixed with horror. *Man, that seems like a lifetime ago. This is the new you, Matt. Make this work, make this work,* was the mantra he used while walking down the stairs to the kitchen.

Holy shit. Matt had seen some big guys in a room before. When he played college ball, the team always had a pre-game meal together the night before a game, but this was an impressive sight to see. Not only was there an incredible amount of food on the buffet, but the size of each of the twelve men there was impressive.

By the looks of these guys, they were pretty much meat and potato guys, definitely on the M&M team, and definitely go-back-for-seconds (or thirds) guys. They must have the groceries delivered more than once a week and by the truckload.

Off we go. Matt kept an eye out for Liz. She was nowhere to be seen. *Shit, now what?*

"Make this work, make this work, make this work," he muttered as he strode semi-confidently to the one end of the buffet table where the plates and utensils were located. He figured that if he took an extraordinary length of time gathering up a plate of food, when he turned around, there would be an empty seat. That was completely wishful thinking, because not only was the room still full and crowded by the time he turned around, but it was also dead silent, with all eyes on him.

One of the seated Henchman spoke, "Looks like College Boy wants to sit and eat with us. Maybe if he followed the

House rules, he would know that dinner started ten minutes ago."

There went the flip-flop in the belly, again. Matt's face went from pale as a ghost, to bright red with embarrassment. There were no open seats. He turned and fumbled one last time and went to take his plate of food up to his room to eat. What other choice did he have? He felt sick and like he had lost his appetite. What the fuck? How is this supposed to work, what fucking kind of team is this? He was the captain of his teams throughout high school and for two years in college. This was not cool, and definitely not how you welcomed a new team member.

Fuck this, I may just try to do this on my own. Who needs this bullshit? I'm going to tell Jimmie to forget the training, or whatever the fuck this is supposed to be, I'm out. I don't want to be part of something like this. I mean, what did I do to deserve this? I'm on their side, right? Matt was so pissed he was close to telling the entire room what dumb pieces of shit they were.

"Bye College Boy, have a good night," sniggered the Henchman from his table.

As Matt was leaving the kitchen, he left so fast that he didn't realize there was anyone else in the hall. Jimmie was standing in the middle of the hallway with his arms crossed over his chest. He looked like a drill sergeant getting ready to bark out orders at his unit.

"Where are you headed, Matt? You don't want to eat with the rest of the Team?" Jimmie asked with his head cocked to one side. Matt was not in the mood for a Jimmie lecture. "In case that was left off your schedule, we all eat together. Why don't you come back in and find yourself a seat?"

"Yeah, no, I'm good. Dinner was on the schedule, but it did not mention that it was a Team dinner. There are no seats, and I wasn't exactly given a warm welcome by your Team. In my world, that is not how you treat team members. That is not how you build trust with each other. You seriously expect me to go out and work with these guys and lay my fucking life on the line, and they either won't even acknowledge me at the dinner table, or they act like assholes? I really don't think so. I would rather take my chances alone out there. What would be the fucking difference at this point? I'm all alone anyway! This really is bullshit," Matt exploded, not even pausing to take a breath.

Jimmie was quiet while Matt ranted, then he said, "Matt, come with me to my office, please. I would like to continue this conversation there." Jimmie looked at Matt like this was not an option, but an order being given. Matt wasn't sure if he had a choice or not, but he figured that going would be the best choice.

Walking to the office, Matt thought about how he was going to tell Jimmie, *Thanks for the opportunity, but I'll take my chances on the outside.* Matt felt like a punch in the gut as he thought about going back to his old life. *Holy shit. I have no house, no car, no job, nothing left.* He could move back home with his mom, and he could find a job and get a new car. He had to remind himself that he was not trapped here; he had options. Though moving back in with his mom wasn't the ideal situation, it was preferable to staying here and being treated like a fucking virus, that was not an option that he would pick. Matt followed Jimmie to his office. It had the same Zen Den vibe as it was the first time he met with Jimmie. That kind helped to dissipate Matt's obvious anger. He sat on a chair this time, not a pillow on the floor. Jimmie took a minute before he spoke.

"Matt, I'm surprised at your reaction to this evening's dinner. I don't think we have ever had a situation like this. In the brief time I have had to reflect on this, I think I understand where the confusion and the hurt feelings came from. Please know that I am not making excuses, but rather explaining their behavior. Keep in mind that I am open to hearing what you think would be a better, more enthusiastic way of welcoming a new guy to the Team. Would it be alright with you if first I shared my view on this?"

Matt wanted to slam his plate of food on the desk, but his manners got the best of him. He was not raised to throw temper tantrums. Pouting was different. His mom used to say he was the easiest kid to raise except for his bouts of pouting. He could put a sneer on his face and look completely uninterested if he tried hard enough.

"Sure whatever, I will sit and listen, not like I have anything else to do," Matt huffed under his breath.

"Thank you, Matt, I really appreciate you having some patience and grace with me. My first thought was this: we have never hired someone who was not already associated with another person on the Team. All the referrals for the positions have been from internal Team members. I'm uncertain that they know how to react or respond to having a new guy who is new to everyone. That is theory one.

"Theory two is this: have you really looked at these guys, sized them up, tried to figure out who they are? If you had, you would recognize that they are as close to a modern-day Neanderthal as you can get. They lack the proper social cues to make it in the traditional sense, they were the boys who were constantly being kicked out of class, in detention, getting in fights, the bullies, the high school dropouts, the 'bad seeds.' They have no way to relate to you. They know what you did at The Basement, they know you are smart and educated, and that really, you are *not* one of them. Maybe they think you have a chip on your shoulder, that you are better than them. You being the stereotypical jock who was unkind to them, made fun of them over the years. Guys like you are not who they have ever befriended or worked with before. Is this making any sense? Again, no excuses, but offering some food for thought."

Matt felt like a shit. First, he had no way of knowing about the hiring pattern of the members of the DMF Team all being from internal references. Still, it was no excuse for them being total assholes to the new guys, but it made a little more sense to him. Jimmie's second theory made complete sense. Matt knew exactly who these guys were in high school. The thing these guys didn't know about Matt was that he wasn't that elitist, super prick of a jock. Matt knew that there was this social stigma that always seems to portray high school jocks in the absolute worst light. Those jocks were always uncaring, egotistical SOBs that only had friends exactly like themselves. Maybe there was a token 'outsider' that they brought in to make them look not as pious. Matt was not that guy. He had many friends in high school, despite being the 'big man' on campus. He was in the local paper after every football game. Everyone knew him, he never had to look for a table to sit at for lunch, even voted as having the 'Best Eyes' in the senior class. There were no strangers to Matt in high school. But now he knew what the guys on the DMF Team were used to expecting from guys like him. He really felt bad now, those guys were probably treated like fucking dirt, laughed at, made fun of, and ignored.

Jimmie added, "Matt, I know you are a good guy. Problem is, they don't know that."

"One thing that my mom taught all of us kids is to not point fingers and not to blame," Matt said, "I will take some personal responsibility for my reaction. I didn't realize I had a part in this, but now I see I do. I get what I have to do now, and I will figure out a way to let them know who I am and what I'm about. I have to say Jimmie, I was this close to walking out the door. I was really disgusted and appalled at their treatment of me. Thank you for putting it into perspective. I don't think I would have been able to do that. Do you mind if I eat my dinner here and start fresh again tomorrow? I have a gym session with Franco and David H. in the morning."

Jimmie nodded. "Of course. And Matt, the more I interact with you, the more I see possibilities and potential. I'm not sure what that looks like for your future with DMF, but man, do I feel your potential in my bones. The last thing I want you to reflect on is that the DMF security Team runs like a well-tuned machine. Think of it as each member has an integral part in the Team machine. The gears need to be working in sync with the whole. Does that make sense to you, can you visualize that?"

Matt closed his eyes briefly and pictured a machine with moving parts, all working off the movement of the other parts to make the entire function optimally.

"Makes sense to me. I'll just need to see what part of the machine I end up being," Matt replied.

———

Matt set his alarm for the first time since being in the House. He slept restlessly after his talk with Jimmie, thinking about how to navigate the rest of the Team. He did not want to be late for his morning gym session with Franco and David H. He was eager for a couple reasons. One being that he was going to try a new tactic in his approach to the guys to be more forthcoming and aware of their preconceived ideas of the stereotypical asshole jock they assumed he was. Another reason was he hadn't lifted weights in months. He also knew that these guys, based on looks alone, were in better shape than him, and they were going to make sure Matt knew damn good and well they were in better shape than him. Matt was planning for it to be an all-out ass whopping.

He went down to the kitchen with the thought of just grabbing something light, and no coffee, which was a huge bummer, because he enjoyed the coffee in the morning. He usually would take a cup outside and enjoy nature. Now, looking back on that, he decided would have to put a stop to the ritual. It might look bad to the other guys, like he was a loner or too cool to be inside with the guys.

Matt walked into the kitchen with some hesitation, sort of peeking his head around the corner to see who was there already. During breakfast, people would come and go, it wasn't like dinner where everyone ate together. Still, Matt planned to eat in the kitchen to cover all his bases. Getting the Team to accept him was a new project for him, so looking at all angles of his behavior was a must.

Thankfully, no one from the Team was there, but he got to see the back of the chef/magician who was the creator of all the wonderful meals prepared. He wanted to shout out to them to turn around. He was still sure this was a house-elf that could have these fantastic meals out together all day every day. Matt finished his toast, and his belly did the flip-flop again. In walked Franco and David H. They both had their game faces on and didn't look like they were morning people.

Matt watched them grab some fruit and bars as they walked right out the door. They still had not acknowledged his presence. Matt got up from the table in a flash and took off after them. They had already reached the same black Suburban that they drove in on the first trip to Redd's by the time Matt got out the back door. He scrambled to barely grab open the door and hop in before they took off.

Matt felt the most awkward he had possibly in his entire life. This was game time, the moment to redeem himself with these guys. Neither one had said a word to him or each other. There was music on when they got in the car, something Matt didn't recognize, a heavy metal song from the 80s, the kind that you just automatically start bobbing your head up and down to. Matt just could not think of anything to say, so he sat in silence on the way to the gym.

The gym was a short drive from the House in the opposite direction of Redd's. Matt had never been to this side of town before and was not familiar with the gym. By the name, he was certain that it was not a chain franchise. Matt did a double take to make sure they were actually walking into the right place, because when he looked up and saw 'Pinky's' as the name of the gym, he just grinned. *Who calls their gym Pinky's?* Matt almost said out loud, then he remembered he needed to show them he was not a judgy person. Instead, he said casually, "Hey, I just wanted to say thanks for the lift here, I appreciate being able to get out of the house. I guess you guys know I'm stuck there for a bit. It's nice to be out in the world again."

Franco and David H. both turned and looked at each other with the 'are you fucking kidding me' look. "You sure about that College Boy?" Franco turned to say. "We're going to see what you're made of."

"From what I can see, he looks like an out of shape gamer, this should be fun. Look, he's already shaking in his boots!" David H. sneered at Matt.

Great, they are going to kick my ass, but they also spoke to me, so that's a start, and I will take it!

Pinky's was at the end of a strip mall and was just like any other gym Matt had ever been in. It was sectioned off into cardio, free weights, machines, and a place to stretch pre or post workout. Nothing fancy, but it got the job done. It was certainly not one of the huge chain gyms with thousands of square feet with every piece of equipment a person could ever need to work out, filled with lots of pretty, perfect people. Matt wondered if there was a real Pinky, and if so, was it a girl or a guy?

He didn't have to wonder long, because as they walked in the door and flashed their keychain membership cards on the scanner, a woman who looked about sixty, and incredibly fit, with very blonde hair, long pink fingernails, and matching pink lipstick came over to say hello to Franco and David H. Matt felt like he was in a video game, adding another character to his collection. The name embroidered on her shirt was Pinky, with a heart at the end of her name.

"Well, hello gentleman! What a pleasure to see you on this fine day. I trust that all is well with you and Eddie? How is my little sweet Eddie doing? I've been meaning to come and pay him a visit, I just wasn't sure he could have visitors," she roared.

"Fowler is doing well," Franco responded shortly.

"Oh, good! And I see you have a guest with you today. Is he going to be a permanent guest? Is this someone I need to get a card for?"

"Yes, ma'am," Matt spoke up.

"Sweetie, come over here and I can get you set up so next time you can come alone, and not with these two big muscle heads," she said. She spoke a million miles a minute as she guided Matt over to the front desk. She turned back to Franco and David H. "This is *the guy*, right?"

"Yep," Franco replied. "He is going to be working with us from now on. It wasn't my idea. College Boy here thinks he is one of us now because he got really lucky."

David H. chimed in with, "Yeah, beginner's luck, big time beginner's fucking luck."

They couldn't actually be thinking he was lucky? *What the fuck? This is lucky? How could they think I wanted to do this?* Matt could not even find the words. At least he knew where they were coming from after hearing how Jimmie explained it.

Matt got the feeling that getting a job on the Team was a huge deal. *So, they think I am not worthy of this, and I just got lucky, huh?* It probably was a desirable job if you were a guy like that. What other jobs would be more perfect for guys like them? Not to sound all high and mighty, but in this world nowadays, for a guy with maybe a high school education, no skills to speak of, maybe a criminal record, getting a job like this must feel like you hit the lotto.

Matt figured this was a matter of perspective. It helped to put himself in their shoes for a second to see things from where they stood. Matt certainly wasn't as aware of that as he should have been. He had become a Henchman despite having a college degree. He had never dreamed of this as his career path, it's not exactly a major you could choose from in school. He may have come into this job very differently than the other guys, and he would need to learn what he didn't know about being a Henchman, which was a lot. But maybe he could help them with some things the Team didn't know. This could be a good fit, in Matt's opinion. He would just have to figure out how to translate his skills into the job on the Team. If conversations didn't work, there were plenty of options to take instead of going straight to violence. Maybe that would be something he could weave into the Henchman?

It was the ass-kicking workout he had been expecting, but Matt was proud of himself, as he hung in there with them longer than he thought he was going to. He was, however, not looking forward to trying to walk down the stairs tomorrow.

Matt's goal for this first workout was to slowly begin to earn respect. When it was his turn for reps, he quietly and respect-fully moved the plates off the bar or the pin up on the machine to a weight that was manageable for him. The first time he did that, he noticed the guys give each other a look and approving head nods. Not to Matt, but to each other. Still, work to be done.

The workout also proved to be insightful for Matt. He got to observe the guys' behavior out in public when they were not at work. Matt had made some comments that they responded to. He also found out that he would be called College Boy from now on. He didn't mind it; he was sure there were a lot worse nicknames to be called.

The entire front of the gym was floor-to-ceiling windows, which allowed both Franco and David H. to do regular checks to see who was in the parking lot, frequently watching the front doors to make sure they saw every person who checked in. Matt wondered how they would protect themselves if something were to go wrong. They obviously didn't have Suit coats on, so what would happen if . . . then he realized that they had been carrying a gym bag around with them to each station. They would reach in and grab a drink and look at their phones, but Matt was getting the hang of things and he knew these guys wouldn't go anywhere unarmed.

Toward the end of the workout, Matt was trying to be casual and stood by the bag and tried to look inside. Franco came over to grab his drink out of the bag, and that was when Matt saw the weapons. There were two very large guns in the gym bag. So, they do come prepared for anything.

On the way back to the House, they stopped at the Starbucks drive-thru for a coffee. The stop made him feel a little more at ease and like life was actually going to be ok again. Matt ordered his venti Americano with cream and three Splenda, while both Franco and David H. got venti vanilla bean Frappuccinos. It amused Matt to see those two large men drinking anything with whipped cream and a caramel drizzle on the top.

Walking back to the House, Franco turned back to Matt

and said, "College Boy, you did real good in there today. Don't think you are all sly though, I saw you checking out what was in the bag. But good on you for being observant and getting your head in the right place. You need to think like one of us if you're going to be part of this Team."

Matt nodded. "Thanks for the tough workout, man. I can hardly walk straight; I'm going to be hurting tomorrow."

Franco half-smiled smugly. "You should expect to feel like that every time you work out with us." They walked away, then Franco turned back, "Oh, and just in case you didn't know, we can book massages here in the House. You may want one, 'cause you are going to be sore as shit tomorrow!"

David H. just snorted and laughed, then said, "Yeah, College Boy, sore as shit!"

Matt knew they were right about both things. That he had to think more like them, and that he was going to be sore as shit tomorrow. A maid, a chef, and now a masseuse? Matt was really wondering what the salary was for this job, and if he was going to have to pay for this stuff?

Matt hurried up to his room to clean up, grab some food, and be ready for his meeting with Jimmie. He was looking forward to it since he had something positive to report back. If Jimmie hadn't pulled Matt out of his whiny little funk last night, he might be sleeping on someone's couch with one eye open, wondering who was coming after him and his family. He would always be grateful for that conversation.

After a quick shower, Matt quickly got dressed and noticed the time. It was 9:50. He had just enough time to run down and grab a bagel or something. Matt had lots of energy and he wanted to keep it that way. He felt his legs quiver as he walked down the stairs. He made a mental reminder to ask Jimmie how to book a massage.

CHAPTER 11
THE WISDOM OF JIMMIE

Matt arrived at Jimmie's office right at 10. He had enough time to grab a bagel but was disappointed that there was no sighting of the ever-elusive house-elf. Arriving at Jimmie's office, the door was open. Matt could hear the trickle of the water feature in his office. Jimmie must have heard him coming down the hall.

"Come in, Matt," he called. Matt pushed the door open. He thought that this would be a sit-on-the-pillow with a cup of a tea kind of talk but waited for Jimmie's cue. It still made little sense to him why someone with this chill and peaceful world view would be in the business of usually violent and dangerous 'security.' Matt was hoping to learn more about Jimmie and how he was able to stay so calm and peaceful in the midst of such violent guys. "So, I heard you got to meet Pinky this morning. Tell me, how was it?"

"Um, yes, I got to meet her. The workout was tough. I'm going to be sore tomorrow. We stopped at Starbucks, which was a treat for me. I think it went well, Franco talked a little to me. They call me College Boy now."

"That is what I heard too. Pinky was keeping an eye out for

me. You never know who's watching, Matt." Jimmie smiled. "Have a seat over here."

Matt guessed right, it was a pillow and tea talk day. *See, I am getting the hang of this*, Matt thought. Matt was proud of himself for being able to predict something. He would not get too cocky about it though, since he hadn't noticed Pinky had been watching him and reporting back to Jimmie. Matt was looking forward to more words of wisdom from Jimmie, as he seemed like he knew everything that went on in the House.

"I hope you don't mind if we jump into something I spoke to Garrett about. It seems like it may be helpful to everyone," Matt said.

"Sure thing. What did you and Garrett talk about?"

"By the way, I enjoyed meeting him. I guess he is part of your family as well," Matt said. He paused, then continued, "I have been meaning to ask how Mr. Fowler is doing. I haven't seen him for a few days. I hope he's on the mend. Pinky asking about him made me realize I hadn't seen him," Matt said, taking a sip of tea. He was glad he brought tea with him this time, though he already had a coffee this morning.

"Mr. Fowler is healing well. He has been out of the country for the last few days. He and Liz had some business to take care of. After the incident at The Basement, I decided that Mr. Fowler's security needed to be upgraded. Liz can take excellent care of him, but I added a few extra Henchmen this time."

"Liz goes with?"

"Yes, Liz travels with him most times, especially when he needs a little TLC. She is the only one he would allow to give him that. They are very close. They always were, but when Elizabeth passed, they only had each other." Jimmie paused, looking at Matt. "You know that we three are related, right? Liz is my niece."

"I didn't know that," Matt replied, a little surprised. Though now that he thought about it, they bore some resemblance.

"Yes, Eddie was married to my younger sister Elizabeth," Jimmie said. Matt could detect some sadness in Jimmie's voice. He sat taller, his tone softer. "Ed and I grew up together, we were neighbors. I have known him since we were in the third grade."

"I don't have friends like that, I mean that I have known for as long as you two have known each other," Matt said, stretching his legs out in front of him.

"Ed actually enlisted in the Army with me, but he stayed for five years. I did my twenty years. As kids we—Eddie, myself, and Elizabeth—spent most of our time together. After Ed got out of the Army, I went home for a visit. While there, I noticed a slight shift in the body language between Eddie and Elizabeth. I knew something different about her. She was lighter, happier, and smiled more than usual. I thought to myself she must have gotten a boyfriend, but if she did, why hadn't she told me? We'd always shared those juicy little secrets with each other." Jimmie said.

"So, they didn't tell you right away? I guess I can see why. I am not sure how I would take it if one of my friends started dating one of my sisters," Matt said.

"No, they didn't, I think it was for the best at that time. They were very happy together; they had a lovely marriage. My heart still hurts when I think of the phone call I got from Elizabeth telling me she was sick," Jimmie said.

"I am sorry about your sister, that must have been really hard on everyone. How long ago was that?" Matt asked.

"Elizabeth got sick when Liz was ten. Cancer. It was heartbreaking. I was still in the Army, stationed at Fort Sam Houston, so I wasn't around like I should have been. Elizabeth fought hard, but the horrid disease took her from us after a relatively short but mighty battle. As with most healing, time is key."

"I can't imagine dealing with that," Matt said, shaking his head. He thought of young Liz and what it must have been like for her to have to grow up without her mom.

"Losing Elizabeth was, well, just awful. Especially losing her before I had really come to terms with death, and what it all means, the permanency of it," Jimmie said.

"Well, isn't death permanent? Isn't that the whole concept around death, that it is an ending?" Matt questioned.

"Not so much, in my eyes. I have a concept surrounding death that I work off of. I will talk to you about that at a later time, too much to go into now." Jimmie smiled.

"That would be great, I would love to hear more about death," Matt laughed. Sensing it time to change the subject, he asked, "Did you enjoy your time in the Army?"

"At the time it served me well. I was sent to Security Forces Assistance Brigades, SFAB. These guys are an elite division and one of the top tactical units in the Army. It taught me how to fit in places discreetly, as well as other skills that showcased the fearlessness I now can face the world with."

"I have heard that there are those special secretive units that keep the world in check. I bet you have some crazy stories to tell."

"I have had some crazy adventures, yes. As the years passed, I advanced through the ranks of the Army. I was surprised that I thrived with the structure and routine offered by the military. Most people know there is some dark shit and bad things going on, but the rose-colored glasses stay on. Rose colored glasses were not standard issue in my unit."

"So, when you left, or retired, from the Army, you started working with Fowler?" Matt asked.

"Yes. I went to live near him so I could help out with Liz. It was a natural fit for me to use what I learned in the Army to create the Team that we now have. That is just a bit of background for you to get to know us all a little better." Jimmie smiled while taking a long sip of now lukewarm tea.

"It does help me put all the pieces of the puzzle together when I hear about how everyone fits together," Matt said.

"We have an incredible bond, the three of us. I'm not sure why I told you all of that, except to say that it felt like the right thing to do," Jimmie said.

"I'm glad you did, and I feel it will help me find my place here at DMF," Matt replied. He was still thinking about death, about losing his sister or mom as Jimmie and Liz had. When he thought about how close he was to his family, the thought of anything happening to his sisters, brother, or his mom, made his stomach hurt. "I wanted to ask how the 'eliminating the problem' situation is going? I know you said you would let me know, but I wanted to check in to see if there was anything to report?"

"Matt, you read my mind. There have been some recent developments in that situation that I was going to share with you this morning. It's nothing to be alarmed about, just an update. I guess there is some good news for you in all of this. The day in The Basement, the man you shot was hired by the boss of the competing organization, the OT. Well, you didn't actually kill him, he's still alive. Not that they are not still extremely pissed at you, they are, but the asshole is alive. It takes down the revenge aspect a notch. So, you haven't popped your killer cherry yet, you are still a virgin in the mysterious world of the Henchmen.

"With that said," Jimmie continued, "we are still following strict guidelines with your protection and that of your family and friends. The safety plan had to be reviewed, but it is all in place and our efforts haven't changed. Setting up plans like this is the part of my job that I get a real kick out of. Reminds me of the old days when I was in the Army. Being a security expert is a very niche role, few people in the world could compete with what I know. I hope that gives you some comfort."

Matt sat back in the chair feeling a little conflicted. "Well shit. I had been processing the fact that I had killed a man, and pretty much had come to terms with it. I could never get to the place where I felt bad about it, which was strange, but at least I know who the guy was. Somehow I don't think that will be my last chance to defend myself with a weapon."

"I will agree with you on that point. But I did want to chat also about how you see yourself fitting in here. What do you think a day in life looks like for you?"

Matt had not really thought about this. What did the other Henchmen do all day? He wasn't sure how to answer this and was a little embarrassed about it.

"Honestly, all of what I know about being a Henchman is limited to what I have seen in the movies and TV and the few interactions I have had here. I can guess that we would travel with Mr. Fowler to meetings, keep an eye out for things, go to the gym, but apart from that, I don't really know."

"Don't be so hard on yourself, how would you know what goes on in a world you have had no part in? All the other Team members have had some experience, and I have not had to break down the job. There isn't really a written job description like you are probably used to having. However, there is a code. Of course, it isn't written anywhere, an unspoken code. Have you seen the movie, *Fight Club*? They had rules, everyone knew them and followed them. It is like being on this Team, and for Henchmen. The number one rule that was the most important was, 'You don't talk about Fight Club.' Do you know what the second rule was, Matt?"

"It was, 'You don't talk about Fight Club,'" Matt replied.

"Correct," Jimmie said with a smile. "There are eight rules of Fight Club and five rules of being a Henchman. Take note Matt, write this down, or put it in your phone as you people do nowadays. Learning these could literally save your life someday."

At the end of Jimmie's speech, Matt had written down five rules in the notes on his phone:

1. Never speak on the job.
2. Never do an errand on your own.
3. Never argue with an order.
4. Never hesitate.
5. Know your role, stay in your lane.

"I think it's time you start with some on-the-job training Matt, you up for that?"

"Heck yeah! I'm ready, you tell me when! I want to learn all this new stuff. In all honesty, learning to be a Henchman should be a piece of cake," Matt replied.

Jimmie frowned at Matt's response. "I know your new nickname around here is College Boy, those kinds of smarts are valued in many places. Here, we just don't have anyone else like you. Figuring out how to incorporate your skill set may be challenging. The guys on the Team have experience in what it takes to do this job. I'm not saying you won't be able to figure it out, but it will take some time to see how we can use your strengths. I'm leaning towards this being an excellent thing. You will bring a new perspective to this job, which is something that I feel is needed. For now, it will be for on-the-job-training. I have been thinking about how best to educate you on the role of a Henchman. There are no training manuals to read on this. Are you the watch-and-learn kind of guy?"

"Yes, I am a visual learner." In a way, Matt was relieved that he didn't have to figure out what he would do all day, or if he would be any good at it. He nodded at Jimmie. "I think that sounds perfect. I don't know of a better way to start than that. I need to wrap my head around what goes on here on a daily basis. Since there isn't a training manual, then I guess hopping right in is best," Matt said with some pride. "My suits should be done now; can I go pick them up at Redd's? Or wait, would that be considered doing an errand, not something I should do alone?"

"Yes, I'm glad you brought that up. You can't start a new job here without a suit, those are one of our biggest traditions here. Our dress code is a suit, that's what the Team wears to run errands. You are correct in thinking that going to Redd's alone would be a breach of the Five Henchman rules," Jimmie said.

They decided that tomorrow would be a good day to start. Jimmie would let Franco and David H. know that Matt would ride along.

"I think those two would be the best for you to start off with. They have a couple of errands to run tomorrow, nothing too intense, so that should be a good place to begin," Jimmie said. "They can take you to Redd's beforehand and get you those suits. Redd usually does a good job, so you should be able to wear them the same day."

"Can I just ask quickly, what exactly is an errand? I've heard that term tossed around, but I'm not clear on what that is."

"That is a term that someone came up with years ago. *Going on an errand is* what the Henchman says when they are referring to going out and working a job. Now, I know you aren't familiar with what that even means either. Our roles are diverse, and I won't get into everything right now. But some examples of what an errand would be are making a visit to a potential competitor, visiting with a startup, or providing security for anyone who needs it. That is a dumbed down answer, but I hope it gives you room to use your imagination," Jimmie answered.

Running errands in his past life meant filling up the gas tank, grabbing groceries, that kind of stuff. Running errands while working for the Team meant something very different. "That helps me to feel a little less lost, I'm trying to make sense of this new work culture. And I would like to spend more time with Franco and David H., getting to know their style of work would be appreciated. I just wanted to thank you for all of the generosity you have shown me, but I realized that when we went to Starbucks, I didn't even have any money on me. I don't know if my debit card works. I know I'm not supposed to use my credit cards, I'm just wondering if I will get paid or not?"

Jimmie laughed out loud. Matt didn't understand why Jimmie found this statement to be humorous. Hopefully he wasn't laughing because he had the gall to even ask about that, or if it was just a completely stupid question. Matt waited until Jimmie gathered himself with his eyebrows raised and head tilted, waiting for an answer.

"That was just funny because I thought Liz had already talked to you about that. I apologize for not making that clearer sooner. Your onboarding has not been traditional. Since she hasn't already, I'm sure she will meet with you tomorrow to hammer out the details. Good question to ask, Matt."

"Great, thank you, I look forward to meeting with her too," Matt said, rising to leave. He turned back, having almost forgotten to ask. "Oh, and Jimmie? Were the guys just busting my balls, or can we really book a massage? Because just sitting here for this short amount of time, I have gotten really stiff, and tomorrow won't be fun at all."

Jimmie smiled, pulling a business card from his desk

drawer. "Here is the number to book that, yes we have a masseuse on site. One of the many perks about being on the Team. I'm a firm believer in self-care. Oh, and here is $40 so you can treat the guys to Starbucks tomorrow. When you meet with Liz, she'll have some good news for you."

CHAPTER 12
SHOW ME THE MONEY

Matt was not going to let an in-house massage go without giving it a try. Immediately after leaving Jimmie's office, he curiously called the number to book a massage. The woman on the phone said he could come immediately.

The massage room was a small room on the second floor. It was similar to Jimmie's office in a lot of ways, the smell, the dim lighting, the slow, wordless music.

————

After the massage, it took Matt a couple of minutes to realize where he was. He had gone into a deep relaxed state. His world came back into focus. This was definitely a perk of this job that he was going to utilize often.

Matt thanked the masseuse, Dorothea, on his way out. If he'd had any money on him, he would've tipped her. He made a mental note to bring extra next time he came.

When he got back to his room, feeling relaxed, he felt a jolt of excitement when he remembered that he would soon be finding out what his salary and benefits were with this new job.

He had no clue what to expect. What benefits are

included? He didn't want to shoot too high and embarrass himself, especially with Liz. He wanted to impress her with how well he had acclimated to life here in the House. He was excited to share all the things he had figured out, and how he almost left the House the other night. It was important to him he stopped looking so much like a newbie and moved into a more comfortable position.

He thought he would Google it. Isn't that what you did with anything you wanted to know? He took out his phone and first asked Siri, "What is the average salary of a Henchman?"

Siri couldn't come up with any real numbers, instead, it appeared as though even Siri was making a joke of his question and only came up with no concrete answers: "Pay for the ones that actually hit the target, and not collateral damage. This pay structure would save all of us bosses money." "The bigger the talent needed, the more they should be paid. The more special talents they have, the bigger the pay day. Old fashion ruffing up won't see as big of a pay day as someone who can bring explosives experience to the table." "The pay grade can be negotiated depending on which superhero is involved, and which villain hired you. Some villains pay better than others." "As an unaffiliated Henchman, working for a new villain includes hazard pay."

All the same information came up when he typed in and searched it on Google. Nothing reality-based.

Even Google responded as though Henchmen were only in superhero movies or comic books. It was not common knowledge that they were an actual part of society, how did the internet miss that detail? This was blowing Matt's mind. He had been living as a real-life Henchman and it wasn't fantasy or sci-fi. This made his new life even more of an adventure. This still didn't answer the question about what the guys on the Team told people they did for a living. Matt thought he had better come up with a suitable answer for what he did for a living now when asked. He knew he couldn't rely on his 'me time' excuse to his friends and family much longer, they'd be asking about a job sooner or later. He was still confused because both Fowler and Jimmie used the term Henchman. The meeting with Liz should prove enlightening.

Just as Matt had discovered from the internet that being a Henchman was for comic book characters only, Liz knocked on his door. Matt jumped up with excitement to see Liz. She was standing there looking refreshed and in a sharp-looking business suit. Matt cringed when he noticed she had a suit coat on, knowing what she had tucked inside it. Matt wondered if she had just gotten back from a visit somewhere or if she was on the way out to visit with someone.

"Liz! It's great to see you! I'm glad you're back, I have so much to tell you," Matt said enthusiastically. He almost instinctively reached out to hug her, but he stopped before embarrassing himself. Sure, he thought of Liz as a friend, but he wasn't sure if that sentiment was reciprocated.

Liz, looking rather amused, smiled a genuine smile. Matt had never seen her smile like that before. She looked happy, and that made him happy. Before all this, she looked tense and irritated most of the time. This was a different side of Liz.

"Good to see you too, Matt. I've heard about some of your activities around here. You met Pinky too? That woman is a trip."

"Does she always have all the . . ." Matt asked, gesturing to his lips and nails, referring to Pinky's hot pink lipstick and nail polish.

"Always," Liz confirmed with a smirk.

Matt laughed. "You'll have to fill me in on what her story is."

"I don't know if I would ever have the time to do that. She's a hot mess with quite the sordid past."

The smile cleared from Matt's face as he looked Liz up and down and casually said, "What's with the jacket? Are you going somewhere?" He was really hoping that he had correctly expected the reason for her wearing a jacket during the day in the House.

Liz lightly patted the right side of her jacket where she stowed her gun. "Look at you! Little show off you are now, with your keen observation skills, I like it!" Liz exclaimed proudly. "I'm just back from an errand I ran with my dad. Nothing very exciting if that is what you are wondering. I was out of the country for a few days with him. The trip overseas didn't go so well."

Matt's eyebrows raised a bit, "Can you tell me about the trip, what happened?"

She sighed. "Another time, Sport. I can't get into all the details, but my dad is starting a new facet of DMF I'm not too sure about. It's a long story. I don't like the guy he is doing business with there."

He was actually excited to hear what type of errand she was on. Liz sat in the chair that was next to the chest of drawers in Matt's room, and Matt sat on the edge of his bed. Matt noted the informality of this meeting. He wasn't expecting it to be a relaxed conversation, but then he remembered that assuming and having expectations was usually a waste of time and not the best way to go in the House. Rules were very different here most times.

"Jimmie said that we needed to talk about your pay, that you had been asking him about it. I wasn't trying to leave you hanging, just hadn't found the time to sit and discuss," Liz said.

Matt suddenly felt a little tension in Liz's voice. He hoped this would not be an uncomfortable conversation. He really wanted to keep a good relationship open with Liz. Matt wondered if she was technically his boss. That would certainly change things a bit if that was the case. Matt felt a connection with Liz, like a sister–brother connection. She definitely didn't throw off any other vibes than that, and Matt was completely ok with that.

"We don't have a formal contract or anything like that for you to sign as part of employment. We have an NDA that everyone has to sign, similar to the one you signed the first night you arrived. That one covered you not speaking about the location of the House, this one is for all future encounters to come with your new job as a Henchman. As before, this is not negotiable. Before we go any further, are you willing to sign this new one that covers the duties of your new position Matt?"

Matt thought signing it would only lead to the allure of becoming an official member of the Team. Again, *what are my choices now, anyway?* He needed to be safe and so did his family. Strange thing was, Matt was getting so curious about this new job and so hooked on this new TV drama life he was plopped into that he didn't hesitate to offer his signature.

"Do you have a pen?" Matt reached out to Liz to take her pen.

Liz looked surprised, but handed him that pen, "That was quick, Sport, you sure about this? Do you have questions?"

Matt had his head down and was already signing the NDA when Liz asked.

"Is there just this one spot to sign? And no, I don't have any questions about this. I'm ready to get going," Matt said, letting out a long sigh.

Liz cleared her voice before holding up a piece of paper, which seemed to make it a little more formal than any other part of this onboarding process. Matt could see the letterhead on the paper she was reading, and it had Garrett's name on the top. Matt figured that this must be the standard hiring package that the Team was offered. In a monotone, Liz read from the paper, saying that Matt's base pay would be $125k a year. That would include him being able to stay at the House for an indefinite amount of time, meals while there, cleaning service, and the use of certain vehicles.

Matt had to interrupt once the initial shock wore off. "I'm sorry, did you say that my pay was going to start at $125,000? Are you serious?" Matt stammered.

"Listen, Sport, that's what we pay, if you don't like it, you can take it up with Jimmie," Liz said firmly. Matt could detect some defensiveness in her tone.

"No, no, that's fantastic, I just didn't really know what it would be. Trust me, I'm not complaining at all," Matt said. "Shit, that more than doubles what I was making at Tailgaters. I'm just surprised, in a good way."

"Ok, perfect, makes things easier when we have the Team all start out at the same rate. This is a fairly important job, and we feel this pay rate compensates for the position guys can be put in."

Matt stood up from the edge of the bed and began pacing in small circles on the side of the bed. He wondered if it was a good time to ask what he thought were important questions.

"So, given the scope of duties for this job, is the salary, room, and car all that a Team member gets? I don't mean to sound ungrateful, but what about paid-time-off, sick days, holiday pay, health insurance, or even life insurance? I would think the latter two items would be a priority?"

Liz didn't have an immediate response to what Matt had just proposed, but she rolled her eyes.

"Matt, there you go again, earning your College Boy nickname. We don't offer those sorts of benefits; however, we highly encourage the Team to purchase that on their own."

"It's not about me being college educated. I would think more guys would ask about benefits. I don't think these guys even know how to purchase policies on their own. I know I will."

"I'm sure you will, Sport. Anyway, I know Jimmie told you I had some other good news to share with you."

Matt had forgotten about Jimmie's message after hearing what the salary was going to be. The news of his new six-figure salary was in the forefront of his mind.

"Right, yes, he said that. What is the good news?" Matt asked.

"We were able to sell your truck. We put the proceeds of that sale into an account, I think Garrett may have mentioned it to you. Here is the debit card for you," Liz said, handing a surprised Matt the debit card.

"Holy shit! This is awesome! It's nice to have some money in my pocket," Matt said, smiling.

"Glad to help. The sale of your condo is taking a little longer than expected, but once that is sold, that money will be deposited too. More to come on that. I know Jimmie was going to have you pick up your suits from Redd with Franco and David H., but we talked, and I decided I would take you. Are you ready to go?" Liz asked.

Matt nodded, following Liz. "Thanks for the update on the condo. I had put that in the back of my mind. I have never had a custom-made suit. I'm curious how they'd fit."

"Sport, you should be wondering about a lot more than how your suits fit. We are a team here too, just like your football teams, there are certain roles for each of us to play. No one, not even me, is quite sure how you will fit in."

On the way to Redd's, Liz began to have the same conversation that Matt had had with Jimmie, the one about how we all need to work together, for the machine to run efficiently. Matt figured that each new Henchman must hear this story as a way of making them feel useful and that they are a necessary piece to the puzzle, a cog in the gear. It was such a simplistic way of illustrating the importance of their roles, but Matt could only listen to this dumbed-down explanation of teamwork so many times. He started to feel insulted that Liz felt the need to drop to the Henchman's overall lower intellect to impress upon him the need for him to be as good as he could at his particular role within the Team.

"Liz, do you really think I don't get the whole team concept thing? I did play college football. I am not sure what you think I don't get? I really don't get how hard this can be? I mean once you see it a couple of times, isn't that enough?" Matt scoffed.

"Wow, no wonder the guys are not ready to talk to you. That was condescending. Do I look like an idiot? Do I speak like I am an idiot? We use the team metaphor to illustrate how we all fit in; all serve a purpose. For you to think that you got it all figured out can be dangerous. We play with guns and people's lives, not insurance policies," Liz said without looking at Matt.

The two sat in silence the rest of the trip to Redd's, each lost in their own thoughts about the comments made. Matt didn't feel good about pissing Liz off, and he wondered if Liz felt like he may end up being a liability for the Team.

After entering Redd's and pushing the secret button that invited them into the Suit Lair, Redd welcomed them into his studio with warm embraces, for both Matt and Liz. He had Matt's suits hanging on the rack near the front counter, indicating that he was expecting them to stop in.

"Matt, head on over to the fitting room, and let me see what we got," Redd instructed.

As Matt emerged from the fitting room, Redd smiled and

looked pleased with how the suit fit. Liz briefly looked up from her phone, still not speaking.

"This feels great, Redd, thank you. Liz, what do you think?" Matt asked.

Liz's only acknowledgement was an unenthusiastic thumbs up. Matt realized that her silent treatment was making him uncomfortable. In an effort to get her to speak, Matt thought he would offer to buy her lunch with his newly acquired debit card.

After saying their farewells to Redd, Matt and Liz walked back to the car. *Still nothing*, Matt thought. Deciding he needed to be the one to repair their new friendship, Matt cleared his throat and asked Liz to lunch and to offer an apology.

"I think I said some stupid shit earlier. I just don't get it yet, and I should be more aware of that. I have been an official Henchman for a few hours, how could I possibly know what the job really looks like. But, since I am a rich man now, with my new debit card, I would sure like to buy you lunch and try and start over," Matt said in a gentle, sincere tone.

"You are an asshole, Matt. But yes, I will take that lunch, and I am picking where we will go," Liz said with a slight smile.

———

After lunch at Taco Bell with Liz, he felt like garbage, physically. How was he ever going to be able to keep up physically if he ate shit food? Going to the gym was going to be as important as when he played college ball. He was going to have to spend some serious time in the gym. He needed to get in game-day shape, which meant doing some serious cardio and lifting more weights.

Now that he was official and had his suits, Matt wanted to

prepare himself to actually start his new job. It was going to be more difficult than he'd ever imagined. After his fruitless Google search on what a Henchman gets paid, he knew he was going to have to rely on his keen observation skills to get him up to speed, as there was no proper job description. He still wasn't sure when he could go out alone again. Matt mentally added it to the ever-growing list of questions he would ask the next time he spoke with Liz. It seemed like every time Liz left, he thought of more questions only minutes later.

As far as leaving the house by himself, Matt understood the need to travel in groups for his protection, but it was strange for him to be a grown ass man and not be able to take a simple drive. Things certainly weren't simple anymore. He wondered what would happen if he just casually strolled down to the kitchen and grabbed a set of keys.

Matt had nothing to do the rest of the day, so he thought he would give it a shot. He knew where the keys were kept, and just grabbing a set would work, right? All he would have to do is push the unlock button on whichever set he grabbed and see which car lit up. All he wanted was a quick drive around the block, just to remind himself that he was not a prisoner, nor a grounded teenager. *I'm officially on the Team now, shouldn't I be able to come and go like the other guys?*

Once he got to the kitchen, he noticed there were no one in the kitchen, which he took as a good omen. This was his chance. His heart was racing like a teenager sneaking out of the house in the middle of the night. It felt like he was about to do something very dangerous, which had become something he wanted to feel again. The adrenaline was a little addicting.

With the key fob in hand, he walked out the back door, still not having seen a soul. The lights on the Audi RS flashed, Matt grinned. *Nice choice.* He could get used to having a wide variety of luxury vehicles at his disposal.

Matt walked over to the Audi, took one last look around, opened the driver's side door, and hopped in. This was absolutely the nicest ride he had ever been in. It would have taken his entire career in insurance sales to afford to drive this kind of car. The smell of leather and men's aftershave permeated the warm air in the car. Matt took a deep breath and pressed the ignition. Matt felt the power of the engine roar, his heart still beating fast, still no one around. So far, so good. Putting the Audi in reverse, he made a quick turn to drive the Audi straight down the long driveway to the street. He figured the gates at the end of the drive would just open, that was what they did when he had left before with Liz, and with Franco and David H.

Only this time, they didn't. Instead, out of nowhere, Jimmie appeared. *Where in the hell did he come from?*

Matt almost had a heart attack from seeing the look on Jimmie's face. It was a look Matt had never seen and hoped he never would again. *Jesus, if looks could kill.* Jimmie had perfected the complete badass, 'I will kill you with my bare hands,' look. Matt felt like he was three years old and had broken some expensive family heirloom.

All Jimmie did was stand there and raise a hand with his finger pointed back at the garage and parking area. Matt fumbled with the gears to get it in reverse so that he could get the car back as fast as humanly possible. He wanted to put the car back fast, but then again, what was Jimmie going to do to him once he did? He shuddered to think about it. He knew he was in trouble. Despite Jimmie being older than his parents, he knew that Jimmie could take him in a fight. He would probably do some special Henchman hold or punch that Matt wouldn't even see coming.

As soon as Matt got the car parked, he wondered how bad of a mistake he had just made. He slowly opened the door and got out of the Audi. He wanted to run and hide in his room and forget that this had ever happened. That wasn't an option. What was an option was to get out of the car and wait like a guilty dog who just chewed his owner's shoe for Jimmie to walk up the driveway to greet him. Matt stood leaning against the Audi with his head down, fidgeting with the set of keys. With his eyes trained on his feet, he heard Jimmie arrive.

"Matt, come inside so we can talk," Jimmie said in a calm but strong tone.

Matt didn't even look up, he walked over to Jimmie and just handed him the key set. Matt slid his hands in his pockets and followed Jimmie into the House. Jimmie stopped briefly to hang the key set back on the rack. Not saying a word, he continued the walk of shame to his office. Matt still had his head down, and wouldn't you know, of course there was a fucking crowd in the kitchen. *Where were all these guys before?* Matt knew he would have never pulled this stunt if he would have seen anyone. All eyes were trained on Matt, he could feel it. Christ, even Liz was there to watch.

"Hey College Boy, way to completely fuck up!" Matt heard someone shout.

"Nice job, asshole," sneered David H. as he walked by.

Matt knew David H. was right. What in the hell was he thinking? He looked up just enough to see Liz. She had her arms crossed across her chest and gave him a no-no head shake.

CHAPTER 13
THE TALK

M<small>ATT KNEW</small> for sure that he and Jimmie would not be sitting on any pillows this afternoon. Jimmie walked into his office first. He made sure Matt had taken a seat in one chair across from his desk before he shut the door to the office. *Ugh, the door had always been open in the previous meetings . . . Is he going to kick my ass, or what?* Matt wondered, and if so, there would be no one to come to his rescue, and no one who really knew whatever happened to him, except for those in the House.

Jimmie slowly and deliberately walked to his seat behind the desk, Matt still sitting with his head down and shoulders slumped.

Matt heard Jimmie take a long, slow, deep breath and exhale before he spoke.

"Matt, I wanted to thank you for what you did today," Jimmie said quietly.

Matt's head shot up with a confused look on his face. He pushed himself up to more of an upright position in his chair.

"Why's that?" Matt asked. He was half expecting Jimmie to say, *nope, only kidding College Boy, you're fired!*

"I mean it, Matt. I see that I have not done a very good job of explaining to you the situation you are in. I take responsibility for underestimating your own desire to be free once again. This was a gift for both of us. I can correct it now and save both of us from any further confusion. I thought you understood on a deeper level the importance of following our rules."

Matt sat up even straighter with a slight lean forward. He wanted to make sure he was not getting punked or something. "I'm not sure I'm following what you are saying Jimmie, and I mean that with no disrespect."

Jimmie leaned back in his chair, laced his fingers behind his head for a moment, then slid his hands down his face, stopping briefly at his mouth, eventually landing in his lap. "I failed, because if I had done a better job explaining things to you, this would have never happened. But I want it to be clear, I wasn't the only failure in this situation. I had higher expectations of you, Matt."

There was disappointment in Jimmie's eyes as he peered into Matt's. It made him want to barf.

Jimmie continued, "I know for a fact you were told about the rules that the Henchman follows, because I told you myself. Is that correct?" Matt nodded. "I will take responsibility in my part of this, but I have to say, I am extremely disheartened because you showed blatant disregard for rules that we take seriously. The amount of disrespect is off the charts. Now tell me. Which one of them did you break?"

The tone of voice Jimmie used gave Matt the creeps. He had a look of compassion and understanding on his face, but the tone and words he used were intimidating. Matt felt like shit. First, he insulted Liz, now he disappointed Jimmie. Knots formed in his stomach and bile drifted up to the back of his throat. "Um, well I guess it would have been rule number two, never do an errand by yourself?"

"That's right, have you ever seen anyone else on the Team

leave alone? These rules are really not something that we put together for shits and giggles. They are a creed that we live by, they keep us alive most days. I get they don't mean that much to you just yet but believe me when I tell you they will one day."

Matt felt even dumber than he had when he walked through the kitchen a few minutes ago. "I really feel like an asshole, Jimmie. You did nothing wrong, you explained it well enough. I could sit here and try to explain, but I'm not sure it would do any good. I guess I don't get it, it doesn't seem that difficult at first glance, but somehow I keep fucking up."

Jimmie's face softened a bit. "I believe that everyone learns from their mistakes. With all that said, however, I am not sure you are ready to begin the on-the-job training that we discussed. I'm not sure it would be safe for you or for the Team members you would go out with."

That was the worst news Matt could have ever heard. He was bored out of his mind; he had to get out of the House. "Are you serious? Look, I'm not a moron, really, I get it. I will not fuck up like that again. I need to get out of the House. Is there something I can do to change your mind?" Matt pleaded.

Jimmie was already shaking his head, no. "I am going to err on the side of caution on this. My gut tells me you need some time. I think that it would be best for you to start by watching some 'training videos' on the subject. Once you have done that, we can discuss further. But for now, it is a no. You are grounded here at the House. There will be an exception to go to the gym with the fellas."

Wait, what? There are training videos? How come Matt had never heard of these before? Matt knew that if he had heard of these, he would have been all over that. Google didn't bring up any results like that, and Liz had never mentioned it. Why was this the first he was hearing of them?

"There are training videos? Of course, I would love to watch those. I really want to learn what the hell I'm supposed to be doing," Matt said enthusiastically.

Jimmie laughed a bit and shook his head. "They are not exactly training videos that DMF has put together, they are movies and TV shows that have Henchmen in them. Mostly, they are pretty accurate."

Matt sat back and waited for the punchline, but there was none. Jimmie was completely serious.

"Are we good, Matt? I don't have to hide the car keys from you, do I?" Jimmie joked.

Matt smiled sheepishly. "No, Jimmie, you won't have to hide them, the car keys will be safe. I can live the rest of my life without getting that death stare from you ever again."

"I am glad that was all it took. Liz will get you the list of videos to watch. Once you have spent some time analyzing and observing them, I would like to set up a time to talk with you to go over your thoughts on what you noticed, patterns, etcetera," Jimmie said, barely looking up, already preoccupied with his next meeting of the day.

Matt got up slowly from his chair. He wanted to make sure that he and Jimmie were good, that this really wasn't code for something worse. He could see that Jimmie's attention was focused on the next task at hand and didn't look up as Matt left.

"Jimmie? I want to make sure you know I know I made a mistake," Matt almost pleaded with Jimmie.

"It sounds to me like you understand the gravity of the situation. Let's see how it goes with the training videos," Jimmie said in a much gentler tone.

He really wanted to get back in Jimmie's good graces and show him he had what it took to be a Henchman. He was going to make it a goal for himself to not be just an ordinary Henchman. Once he figured out the hierarchy of the Team, he would plot out his way to becoming a leader within the ranks of the Team. Someone who could actually train a new guy, who could cut costs and lead efficiently.

———

After his talk with Jimmie, Matt got a little panicked about not being able to leave the House except to go to the gym. The thought of sitting in his room for an indefinite amount of time made him a little depressed.

The next day, instead of sulking in his room, he decided to explore the side of the house he'd never been to. Having a change of scenery may be just what it took for him to feel less restricted. He justified that wandering on the other side of the house wasn't leaving, just exploring his new home.

The House was deceptive in that it had so many hallways and shut doors. On the way to Pinky's, Matt had finally inspected the House from the outside and noticed that from what he could tell, it had once been two houses independent of each other. There had been a sort of atrium built to connect the two buildings. The inside of the House had been completely renovated, and with the two larger old homes combined as one, it was truly an impressive structure.

He quietly left his room, and instead of staying on the right side of the house, he crossed the threshold into the unknown left side. As Matt was walking through the atrium, he saw Franco and David H. walking toward him.

Oh shit, I must have fucked up again, and they sent them to come find me and tell me I had crossed the line, again. However, they just kept walking and didn't even really acknowledge him. They both gave a very slight side-eye glance, and that was it.

Matt was relieved that he hadn't broken some other code by

going exploring to the other side of the house. He thought about asking them the next time they were planning on heading to the gym. Having that to look forward to each day would reduce the boredom of being grounded. He didn't want to sound desperate or like he was begging, even though he kind of was. He forgot how fast the two of them walked and had to almost run to catch up to them, leaving him breathless once he reached them.

"Hey guys, whatcha doing?" Matt stammered.

Franco and David H. both stopped briefly to assess whether or not they would acknowledge or respond to him. David H. was the first to speak.

"Why do you care, College Boy? We weren't good enough to ask earlier when you just fucking took off alone. No one here is good enough for you, is that it? Now you want to speak to us? Maybe we have nothing to say, isn't that right?" He raised his elbow to tap Franco on the arm.

Franco just raised his eyebrows, took a step back, and spun around on his heel to head back down the hall.

"Wait! I can explain," Matt shouted to them.

Matt ran past them and stopped suddenly and forcefully in front of them. He put his arms out straight in front of him as if to say, *stop right there, I am not finished with you!*

Matt didn't realize his actions before it was too late. David H. had grabbed Matt so quickly that before he knew it, he was face-first against the wall, arm pinned behind him. David H. used his right hand to take Matt's arm and twisted it so far behind his back, he thought for sure it was going to break. David H.'s left hand was on the back of Matt's skull, pushing his face violently into the wall. This was much like the position he'd been in when he first entered the House. It was the same hold Snoop used on him the firsts night at the House.

Matt's head was turned slightly to the left, so he could

speak, just enough to ask for forgiveness for his most recent faux pas. Through a very crooked, tight-lipped mouth, Matt managed garbled words to Franco. "Please dude, that was my bad, I meant no disrespect. I just want to talk to you guys," he gasped under duress and lack of oxygen. "I want to explain, please, just let me explain."

Franco motioned to David H. to let Matt go. Without hesitating or questioning, David H. released his grip on Matt. Matt stayed semi-stuck to the wall in the same shape he was in while David H. was holding him there. Ever so slowly, he lifted his face off the wall. He noticed there was blood on the wall, and tried to wipe it off, which was when he noticed how his arm felt. His arm, although extremely bruised, did not feel broken. He balanced himself by holding onto the chair rail molding on the wall.

Taking a deep breath, Matt started to speak, but before he could do that, Franco walked close to him, so close that Matt could smell his breath and see the pores in his skin. Matt wanted to close his eyes, because he felt like Franco was looking right through his soul. It scared the shit out of him. Not that it was an evil look, it was a look like, 'I will fucking kill you right now and never think about it again.' Matt didn't close his eyes though, he wanted to somehow redeem himself.

"What the actual fuck was that College Boy?" asked David H. "It seems like you really want to fail. Do you think your football tackling skills will save your dumb ass here? Not going to work, College Boy."

"Can I speak now?" Matt pleaded. "Can we go sit someplace? I would like to explain. Again, I mean no disrespect to either of you."

"I don't know, what do you think David? Should we let this asshole speak to us? I'm not sure I want to hear what he has to say," Franco said with utter disgust.

"Dude, it's your call on this. I'll go talk, beat his ass, or whatever you want. I think it's funny that he thinks he's so smart, and all he does is fuck up one thing after another. Maybe let's give him a chance, maybe we owe him that. I mean, he had Fowler's back and was smart enough to bring him here. Maybe he isn't all that bad."

Franco gave a slight nod and headed down the hall. Matt wondered how things had got so bad so quickly. He just was going to ask for a ride to the gym, and then all this went down. They walked toward the side of the House that Matt was familiar with. There was a door down the main hall that he had never seen open where Franco stopped. He gently knocked on the door, and when there was no answer, he opened the door.

The room looked like some sort of high-tech meeting room. There was a conference table in the center of the room that had four chairs on each side, and one at each end of the table. There were four huge TV screens at least seventy inches each on all four walls, a speaker sitting on the center of the table with a dozen lines, a laptop at each end of the table, and a video camera set up in the corner, with what looked to be a green screen behind it.

"Sit," instructed Franco.

Both Franco and David H. took the chairs facing the door next to each other. Matt thought the most logical place for him to sit was across the table from them. Matt felt a little more at ease to have the width of the conference table between him and the guys. Franco's death stare lingered, and Matt could still see a bit of the tension, but it had shifted ever so slightly.

"How do you want to do this?" Matt asked as soon as they got settled.

He was leaning forward in his chair, ripe with anticipation of the positive vibe he thought the conversation would have. At long last, Matt could explain himself to the guys. There was no doubt in his mind that once he explained, they would welcome him with open arms as a full-fledged member of the Team.

Franco was the first to respond, "I'll go first. Let me just put it out there for you, College Boy: the entire Team thinks you are a lucky, entitled, piece of shit. Guys like you will never fit in here, no matter how much you explain to us. We think it is a bad idea to have you anywhere near our business. How's that for a place to start? That's how I want to do this, College Boy."

Matt shifted his weight back in the chair, disappointed. This was not how he thought this was going to go down. Quickly, he thought of a better strategy than just trying to explain away his behaviors. He thought he would just plead stupidity, nothing more. He knew that this conversation was pivotal in developing a halfway decent relationship with the rest of the guys.

David H. sat with a smirk on his face and picked at his fingernails instead of paying any attention to Matt as he spoke.

"Ok, ok, so I know that without a doubt, I fucked up," Matt said, looking at them both, first at Franco and then at David H.

"You think? Which fuck up are you referring to? We're losing count," David H. spat. "If it was any of us doing the shit you did, we'd be gone."

"We just don't get chance after chance to fuck up like you have," Franco added.

Matt thought to himself that this was actually the longest conversation he had ever had with them, and he wanted it to go longer. He wasn't sure how to play it, but then he thought about how Jimmie spoke to him yesterday, thanking him for showing him more of what he needed to learn after he tried to leave.

"Just hear me out for just a second," Matt said. He got up from his seat, walked around the back of the chair and placed his hands on the back of the chair. Taking a deep breath, head down, he looked up and said, "I really need your help."

Franco and David H. exchanged surprised looks.

Matt paced around the room. "Look, I thought that explaining to you the whys of my actions would help. But I know that any explanation fixes nothing. The truth is, I just don't get it. I don't know what I'm doing. I keep screwing up in ways I didn't know I could screw up, but I don't want to be that guy. I'm not smart in the way you guys are smart. I won't explain my world to you. That is not my place; my place is to learn your world."

With that said, both Franco and David H. looked up at Matt, who was still pacing around the edge of the table, staying on his side of the room.

"Go on, College Boy," David H. commanded.

Matt continued, "Every time I think I'm getting the hang of this life, I quickly get reminded that I have no fucking clue. I want to know more, but trying to learn this on my own or by watching movies will not cut it. I really need to be taught by guys like you who are experts."

"Ha! Experts, I don't think I've ever been called an expert in anything!" snorted David H.

Matt could see that Franco was contemplating whether to believe what Matt was saying, wondering if he was just blowing smoke up their ass. Matt thought it best to not pile on any more compliments.

"Jimmie has me grounded right now," Matt stammered like a little boy.

Lightening the mood, both Franco and David H. laughed out loud.

"Shit, Jimmie's the man!" David H. proclaimed as Franco nodded.

Matt smiled at their reaction. "Like I was saying, Jimmie

has me doing research, and once I'm done with that, I can go out on the job with you and the Team. Obviously, I'll only do ride-alongs. How about we start there?" Matt asked diplomatically.

"A what? A ride-along? What the fuck is that? I have never heard of that?" David H. said with a raised eyebrow.

"I am guessing it is for douchebags who don't have a clue what's going on. They sit in the back seat, don't do *anything* except just watch us real men do the work," Franco said.

"Nice, so College Boy is getting more special treatment," David H. said.

Matt continued, "Yeah, it is something like that. I just come alone, ride along, and observe. I'm asking for you guys to give me a chance. If I go out with you, and I still fuck up, then we can have this talk again, or if I become less of a fuckup, we can also have this conversation in a different context."

Matt pulled the chair out so that he could sit down again. His heart was beating faster than normal. Was he able to pull this off? Was he able to convince them to give him a chance? He knew that he desperately needed training; he thought that would be the key to learning how to be a true Henchman, not just a lucky Henchman.

"How about this, College Boy, I talk to the others about your request. I'm not promising anything, do you understand that?" Franco said, looking at Matt with the death stare back in full force.

Matt was going to make a crack about the death stare that Franco had perfected. Something like, *I hope there is training on how to cultivate that look.* But he thought better of that—now was not the time. But he really wanted to learn how to do that, it was very effective.

"I'm cool with that," Matt said, unable to hide his smile.

"You better be proud of that College Boy, 'cause that's all

148

you're getting," David H. said loudly, almost violently, if words could produce energy.

Matt went to stand up. As he got halfway to a full stand, he said, "Do you want to hear something funny?"

Franco and David H. looked at each other with a look of 'not really, but ok.'

"I was just out walking around the house, actually looking for you. I wanted to ask if you were headed to the gym at some point. Jimmie said I should tag along with you guys. That really was all I wanted to ask this morning," Matt said, laughing a little, hoping to end the meeting with a little levity.

Franco was the first to answer, "Sure, dude, you can come with us again. We go in the mornings, around eight."

"We won't go looking for you, if you aren't there, then tough shit for you," David H. said.

"Plus, Pinky keeps asking when you are coming back," Franco added.

"What's the deal with her? She seems super cool and like she knows, well, everything. Is she related to anyone here?" Matt asked.

Franco and David H. both smiled, shaking their heads. "You've seen her ask about *her Eddie*, haven't you? Christ, it doesn't take a genius to figure out that they were a thing, does it?" David H. replied.

"Dude, I don't know if they were a thing or *are* a thing. No one has ever had the balls to ask for sure. The story we are told is that Pinky and Fowler have known each other for years. I guess Pinky was Liz's mom's friend. Pinky helped them get through some tough times after she died. She was the one person Fowler got, or gets, 'comfort' from," Franco said with a wink.

"Oh, so they were, or are, friends with benefits then?" Matt said.

"I think they're still a thing. She gets so God damn silly when she says his name," David H. laughed.

"We all pretend it's nothing, so I would suggest you do the same. Don't ask any stupid questions, College Boy," Franco said sternly, rising to his feet. David H. followed suit and they left without another word.

CHAPTER 14
THE RESEARCH BEGINS
IN EARNEST

MATT GOT BACK to his room with a sense of pride, accomplishment, and a bloody nose. The bloody nose was worth it since he had made significant strides in connecting with Franco and David H. If having his face pushed into a wall and having his arm nearly broken was what it was going to take, he was up for the challenge.

When he got to the room, he noticed boxes sitting on the floor near the desk. As he approached, the size of the boxes and the brand on the sides made his knees buckle. *A new computer?*

Matt rushed over to the boxes like it was Christmas Day. The boxes were opened one after the other and the system set up began. Whoever picked this system knew what they were looking for. Matt didn't think he would have picked anything different, especially if money wasn't an issue. This was the latest system from Intel, top of the line. Setting this up was a fantastic way to end the day. Although, he did have a pang of sadness hit him. He wondered how the boys at The Basement were doing. He had this new exciting and challenging life, but what had become of his friends there?

After every box was open, every cord plugged in, every program downloaded, everything set up just right, Matt gathered himself, and got ready to dive into the world he knew and was good at. He grabbed his headphones and logged into his favorite game, COD, aka *Call of Duty*. He had just gotten logged in and ready to go when he noticed movement at his door.

Matt spun around in his new gaming chair to see Liz standing in the doorway. She was holding a pizza and a six-pack of Blue Moon. Matt quickly threw off the headphones and jumped to his feet, completely forgetting the game he had just started.

"Liz! So great to see you! Did you see what I got?" Matt said, pointing to the new system, and smiling ear to ear.

"Down boy, down! Of course, I saw it. Who the fuck do you think went and bought it? Franco and David H.?" Liz rolled her eyes. "I thought you needed something to remind you of home. Does it suit your needs?"

"Hell yes it does! Thank you, Liz," Matt said, resisting yet another urge to hug Liz. Matt was surprised by the way Liz seemed to care that she had picked out the right type of system for him. Matt quickly kicked the empty boxes to the side and asked, "Hey, let me take one of those things from you. Did you bring that for me, for us, are you staying?" He set the pizza on the bed.

Liz sat on the bed in between the pizza and Matt. "Yes, I'm staying, that's why I brought dinner and beer!" Liz said in a mildly agitated tone. "I have the list of your training videos. I actually had some fun going through the list and seeing how others not in our business portray what we do on the Team. It was more or less accurate—generally speaking," Liz noted.

"Sweet! I'm looking forward to seeing the list, and to see if I have already seen some of them," Matt said with excitement.

"Sport, it won't matter if you had seen any of these movies before. You're going to be watching them with a fresh set of eyes this time. This isn't for entertainment; this is to learn. From what I hear, you have a lot riding on this," Liz smirked. She gazed at Matt's arm and said, "How's that arm feeling?"

Matt's face dropped, and he wondered how it was possible that literally everything he did got filtered down to her. It must be her job to know every detail of the House and the Team. Matt thought she should spend some time with Garrett, because from what had Matt gathered from their conversation, Garrett didn't have a clue of the comings and goings in the House.

"It's fine. The good thing is that my nose and arm aren't broken. They both very well could have been," Matt said with an eye-roll. "Those guys have a short fuse, huh?"

"Quick reaction time," Liz corrected.

"I'm not even going to ask, but I'm going to assume you heard we had a conversation too, which ended up being a very positive thing, putting me in a much better place."

"It's about time you spoke to them. They are difficult eggs to crack. But once you're in with them, you're in. You get that? There will never be a time when they don't have your back," Liz said, grabbing a Blue Moon and taking a long drink. "Sometimes this shit tastes so good."

Matt agreed by nodding and grabbing a slice of the pepperoni and sausage pizza. He took a large mouthful of the pizza and said, "Sometimes this shit tastes so good."

Liz started laughing, and then Matt did too. It felt good to laugh, and he hadn't remembered the last time he laughed, or if he had ever seen Liz laugh a genuine laugh.

Liz saw the remote and turned the TV on. She logged into her Netflix account. She went to her 'My List' section. From there, Matt could see that there were a lot of films that he had seen but remembered the 'new set of eyes' comment Liz had made.

"I'm sure you've seen most of these that I picked out. We're here to observe. Jimmie wants a full report back on what you see and what you notice in each of the films." Liz said, still navigating the Netflix screen, scrolling past the titles.

The Princess Bride was the first title that Liz picked to watch. She didn't ask if that was what Matt wanted, she was the lead on this project. Matt would have rather watched any of the Marvel movies with superheroes and villains in them. He noted the *Star Wars* series was on her list and *The Wizard of Oz*. There were even some comedy movies, including the *Austin Powers* trilogy and *Back to the Future*. Who could forget Biff and his gang of Henchmen?

Matt scooted himself back to the top of the bed and stuffed some pillows behind him so he could sit upright while he finished the pizza and drank a few of the beers. Liz followed suit. It felt great to have this feeling of normalcy again, of laying back, drinking a beer with a friend, watching a movie, and eating greasy pizza.

They felt comfortable enough with each other while watching the movie that they both dozed off towards the end. Matt was trying really hard to stay awake just in case Jimmie asked him a specific question about the movie or what the Henchman's role was. What he took away from *The Princess Bride* was the classic good versus evil. The despicable and evil guy had his two Henchmen do the dirty work while the good guy tried to do everything himself, with no Henchman.

As the movie ended, Liz got up to gather her things and leave. "Well Sport, what do you think? Do you have any ideas? Common themes? Those are the things that Jimmie will ask you about," Liz pressed through an enormous yawn.

"No, yeah, I get it, I think. Looks like the Henchmen always works for the bad, evil guy," Matt replied, also yawning.

"You think we are bad or evil?" Liz said, suddenly more

alert, standing with her hands on her hips, not looking pleased with the comment.

Matt's stomach did a flip. *Oh Christ*, he fucked up, again. When will he learn to think before he opens his mouth?

"Um, well, I don't know exactly what you do, but that's what I noticed in the movie. I meant no disrespect, I was just trying to explain . . . " Matt trailed off, looking rather embarrassed.

"How about I never hear, 'I was just trying to explain' from you ever again. That phrase seems to get you in more hot water than if you would just learn when people are busting your balls?" Liz said with a grin on her face.

Thank God. He was relieved that he hadn't made another faux pas today. The one with Franco and David H. earlier was enough for one day.

"Ha ha, hilarious, Liz," Matt said, trying not to smile.

"I'll be here tomorrow night too. Maybe a little earlier so we don't get so sleepy. We can try to squeeze two movies in. If you have time to watch during the day, do that, just let me know. Have fun at the gym tomorrow with the guys, and tell Pinky I said hi," Liz said as she left the room and headed down the hall. She spun back around. "Oh, and I almost forgot to tell you. You have an 'orientation' of sorts tomorrow afternoon with some high-ranking M&Ms. Twelve-o-clock in the meeting room where you met with Franco and David H."

High ranking Henchmen? Matt went to bed that night eager to know what this orientation was all about. He wondered what characters he would meet this time.

CHAPTER 15
INTRODUCTIONS

THE MORNING GYM session was fairly brutal, but Matt enjoyed getting out of the house and hanging out with Franco and David H. After their conversation in the meeting room, things had progressed to a halfway decent point. There would be more actual conversations, a little ball busting, and absolutely no pleading 'let me explain' rants in the future.

Franco and David H. told him on the drive home from Pinky's that the high-ranking Henchmen he would be meeting with were Ricky, master of sarcasm, Skippy, called that because he had a severe leg injury and when he walked he had to skip his one leg, David M.—the original David, David H. told Matt while rolling his eyes—William, don't call him Will or Bill, because he won't answer you, got it? Gabriel, Gabe for short, also Franco's younger brother, and of course, Franco.

"How do you guys get to be called high ranking Henchmen? An evaluation or something?" Matt asked.

"Oh yeah, we all go and take a test in front of Fowler and Jimmie and get points on how quickly we can tie someone up with and without duct tape. Then after that we have an oral exam on a vignette," laughed David H.

"There is nothing in particular they do to be called high

ranking. I would call it more longevity based. Although, evaluations may be a good idea," Franco said.

"Very funny David, But Franco, you are part of this group, correct? Are you, David?"

"Yes, I am probably the longest ranking Henchman on the Team at this point. David isn't quite there yet, but he is working on it, right David?"

"Nope, not yet. With any luck, I will be sitting there with all the big boys sooner than later," David H. said.

"Good for you David, way to have a goal to work toward. I'm confused though, wouldn't Liz be considered a high-ranking Henchman? I have seen her work firsthand, and she can handle her business."

"Liz is a badass without question. She is sort of in a class all by herself. She floats between working with us and being a liaison between us and Fowler," Franco said.

None of the high-ranking Henchmen mentioned had introduced themselves to him up until this point. He had barely started to have civil conversations with Franco and David H., and those had given him hope that he would be able to connect with the rest of the Team.

"I will meet you back in the meeting room around eleven? Any words of advice you can give me when I meet everyone?" Matt asked.

"Don't be an asshole," David H. laughed.

"Got it. True words of wisdom," Matt said.

Entering the meeting room, there were some side glances and whispers from some of the guys. Matt's reputation had preceded him as he was being introduced to the Team.

"Hey guys, thanks for stopping by. I thought it would be good to make an official introduction of Matt, AKA, College Boy. It's cool to still call him that, I don't think anyone except Jimmie calls him by his real name. He's one of us now, and I thought that you guys should have an opportunity to introduce yourselves and to ask him questions, or whatever. I know you all are hungry, so let's get down to it," Franco said, addressing the room.

At first Matt thought about standing to make his intro speech, but thought better of it, not wanting to give the impression that he was above them in any way. "Look, I know that some of you thought it was dumb luck that I was there that day in The Basement and saved Mr. Fowler's life and all. Honestly, I have to agree and say, yes it was dumb luck. I am trying to make my way here now with a fresh start. I know you guys are pros and I would like to learn from you," Matt said.

Ignoring Matt completely, Ricky said, "I think I speak for the rest of us when I say that we don't have questions, we just want to see results. We want to be sure that he is safe to work with and will follow *our* lead. None of us care that he went to college or was captain of his football team."

"Ricky is right. Everything will be fine if he doesn't act like he knows how to be a Henchman, showing us disrespect," William said.

"Those are all valid comments to make, but can I just ask that you speak to him, not me? He is sitting right here," Franco said, nodding in Matt's direction.

"Ass kissing? Is that what this is called Franco? Trying to make nice with the new guy, look, we will figure it out the way we decide. He heard us, and now, we are leaving to go get food," Ricky said, motioning the rest of the five to follow.

The door in the rear of the room opened, and like all good Henchmen, their hands were on the ready, reaching for the butts of their weapons in a split second, until they realized who was coming in the door. They shifted their focus to see Liz, while quietly and mechanically stowing their arsenal. "I see you met the cool kids. Good to see the fellas being so welcoming," Liz laughed.

"We *are* the cool kids, you got that right. We were just leaving, we are done here, isn't that right Franco?" Ricky said loudly.

As the room emptied, Matt stood looking to Franco for a sign that it hadn't been a complete shit show. "What the fuck happened here? What did you say this time?" Liz said.

"Nothing! I swear," Matt stammered.

"He really didn't say anything, they were just playing hard to get. They will be fine. They were just making a point," Franco said.

"What point would that be?" Liz asked.

"They want me to know who's boss and that I need to work with them and not try and be some hotshot who thinks they know it all," Matt said.

"I will round them up and let them know we need to finish the meeting after lunch," Franco said.

"Ok, if that is all, then that would be sort of expected. I am going to give an update to Jimmie and my dad. See you in the kitchen?" Liz asked.

"Don't worry, you can sit by me and David H. until she comes back; let's go eat, I'm starving," Franco said.

"Thanks dude, I'm starving too."

At the buffet, Franco grabbed himself two plates, which had never crossed Matt's mind. He followed suit, loading up two much anticipated plates following their tough morning workout. While in line he noticed Garrett walking randomly from table to table, lingering at each table for a moment, and then moving on. *He must be doing his due diligence and gathering details about the events of the previous day,* Matt thought.

As they sat, Liz returned and pushed her way to take a seat

at the table next to Matt, sipping her coffee, "I think you have a fan club over at the other table."

Matt had noticed the guys at the table across the room had been staring and trying to not be obvious.

"Yeah, I noticed them, who are they? They're not part of the M&M Team, I gather."

"That's the whole CM team right there, all six of them minus Jackson. They're super nerds, but we love them. DMF wouldn't be the company it is without them," Franco added.

"Maybe I should go introduce myself to them," Matt announced.

"God they are going to love the attention," Liz said.

As Matt approached the CM Team's table, half of them pretended to not notice him standing there, the other half fidgeted nervously with their plates of food.

"Hi guys, I wanted to stop by and introduce myself to you. Franco tells me you are the CM Team, and you do really good work here at DMF. Maybe you can show me some of the projects you are working on sometime, I would love to hear about them. Plus, I miss having someone to talk gaming with. Do you guys play anything? I'm a big COD guy."

All six sets of eyes looked up simultaneously. One of the guys eventually broke the silence. "It was nice of you to come by and introduce yourself, Matt. We've heard about you. I'm Harry, the rest of the guys are Finch, Cooper, Caleb, Finn, and Albert." Each gave Matt an awkward wave of the hand, some with more excitement than others.

Matt smiled back. "Nice to meet you all."

Leaning closer to Matt, Harry continued in a lower tone, "Thing is, dude, we've never had anyone ask to see our work. We're pretty independent from what the other guys do. I'll have to check with Jackson, our boss, to see if that's ok. I'll get back with you once I have confirmation. We all are gamers too.

Maybe we can all play together sometime. I'm sure the guys would love it, right guys?"

The CM team all nodded with enthusiasm, but it was Finch who was the second of the CM team to speak, "What is your loadout?"

"Oh yeah, you are speaking my language. I usually run with an M4. What is your tag name Finch? I will look for you the next time I'm on, mine is BigBadBear72."

"Sweet, man. I'm running with an AK-47, that is my favorite. My tag is SBD44, silent but deadly, get it? Like when you fart, and no one else hears it, but only smells it." The rest of the CM team giggled like middle school boys.

"Yup, I have heard that one before. Hope we can play soon. And Harry, if Jackson isn't cool with me shadowing or whatever, it's fine, I didn't know it would be an issue. You can just let me know either way."

Harry nodded and Matt made his way back to the M&M table.

Liz bumped him with her shoulder. "That was your good deed for the day. Now onto the real meat of the day. Are you ready for this? You will have to shake off how they treated you earlier."

"Actually no, not really. I think I'll go throw up first."

Liz rolled her eyes. "Oh, it won't be that bad. They are good guys, being intimidating assholes is part of their jobs. You'll be fine. But if you need to throw up, be my guest. One time a CM guy, Barfy, actually did upchuck during his first briefing, hence the nickname, so you definitely don't want that to be your first impression with them. Just don't keep them waiting."

Matt gulped. Vomiting in front of the high-ranking guys was the last thing he'd want to do. He'd take the nickname College Boy over Barfy any day. He wondered which of the

CM guys he had just met was Barfy. "Thanks for the advice," Matt said, deciding to head to the bathroom before the meeting.

He eyed himself in the bathroom mirror as he dried his hands, practicing his deep breathing. He knew it was going to be a tough sell to get the guys to accept him. He decided he would approach the Team as if it were a sports team. He was going to 'try out' for the Team, at least in his mind. That was how he would approach it. He had done this so many times over the years that he was sure he could ace it. Matt had been playing sports since he was three and a half years old, this was nothing new for him.

Matt tried not to let his nerves show on his face as he lightly knocked on the door of the meeting room. A deep voice growled to come in. Matt opened the door and felt the energy in the room, there was some definite hostility emanating from the five men. As Matt walked in the room, they each looked up from their phones, put their coffees down, and eye-balled Matt up and down, and up again. Even Franco gave him a death stare as if they hadn't been sitting across from each other at lunch ten minutes ago. They did not ask him to take a seat.

Matt thought about turning around and walking out the door, looking for Liz or even Jimmie. The awkwardness set in. The more Matt thought about it, and the whole 'try out' thing was not the best way to think about this. He forgot one big part of it. When he was trying out for a team, he knew what the fuck he was doing, and he was good at it. This shit was something foreign to him and he felt like he was in kindergarten, looking at the big kids and wanting their approval.

Matt took a deep breath. He was going to do what he was taught to do when making an introduction: look the person in the eye and give a firm handshake. This gesture would hopefully be seen as a sort of peace offering. While he walked over to the men, the thought crossed his mind that they may not reach out to return the handshake, then what? He would just be standing there looking like an asshole. *It wouldn't be the first time, or the last time I look like an asshole.*

He walked to Ricky first; he seemed to be the one giving Matt the most eye contact. The offer of a handshake surprised Ricky. He paused and looked around to the others to see their reactions. They gave the shoulders up, the tilt of the head approval. With that handshake, the games began.

"I've seen you around the house. I know these are odd circumstances, having me here, training me and all. This is weird for me too. I just want to learn from the best, and from what I heard, you guys are the best of the best," Matt said as he moved to shake William's hand.

William just scowled, ignoring Matt's hand. "We don't need our asses kissed or smoke blown up our asses. What is it that you want to learn? You apparently can handle a gun and an intense situation. Fowler is alive because of you. That's all the training any of us have ever had."

"That's a great question. What do you want from us? Why are you getting more special treatment? None of us were offered an orientation," Skippy added.

Choosing his words carefully, Matt replied, "I guess what I was hoping to learn from you was more what your day is like, what exactly an errand is, and any tips you can give me. What happened with Fowler was the one and only time I had ever held a gun. The only thing I know about your jobs and lifestyles is from movies."

"Oh, now we're movie stars? He's only seen us in the movies," Gabe snorted.

"Ok, Gabe, I'm sure that isn't what he meant. Let's cut him some slack. He's going to be part of the Team. We may as well make him feel welcome. At some point, we'll be working with him, and we need him to know what the fuck to do," Franco said.

The room was silent for a moment. Matt wasn't sure if it was his turn to jump back into the conversation or if he should let the rest of the Team figure out what was next. He looked up to see Liz sliding her way into the back of the room. *Thank God, Liz had finally shown up.*

"Yeah, I get that. How would you guys describe an errand to this guy?" David M. asked the room.

Franco jumped in, "Basically, errands are small, daily jobs we do. There's an errand board in the office that we look at to see where we're going. Most of the time, it's to pay visits to small, local businesses that Fowler, well DMF, has interest in, or to encourage small start-ups to keep on schedule, or to provide security detail when needed. I think that's all you need to know for now. You can learn more by doing some ride-alongs with us."

"An errand board makes sense. I was wondering how jobs got assigned too. Kind of off the subject, but can you tell me who was assigned to watch over my family? I would like to talk to them about how things are going," Matt said.

"Those guys are separate from us in a way. They are a team within a team, they do long term security. We do more of the day-to-day errands. They don't stay here like we do when we are working. Most times, they get a place near the job and live there while they are on the job. So their names wouldn't be on our errand board," Franco said.

"Interesting. I like that, makes sense to live near the job. Ride-alongs will help, but I was thinking more along the lines of training individually with each of you guys. Like for example, I hear that Franco's a really good shot. Maybe I could start by going to the shooting range or something," Matt suggested.

"Let's start with me first and see how that goes. Is there

anyone else who would volunteer to show him your specialties?" Franco asked.

None of the other Henchmen offered to take Matt with them. The only thing helpful that Matt took away from that 'orientation,' was that there was an office he hadn't been to, and a job posting board. *What the fuck? How do you learn that death stare they all have, or how to intimidate with muscle?*

"You fellas better lighten the fuck up. Listen, I tried to keep out of this and let you figure this out on your own, but this is just stupid. One of you offers to take him or I will make the pick myself," Liz said coldly.

"Aren't you the assertive one today. To get you off your high horse, I will take him with me. Franco isn't shit with shooting. I am better than him any day, I will give him a lesson or two at the range. Maybe you want to come too, Franco, maybe you would learn something," Ricky said.

"Fuck off, Ricky. You take him, that's fine," Franco huffed.

"See, I knew you fellas could work something out," Liz said with a twinkle in her eye.

CHAPTER 16
MATT'S PAID INTERNSHIP

SINCE MATT WAS STILL GROUNDED, he jumped into his new position of a very low-level Henchman with gusto. Matt had done an internship in college, which pretty much just involved getting coffees for the real employees, observing, and the occasional busywork of filing. He thought of this time as an internship with DMF, only now he had movies to watch, and he was required to workout. It definitely wasn't traditional, but then again, he was beginning a new career with a company that didn't even list jobs on its website. Come to think of it, Matt wondered if DMF Enterprises even had a website?

He was spending an extraordinary amount of time either playing COD or watching the 'training videos,' both alone and with Liz. Jimmie had decided he would not ask if he could start his on-the-job training until he had finished the entire list of videos. There were thirty on the list, and he was just about finished. There were only two left: *The Wizard of Oz* and *The Shawshank Redemption*. Matt was curious how both movies could be on the same list. That is, until he watched them again through the eyes of a Henchman.

Oh, I get it now, Matt thought to himself as he watched the flying monkeys in *The Wizard of Oz* take off and defend their leader, the Wicked Witch of the West. Of all the times he watched this movie, Matt never in a million years would have put the flying monkeys in the category of Henchmen. After watching all the films on the list, he had to say that overall, they were some of the best of all the Henchman on screen.

The Shawshank Redemption, though, perplexed him. Before watching it, he wasn't exactly sure who the Henchmen were in that movie. He had seen it before and could not place it. There were no real gangs in the movie, no real bad guy, except for the shitty prison guard and the warden. Matt soon realized that Henchmen come in all shapes and sizes. The asshole guard, Byron Hadley, was a Henchman through and through. Probably one of Matt's least favorite of all the Henchman. He was dedicated to the even bigger asshole, Warden Norton. Karma won in the end with those two.

When Liz stopped by that night, he would subtly let her know the list was complete and he was ready for any sort of quiz that Jimmie may give him. She seemed to be preoccupied and not the usual relaxed friend Matt had gotten used to having as company. She paced around the room before flopping on the bed. She had added just one more flick to the list, *The Chronicles of Narnia*. Matt knew right off the bat the White Witch's army were the Henchmen in this film.

Liz kept sighing loudly and he noticed her knee was bouncing up and down. He could tell there was something on her mind. Matt made a bold move to put the movie on pause. Liz had become a friend to him, and he wanted to ask her what was making her pace and be so distraught.

"Hey! What are you doing?" Liz shouted after Matt had paused the movie. "We are just getting to the good part where Aslan comes to the rescue."

Matt slowly put the remote down on the side table. He looked up to see Liz near tears. She was about to break. Not sure what to do, his instincts told him she needed a hug from a friend more than to answer a bunch of questions. Matt walked over to the edge of the bed where Liz was sitting. She was staring blankly at the floor, slouched in a 'I just can't do it anymore' fashion. Matt sat next to her and in the most tender way he knew, simply put his arm around Liz's shoulder. When she didn't protest, he gently rubbed her arm as if to say, it will all work out, and it will be ok.

In silence, Matt sat holding up his friend, knowing she decided what came next. And what came next were her tears. They started slowly; a couple dropped onto her lap. That was only the beginning. Matt thoughtfully got up to shut the door. He doubted anyone else needed to see Liz having a mini break-down. Almost on cue, as the door shut, the tears turned to heaving sobs.

Matt sat right back down next to her. This time she turned to face him in a way that Matt knew he needed to hug her. She sobbed, sighed, and sniveled. Snot and tears streaked down the whole left side of Matt's shirt. During the entire episode, Matt was silent and just kept a hold on Liz. He vowed to only let go once she did. He wanted to be there for her, for she was his one and only loyal friend.

After a few moments, Liz's breathing changed. It became more rhythmic, and the tears dried up. Matt could see her trying to get herself back together by taking long, deep breaths. As she lifted her head up, her green eyes were even more green if that could be possible. Matt handed her a glass of water, which she gratefully accepted. She got up and walked to the bathroom. She shut the door and turned the faucet on.

"Jesus fucking Christ," Matt could hear Liz saying from

behind the closed bathroom door. "I look like shit. My eyes are going to be so puffy tomorrow, I'll look like I had an allergic reaction to a bee sting or something."

The water from the faucet turned off, the door opened, and Liz came out, looking rather regal and like nothing had happened. She paced around the room for a lap or two and then sat down next to Matt, who was still sitting on the edge of the bed.

"You ok?" Matt asked.

"Yeah, I'm fine."

They both knew that was a lie. No need to state the obvious.

Liz sighed. "Honestly, I'm better than when I walked in here. I cry about one time a year, I guess you got to be included in this year's sob fest. I didn't see that coming."

"Honestly, neither did I." Matt smiled gently at her.

"I suppose you're wondering what that was all about."

"Hey look, I'm cool if I never know. If you want to tell me, that's cool too. Whatever way you want to play this, I'm good with it. This entire scene won't leave my room, you know. It stays here," Matt said in a serious tone.

"I appreciate that, but I may as well spill the beans." Liz sighed. "It's girl trouble. I just hate this shit. I can deal with just about anything, as you may remember, but when it comes to this type of stuff, I'm just such a rookie."

"Girl trouble? What do you mean exactly?' Matt said. He had seen his share of girl trouble from his two sisters, but there was no other girl in the House for Liz to be fighting with.

"Dude, you know I am gay, right?" Liz asked with her eyes wide, a 'duh, how could you not know?' look at her face.

Ah, that kind of girl trouble. Matt hadn't known, but he shrugged. It didn't change his perception of Liz in his head; she was still his friend. "I guess I never really thought about it, but huh, it makes sense," Matt replied.

Liz crossed her arms across her chest and raised her eyebrows. "Makes sense? What the fuck does that mean, Sport?"

Matt's heart raced, worried that he had said the wrong thing once again. He stood up and put his hands out. "Hey, hold on, let me explain. It means that you are a beautiful girl and I have never seen one of the other guys look at you the way guys look at girls who look like you, ok? And for me, I just never felt that vibe from you, which I'm totally fine with. I just figured I was used to my sisters, and that's what it seems like with you, like you're my sister."

"You're a trip, Sport. You really are. I like you anyway, as a brother, and that's it!" Liz said, smiling back as if to say that was as sweet of a compliment as she had ever heard.

"I mean, I might help with girl stuff, just because I have sisters. But not so much in the relationship realm because I haven't been able to have any successful relationships of my own," Matt confessed.

Liz uncrossed her arms and hopped up to take a seat on the edge of the dresser. Her long legs were wagging back and forth with the heels of her black converse hitting the dresser drawers. It was quiet in the room for a moment until Liz looked up and said, "Her name is Mo. I met her the summer after I graduated from high school. It has been a fucking rollercoaster ever since with her. Some days are better than others. She is kind of 'free spirit,' and we don't see each other very often. That's ok sometimes, but sometimes it's not."

What did I get myself into? How was he going to have anything of substance to say to her? How could he actually offer her any advice when he had no clue about successful relationships, much less with a lesbian relationship? After some

170

thought, he decided that bottom line, she was a friend to him. Images of the first night he met her and the night she killed those two goons in his condo ran through his mind. That was who he knew Liz to be, a tough, non-feeling badass living in a world filled with men and no mother around. He wondered if she had ever felt safe enough to show her vulnerability to anyone in the past. He certainly wanted to treat this as a water-shed moment and show compassion. Even if he didn't have the answers, he could listen. He knew sometimes people just wanted to talk. They didn't expect you to have answers, just to listen and validate them.

"So, you've known her for a while, and the long-distance thing is ok on some days, but not others?" Matt offered.

"Yeah, you know what, it's all good, never mind. I just must be PMSing and stressed out about other stuff. It is what it is with her," Liz said quickly.

Matt was not surprised that Liz shut down almost as quickly as she opened up. This time he knew he didn't mess up or say something out of line. What she gave tonight was as much as she could, which was a shit ton for her. Matt felt a sense of honor that she could open up to him as much as she did in the first place. He considered this a win for him. He did, however, feel a pang in his insides. The pang was an intense moment of him missing his sisters; he wondered if he could call them. He knew he'd have to ask first.

"I get it, you were trained, or raised, to stuff emotions. I can see how that can be helpful in your profession. I also know that it's therapeutic to talk about stuff, it helps to let it go. Do you want to just talk, not about your problems, but just talk? I hardly know anything about you, like when you were little. That's how friendships develop in the real world," Matt said.

Letting a deep sigh out, Liz replied, "Sport, as much as you don't get us, I don't get you either. You caught me in an off moment while my guard is down. I've never really let my guard down in front of anyone since her mom passed away." She sighed again. "We can talk, but you can't judge or make faces or look at me with pity, or any of that other softy bullshit, deal?"

"Absolutely no softy bullshit," Matt said and smiled. "Would it be easier if I went first? I can share some of my childhood crap too, we all have some don't we?"

"I really don't know the answer to that. I suppose we do; I was so isolated when I was a kid, I don't know what other people went through," Liz said.

"I guess we all have some sort of growing pains figuring out who we are, and how we fit into the world. You losing your mom is more than any kid should have to go through. I dealt with the loss of a parent, but in a very different way. Mine was more of the dad who walked out and pretended he didn't have kids unless it was convenient for him. It was not the same as your type of loss," Matt said.

"Still shitty though. I don't think I will ever understand how you can bring a human into this world and not think it's the biggest gift you can ever receive."

"Yeah, it isn't cool. At this point, I'm over it. It is his loss. If I am ever a dad, I know I won't ever do this to my kids. Did you ever talk to anyone about her death?"

"Have you not noticed that we aren't a touchy-feely family? 'Suck it up Buttercup' was about all I got. But that didn't do much to cover up our pain. The grief we went through was unbearable at times. It was hard on me to lose my mom, but seeing what it did to my dad was almost just as bad. We were a happy close family," Liz said. "He tried to show a brave face, but I could see it was too painful for him some days."

"I am trying to imagine Fowler dealing with a broken heart. My interactions with him have been few, but he seems like he is as tough as nails. It's so hard to know how to help people through the death of a loved one," Matt said.

"He would just go to work, leaving with the prefabricated smile on his face as he walked out the door. I read books, and the more I read, the more I knew we just had to support each other through the process. It helped to know I wasn't doing anything wrong."

"That is some heavy stuff to deal with. Did it get better when Jimmie came?" Matt asked.

"Yes, it did. He was a good distraction for us. I got to go back to being a kid, playing ball, and hanging out with the wrong kids," Liz laughed.

"Wrong kids huh? Tell me more," Matt said.

"I will think about sharing more of my childhood with you, but not tonight. My walls came down enough for one night. I'm out of here."

"Yeah, I get it. Anyway, you know where I am if you ever want to talk," Matt said, standing up to open the door. It was as if opening the door let out all the emotions that had been released. He could tell Liz was just a bit more free.

"Oh, I forgot to say that since you are done with all the training videos, you can report back to Jimmie. Once you pass that 'test,' you'll probably be ungrounded," Liz said in the commanding tone of voice Matt was used to.

"That's fucking awesome! I'll text him and let him know right now. It would be sweet if he could see me tomorrow after Pinky's." Matt looked like a little boy who found out he got a new puppy or something shiny and new to play with.

Liz was standing by the door, ready to leave. She paused for a moment, seeming to struggle to find words. Taking a deep breath, she simply said, "Thank you." Then she turned and walked out of the room.

Matt flopped on the bed, looking up at the ceiling. He was

pumped for the next chapter in his life. He quickly texted Jimmie, hoping that it wasn't too late to do so. Without a moment passed, Jimmie texted back and said he could meet with him in the morning, after Pinky's. Matt was too excited to sleep, instead he scrolled through Netflix and put on a Harry Potter movie. Matt smiled when the Death Eaters showed up. Now those had to be the worst Henchmen of all.

CHAPTER 17
LET'S GET DOWN TO BUSINESS

JIMMIE WAS SITTING on a floor pillow when Matt arrived for the discussion about the training videos. There was a second pillow already placed on the floor directly across from Jimmie. Matt took that as an invitation. Jimmie nodded in agreement as Matt walked toward the oversized meditation pillow. He tried to suppress his groan on the way down, his legs already aching from the morning lift.

Jimmie started the conversation by thanking Matt for showing up. Matt had gotten used to Jimmie starting each conversation by thanking him for something, even for simply coming to his office. The crazy thing was that the gratitude always felt genuine, which Matt found comforting. Matt actually loved coming to Jimmie's Zen Den. The smells, sounds, and the overall calming effect always left Matt feeling refreshed.

"Matt, I heard you have done a lot of work by paying close attention to the training videos you watched. That's good to hear, it says to me you are serious about this and in it for the long haul."

Matt nodded his head in agreement and added that he

found it an interesting study to watch movies he had seen many times before, but to look at them from a learning standpoint.

"I enjoyed the exercise, and I'm excited to share what I learned," Matt said, feeling proud and like he could contribute to this conversation in a meaningfully way.

Jimmie shifted on his pillow and took a sip of his chamomile tea. "Let's hear what you have to say. What is your overall impression, what did you notice?"

Matt sat up from the slouched position he was in while on the floor pillows.

"What I noticed most of all is how loyal Henchmen are. Loyal to the Team, to the mission, and to their roles. And their roles are integral to the overall success, just behind the scenes."

"Behind the scenes?" Jimmie questioned.

"Well, not behind, that may not be the best word to use, but they aren't front and center. They stay behind and follow with unquestioned motives. That's more what I meant. They're there to support without question or hesitation," Matt answered.

"Ah, I see, I think I understand what you are saying now," Jimmie said. "That is a wise observation to make. What else did you notice?"

"Well, most times, there is an identified leader within the Henchman. The one I thought was amazing was Luca Brasi from the old *Godfather* movie. That movie had tons of Henchmen, but because of his immense loyalty to the Corleone family, he was trusted to do really important jobs for them. He knew the rules of being a role model Henchman."

"Interesting. I hadn't thought about him in that movie in a long time. We should have the Team watch that, as inspiration."

"Luca does have some impressive skills," Matt agreed.

"Which of the Henchmen surprised you? Is there one that stood out more than others?"

Matt smiled. "I've seen *The Wizard of Oz* many times, like most people, but never thought of the flying monkeys as Henchmen. I think they were my favorite."

"Why is that? What did you like about them?" Jimmie asked.

Matt began, "I think they are the best at their job. The witch tells them to capture Dorothy and Toto, they do exactly that, with no fuss, no getting outsmarted, no trying to grab them and failing over and over. They do exactly what they are asked to do, like all good Henchmen should."

"Don't you find it interesting that you picked them, and they literally don't speak? Yet they are able to diligently follow orders and complete them," Jimmie added.

"I didn't really think about that, but yeah, even more amazing and evidence of how rule number one applies: Never speak on the job."

Jimmie smiled. "Touché"

Matt had another question and wasn't sure how to bring it up or how it would be received once the words came out of his mouth. He deduced that this was as good a time as any to ask. Taking a deep breath and pause, Matt then said, "There are a couple of other themes in each of the videos. One, the most obvious, is that most of the Henchmen are not all that bright. They are reactive and not portrayed as being able to think through situations. The second is that they all work for the 'bad' guys. There are not really any Henchmen who work for the 'good' guys. Are we the bad guys, Jimmie? Is that who we are?"

"Ah, I was waiting for that question," Jimmie said. "I have given some thought to that myself in the years since I have been in the field. If you have some time, I would be happy to share part of my life philosophy. It may not answer the question, but it would give you something to think about."

Assuming this discussion would be here for longer than usual, he pulled up his pillow from the floor to move it against the wall, to be more comfortable. "Yes, I would like to hear what you have to say. The more I thought about it, the more I was undecided about how comfortable I would be, being on the bad side, on the side of evil. That is not who I am, or who I ever strived to be."

"I'm always up for a healthy dose of good versus evil discussion," Jimmie said enthusiastically. He cleared his throat. "I have been in this job for a long time. When I started, too many years ago to even remember, I was a sassy punk who thought I was invincible. I was mean and self-centered, basically a first-class asshole. I thought the tougher I was, the better it made me at my job. Having no fear of anything or any sort of consequences was my life force.

"You can throw off that vibe, I have felt it. But it also seems controlled now," Matt said.

"A lot of work went into that control. To get to this point, I fucked up a lot of lives, families, and karma for many years. I lived life with gusto, but only on the outside. No one would have ever known the absolute pain and anguish I was feeling. I walked around so cocky and full of myself that it was enough to make you sick. I had barricaded my emotions so far down. Now that I can reflect, I know it was a coping mechanism for me."

Matt was seeing the theme of shoving emotions, hiding them, locking them up to where they couldn't be reached. That's how Jimmie has trained the guys to cope and survive in this business. *Is that healthy?* Matt wondered. Aren't emotionally healthy people supposed to deal and feel to move on? A human being isn't wired to keep things pent up, especially when in the business of hurting people for the survival of DMF.

"A few years after I left the Army and was working here, I was going about my business, just like any other day. I would get my assignments for the day and did them with no hesitation at all. On this day, my assignment was to have a 'talk' with some guys with another organization who we were having some technical issues with, a very routine visit."

"This is before visits were called errands," Matt observed.

"Yes, they were called visits back in the day. On my drive there, I saw a squirrel. Yes, a squirrel, in the road. It was alive, so not a big deal, right? Thing is, the squirrel was not alone. He or she was literally trying to drag its injured squirrel friend out of the street. He had his little arms wrapped around the chest of his friend. This little guy was fighting and trying so hard to pull what was left of his friend out of harm's way. It was the most beautiful thing I had ever seen, and my heart and walls burst open at that very moment. I cried, heaving sobs, the kind where you can't catch your breath. There must have been at least twenty years of tears that followed. Those fucking squirrels got me, you know? It was the partnership, the love, the connection that I was privileged to witness that day. In life, there are no coincidences, only fate. I know there is a Higher Power that guides us and directs us throughout our lives. Those squirrels were there for me to see that day. I could have driven a million different ways to my job that day, but I was divinely guided to drive that route."

Matt wondered silently what it would have looked like to see Jimmie sobbing. He couldn't imagine Jimmie's kind, but tough face consumed by tears. He had been a difficult one to read, but he could certainly see both sides of Jimmie now. Matt shifted slightly in his seat as a sign of paying strict attention to the rest of Jimmie's tale.

179

Jimmie took another sip of his tea and uncrossed his legs to change up which leg was in front. "Have you ever noticed how something that is as simple as changing how you cross your legs can feel so unnatural?"

"So, you're saying that getting out of your comfort zone is what it takes to see how what we do isn't a bad thing?"

Jimmie nodded. "Changing perspective more so than sitting in comfort. In the years since, I have become a student of many spiritual things. I have gone on retreats and traveled the world hoping to find answers to life's questions. I wanted to have a better understanding about how I fit into the world and to make peace with my past. I incorporated the practice of meditation, mindfulness, yoga, gratitude, and veganism into my daily routine. I became a more centered and grounded soul. I wear my Malas as a reminder of my divine connection to all beings, *we are one.* I touch and hold these beads throughout the day, and I cannot explain the peace I feel. This is a huge deal in the work we do, finding calm in all things can save you."

Matt always wondered what those damn beads were that he wore all the time. It made sense to him now; they were a grounding mechanism. "I wondered what those beads were for. I remember noticing them the first night I was here. You were the only one I saw who didn't have a gun, just beads. I have to ask, in your spiritual studies, you found it was justifiable for there to be good and bad in the world?"

"In a sense, yes, that is how I understand things now. But to me bad, or evil as you say, is more a good person who is confused, not evil. You may wonder how I can continue performing my assigned job duties with all the woo woo I have just laid on you. I will be honest and say it took me a minute to realize how my two worlds could live in harmony. One day, I heard it loud and clear: Humans have free will, they have a destiny. That was it! At that point, my life made absolute, complete sense. The guilt I had carried, the weight, the burden of my past, was instantly lifted and I felt reborn."

"So, you're telling me that because humans have free will, and an encounter with you however violent or deadly it is, part of their karma, that makes it all ok then? More like, this was who they are meant to be, and they are fulfilling their destiny? Choices we make?" Matt asked.

"You're with me so far, kid, that is brilliant. You have the basic concept down, which leads me to why I am a vegan. I never ate another piece of flesh after I saw the squirrels that day. That is because animals do not have free will, as we do as human beings."

Matt let out a breath he hadn't realized he'd been holding. "That is some heavy shit, Jimmie. I'm going to need a minute to process all of that. I guess it addresses some concerns I had as you spoke. I thought that if in fact our lives revolve around karma, good and bad, all that, then we are all fucked. Our jobs are to hurt and kill. But as a fascinating reframe, we 'signed up' for this life, as did the people we defend DMF from. We are doing what we karmically are 'supposed to.' With that, there is nothing to lock down emotionally, as we are following our paths, which is not evil, it is our destiny."

"Yes! That's it. In simple terms, yes, you are fulfilling your karma, which is all we can ask for."

"Then there are no bad guys. No evil?" Matt questioned.

"I think there is evil, Matt. Evil rears its head when people become confused, obsessed with power, greed, and hate. When they become confused and so unbalanced and unconnected to their own truth. That is when there is evil," Jimmie said.

It explained so much to him about the way Jimmie worked, and how he saw life. It was actually fascinating. Matt felt a sort of privilege that Jimmie was sharing this much with him. He had to wonder if all the guys on the Team had heard this. Was there a reason for them to hear it? He didn't think many would appreciate it or understand it at all. *The stereotypical idiot Henchman.* At least he knew he wasn't a typical Henchman, at least not yet. Matt was counting on learning what style of Henchman he would become. The role models he was leaning toward were a mix of Franco's firm leadership and Liz's slick, calm style.

As the meeting concluded, Jimmie explained, "I'm not an educated man, no college degree, but I've been around business long enough to know where there is an underlying flaw in the traditional way Henchmen's roles are defined. During my morning meditation I've had a vision of lightness and a new direction in my work. Divine timing is something that I take seriously. I have to ponder the question, are you the lightness in my vision?"

CHAPTER 18
FIRST TIME JITTERS

LIZ HAD RECENTLY SET up a group text for the Team. Most of the guys knew how to follow a thread, but there were a few who had to be taught the importance of keeping a thread going. Not all the Henchman were pros at responding to text messages in a timely manner. There was a near fatal mistake made, when one of the Henchman hit a 'reply all' in the group text chat, that said some unflattering things about Liz. After that mess was sorted out, the group chat worked well to keep people informed.

The Tuesday Matt officially started on the Team, he got a 911 text, meaning to respond immediately. Quickly responding to the text, Matt was told he needed to fill in for one of the guys who was ill that day. Jumping right into on-the-job training, he had mentally prepped for this day, but when he did, it was not in such an emergency fashion. Matt had eyeballed his new suits many times, longing for the day he got to put one on and head off to work. This was the day. Grabbing the dark navy suit, he rushed to get dressed and ready in the ten minutes they gave him.

One glance in the bathroom mirror, and he was off to the kitchen. He hadn't officially met the Henchman he was partnered with for the errand, although Matt knew exactly who he was as he arrived in the kitchen. Liz was already there, speaking to Aaron. She motioned Matt to join them. Physically, he was the same size as the Henchmen Matt had already met, but what stood out the most on him was his mohawk haircut and his face tattoos. The words "Sinners Never Win" were artfully drawn across his forehead. Matt had never gotten close enough to read his forehead until now. He was grateful they were on the same team. He was the most intimidating guy he has ever met.

"Matt, this is Aaron, Aaron, this is Matt."

"I know who he is, what's up dude," Aaron replied.

Matt went to offer a handshake, but Aaron had already turned back toward Liz to continue the conversation. Matt fumbled to take his hand back and wondered what social skills these guys have. *Neanderthal.*

Liz continued to give Aaron cues and tips about how to incorporate Matt into the errand for the safety of them both.

"You've got to take the lead in this. I know you're usually number two and not the lead, but this isn't anything too intense, so I'm trusting you to go alone on this one," Liz said authoritatively.

"You aren't coming?" Matt asked, shooting a wide-eyed glance at Liz.

"College Boy, I got this, let's go!" shouted Aaron as he started walking out the back door.

Liz grabbed Matt's arm as he walked by. "Just follow his lead, don't try to be a smart guy, ok? Don't fuck this up, it would set you way back," Liz whispered, "and you look the part, love the suit."

"Thanks for the confidence boost," Matt sighed.

The task for the errand was simple, straight to the point. Visit the self-storage site, go straight to the office in the back, not the front office, have a talk with the dipshit that was running the software development in the back, and go. Aaron said nothing else but what was on the agenda for their visit.

"Dude, don't fuck this up, ok? It would fucking suck if you screwed up something as easy as this," huffed Aaron.

Until that point, Matt was actually feeling like a million bucks. *Having a suit that fits this well, riding in a luxury car, working for an hour or two at a time, making six figures, what could top this?*

"Why does everyone think I'm such a loser?" snapped Matt.

"Because you are, I guess." After a slight pause, Aaron continued, "Just playing, it may be a good thing for you to lighten up a little. Ball busting is part of the onboarding process as you call it, didn't you see that part? You think we're so stupid, but I suppose it would come as a surprise to you that we are smart enough to care that you are trained well."

"I don't think you guys are stupid. You think I think you're stupid because I went to college. Maybe I am smarter, but only in some ways, like book smart, but you guys know this shit so well. Hands down, you're the experts. Clearly, we're all gears in a machine that makes the entire Team work efficiently," Matt said.

Aaron scoffed. "See, it's that kind of shit that gives you a bad rep."

"What, what did I say? Christ, I never know what I say to piss you guys off," Matt said, wide-eyed.

"You had me going until you start with the gears in the machine bullshit, Team running efficiently, blah blah blah. No one talks like that. You should have left it alone with the 'we're the experts' part."

"I used that analogy because that's what Jimmie and Liz used," Matt said, looking rather sullen.

"Exactly, my man. But you're part of the Team; you're not Jimmie or Liz. Don't get too ahead of yourself." Aaron pulled into an office building parking lot. "We're here. Are you good, done pouting?"

Aaron didn't wait for an answer, getting out of the car immediately after he put it in park. *How do these fucking guys walk so fast?* Matt wondered as he almost ran to catch up. Aaron walked with purpose and confidence. Matt was already taking note on how to improve his 'business walk.' Once at the back office, Aaron threw open the door, startling the man behind the computer screen.

"Fuck, you scared the shit out of me. What are you doing here?" the man behind the computer screen shouted. The nameplate on the front of the desk displayed *Randy*.

"Look asshole, I told you the last time I was here that if you didn't start producing and giving Fowler the data and code he needed, then I would come back here and not be in a good mood. Guess what, you can tell that I'm pissed right now," Aaron said through the patented DMF death stare.

"What are you talking about? I've done more than he originally asked me for," Randy protested. He took a loud sip out of a nearly empty McDonald's cup, the straw loudly scraping the bottom.

"Is that right? Well, things are not looking good for you to continue at this slow pace. Fowler even had me bring another guy with me, just to witness what kind of carnage I can leave behind when I get pissed," Aaron said.

Matt was thrown with him being included in the conversation. He panicked. Should he answer, should he remain silent, what should his response be? He was told rule number one was to not speak on the job. His confidence was rocked with the conversation he had just had with Aaron, and he didn't want to fuck up again. He thought it through in a split second.

They couldn't call him a fuck up if he followed the rules, right?

He chose silence and tried to muster up a decent death stare. Matt walked over to the fidgety Randy, staring directly at him. As his instincts kicked in, he knocked the McDonald's cup from Randy's hand, ice and soda trickling onto the floor. Then Matt took his arm and cleared off the desk. Papers, food wrappers, old coffee cups, Randy's phone, the laptop he had been working on, all on the floor.

"What the fuck, dude! Jesus Christ, all my shit is fucked! Why do that? Oh man," shouted a surprised Randy.

Never saying a word, Matt turned and walked out of the office. He did that for effect; however, he was also trembling and didn't want the other two men to see his hands shaking, or that he could barely breathe. Matt took some deep breaths until Aaron emerged from the office.

"Now that was fucking funny. I didn't see that coming," Aaron laughed as he walked back to the car.

Once in the car, Matt's nervous system had to reset, and he could speak in a voice that moments before would have been shaky and embarrassed him.

"I wasn't going for funny. I was going for not fucking it up. Was I successful at that?" Matt asked.

"I would call it a success, yes," Aaron said.

"Did I break the laptop? I was worried that if I did, it would have taken more time away from what he has to do," Matt rambled.

"Dude, you still don't get it. This errand was to keep him on track. He hasn't under-produced, the guy is killing it. We just went there to make sure he keeps up the pace," Aaron said with a slight hint of disgust.

"Then why don't you tell him good job, encourage him, be positive?" Matt questioned.

187

Aaron rolled his eyes. "That's not the way Henchmen work. Did you ever see a Henchman be soft and mushy and tell people how great they are in the training videos you watched? No, that is not how things get done. We are all taught that fear is the number one motivator."

"Fear doesn't have to be used that way. Plenty of people respond with praise," Matt argued back, knowing that the conversation was over.

As was expected, Aaron ignored his comment, looking straight ahead as he pulled back onto the highway.

————

Aaron had not wanted to debrief with Matt after their errand, so they parted ways. Before Matt headed up to his room, he stopped to grab a couple of apples and a bag of pretzels. Matt had regularly been taking advantage of the open kitchen in the House. The variety of food left out to snack on rivaled a small grocery store.

As he was about to return to his room, he noticed that Fowler was back in his office. He had not been around much the last few months. No one seemed to speak about him or his absence. Was he gone for business or pleasure? It seemed that DMF continued to be productive whether he was here or not.

Matt noticed that Liz and Jimmie were in the office, and he could hear some conversations taking place. With the door to Fowler's office being opened, Matt thought it safe to do a little eavesdropping while wandering past, being curious about what went on in those meetings. The couch across from the open office door gave Matt a perfect place to sit inconspicuously and scroll through his phone while listening intently to the top three at DMF discuss next steps.

"I had a fascinating discussion with the folks in Italy. This new angle is the next step for us to take," Fowler said.

"Will this new venture diversify us at all, or is it more in line with the cyber division?" Jimmie asked.

"This will just take us to the next level. It's pretty incredible. Have you heard of NFT's? It is enough to make your fucking head hurt. In a nutshell, it's a new way to create, buy, and sell digital art. It's a lot to wrap your head around," Fowler said.

"NFT? I have, but I don't understand exactly what and how it works. NFT is an acronym for 'non-fungible token,' if I am not mistaken. But I couldn't intellectually explain what that is," Jimmie laughed.

"You two old goats will need a lot of tutorials on the whole concept. I can set that up so that you will be able to have an educated conversation about it, when the time comes," Liz said.

"This sounds like what you have been looking for, Ed. I think you're right; I will need to educate myself on this," Jimmie said.

Growing with enthusiasm, Fowler continued, "Think about it. We started with hacking into the ATMs when they first came out and we thought we were big shit. Making forgeries of art has been around since the beginning of time. I know our cyber team will be able to work this angle with gusto. This makes that old ATM bullshit seem like child's play. I know now we have been able to capitalize on our ransomware, and 'insurance,' but I think this will blow that out of the water too."

"This is so new to the world, if DMF becomes the first forgers of NFT's, the payout is gonna be mind-blowing," Jimmie said.

"Do you see DMF staying in the ransomware business, or would we just turn our focus to the digital art world?" Liz asked.

"Definitely stay put. I think if anything, we will just need to expand the CM Team. That may be something that Matt helps with."

"Why Matt? Jimmie asked.

When Matt heard his name come up in the meeting, he stopped chewing the apple and chills ran down his spine. This was going to get awkward with him sitting here, eavesdropping.

"Honestly, I'm not sure how he'll do as a Henchman. I'm not writing him off, I saw firsthand how he handles himself. I just don't know if it is in his blood, so to speak," Fowler answered.

"Let's not rush to any conclusions about his role here, he hasn't even gotten started," Liz reasoned.

Jimmie continued, "I will give him credit for the dedication he has put into learning the way of the Henchman. There is no telling at this point how he will fit into the Team. Like Liz said, he is just getting started."

"I hear that you and Matt have become close, and maybe friends?" Fowler asked Liz.

"You could say that. He's a dork, it's refreshing."

"There is something about that kid, I don't know what it is. Maybe I'm getting older, softer—no comment! You know the kid would not be here today if he had left that night," Fowler said.

"Hey, business is business. He's a work in progress, but I think he is worth the time to get him up to speed," Jimmie commented.

Liz's voice interrupted Jimmie and Fowler. "Stop you two with the 'business is business' shit. Can you both just admit that he is also here for another reason? You both know damn good and well that he is the only link to the OT we have right now."

What the fuck are they talking about, the OT? They were

going to kill me if I left? Matt wasn't sure what to do next. Was it best to come clean and admit he was listening? Should he pretend he didn't hear? He had no one to ask. He was frozen with fear and unable to move from the couch. His one friend was part of the discussion that they would have killed him! He continued to listen, deciding the more he heard the better.

"Not trying to change the subject on your old soft ass, but I have some concerns about Matt being able to fully embrace the entire life as a Henchman. He has a kind soul, and it is clear he did not come up in our world," Jimmie said.

"I say we keep our eye on him, more than usual. I hear what you're saying, and if stepping into a full-time Henchman position doesn't work out, perhaps there would be another place to put him," Fowler said.

"Liz, will you be able to help with observing him? I think you will know what to look for," Jimmie said, turning to Liz.

"Yes, I can keep an eye on him, like I have been. But I want to make this very clear to both of you. There is to be nothing, I mean nothing, decided about him unless you discuss it with me. I know we aren't supposed to get attached to anything or anyone, but Matt *has* become my friend. I will have his back, I want you to know that," Liz said in a tone that left nothing to be questioned.

"Good to be back. I gotta say that this new direction we are taking within the cyber division is exciting, and potentially, very profitable," Fowler said.

Matt heard the meeting ending and was going to try and leave the couch and make a run for it so he would not be found out. In a way, he wasn't not surprised that Liz had his back, he had a deep knowing that she was a lifelong friend. But the uncertainty of his future with DMF gave him anxiety. He wondered how heavily Liz's opinions weighed in the grand scheme of things. *I would sure like to show them I have other skills that would be valued here, not just being a Henchman.*

Liz was the first to leave the office. She immediately looked up and saw Matt. The two locked eyes as Jimmie made his way through the door.

"I got this Jimmie, let me handle this," Liz said without turning to look at Jimmie.

"Let me know if you need anything, Liz," Jimmie said.

Liz nodded and walked over to sit near Matt on the couch.

"We aren't used to having to close the door," Liz said, searching Matt's face for any sign of panic.

"This was one of those times the door maybe should have been closed. Although, I must say, it was interesting to get the inside scoop on what you all think of me. I'm glad I heard. Now I know that the 'choice' you all gave me wasn't much of a choice at all. Stay here, or me and my family are fed to the wolves."

"I agree that the door should have been closed. But let me make this short and to the point. No one was going to hurt you if you left that night, that wasn't what that was about. You would have been free to leave, but with no protection from anyone from DMF."

"Well, isn't that nice, no one here was going to kill me, just would have sent me out with no way for me to know how to keep myself safe. I'm not sure how that feels."

Liz sighed. "I'm glad you're here, Matt. You've brought a lot to the Team, believe it or not. The OT is after you, and we are after him. You are here for a couple of reasons, one being that you are bait. The OT has made himself invisible, but now we know he is after you."

"Bait, I'm bait? I thought I was part of the Team, was that bullshit?" Matt asked.

"It's not bullshit. You are bait, but you are also part of the Team. This is something we have never expected to have to do, train a complete outsider, and keep him safe. I hope you heard the part where I called you my friend too," Liz said, quickly changing the subject.

"I heard that. I don't think that part was bullshit," Matt said.

"It wasn't, Sport. I don't bullshit about friends. I don't have that many to play games with. It means something to me," Liz replied.

CHAPTER 19
AND THE MONTHS
GO BY

MATT HAD LEARNED MORE about being a Henchman since his first errand. He was enthusiastic about learning how to be successful in his new career, which he quickly discovered was counterintuitive to how he had been coached. From Matt's experience, to be successful at a career, one had to lead and stand out, but that was not the case as a Henchman. From a little boy, he was encouraged to lead and be noticed. He had to put all of that on the back burner. Once he realized he would not be praised for doing what he was supposed to do, he could make peace with a new meaning of success.

Matt's chief aim for his days was to follow all the rules and take a back seat to the real action. Problem was, he didn't always know all the rules. The best way to not fuck up again was to literally just stand around, and not speak or do anything until asked. This was a tremendous challenge. It meant him following the lead and not trying to be the lead for the first time in his life. He had never been in a position where he knew so little, and where it, most times, could be a life-or-death situation. It wasn't like screwing up data on a spreadsheet or losing an account. If he made a mistake, there were actual lives at stake.

He had begun to notice during his on-the-job training that there continued to be significant collateral damage. He was also guilty of that when he destroyed the programmer's laptop on his first errand. He also noted that people were getting hurt unnecessarily during most of the errands. The whole laptop incident didn't sit well with Matt. His thinking, from a business perspective, was that it was such a waste of time and money. DMF had to now purchase a new laptop, and hours of work were lost. All for what? To tell him he sucks, but in reality, he was doing a good job? This made no business sense at all. What would it look like if the Henchmen changed their roles, somewhat? Matt often wondered. His laptop destruction was only one example of how they lose revenue out of many each week.

There was the time Matt was riding along with Ricky and his second, Damon. It horrified Matt at the disconnect between what the actual errand was, and what actually happened. The three men went in to visit a couple of guys who were working on some code for the ransomware updates. The visit went as planned, however, upon exiting the shop, while Damon was absentmindedly chatting to Ricky, he stepped into the path of a couple random men.

"What the fuck, dude? Watch where you're going, asshole," shouted Damon to the guy he'd cut off outside the office.

"Hold on, you're telling me to watch out? You're the dumbass that walked into me, so fuck you, man," said the blonde man.

The explosion of testosterone was instant. Ricky and Damon pounced on the blonde and his companion while Matt watched with shock and awe. He heard the bones in the two strangers' arms break—it was a horrific sound, but not worse than the cries of agony from the two injured men.

Back in the Suburban, Ricky asked, "You hungry? I feel like some drive-thru. You guys up for that?"

"Yeah, dude, I'm hungry, let's hit it," Damon said.

Matt couldn't believe that these guys had just seriously injured two random guys for no reason and were having this conversation as if nothing had happened.

"Guys, what the fuck was that? You just broke those guys' arms, why did you do that? Couldn't you have just said, 'excuse me, my bad,' and been done with it?" Matt asked.

Both Ricky and Damon laughed out loud and turned up the music on the radio without giving Matt an explanation.

———

Matt looked forward to going to Pinky's, it had become a welcome part of his routine. Before becoming a Henchman, he hadn't been diligent about going to the gym since college, when it had been a requirement. It helped to remind him of the good old days when he played football, and life was different.

Matt had gotten more comfortable with the flow of it and the goings on. He wasn't as lonely as he had been. The guys on the CM Team, especially Harry, had been a large part of him finding connection in the House. At the beginning, he often felt out of place, like he landed in a foreign country, while other times he felt like he had been here forever. The CM Team were just as thrilled to be spending time with Matt. They would always offer him a seat for meals, which he gratefully accepted. There were days when he had more than one seat offered, which was quite a turnaround from the early days in the House.

Matt found himself spending a few moments a day reminiscing about his old life, his condo, his job, a lot of what ifs; what if he hadn't gone to The Basement that day? His life would be the same old, uninteresting, day-to-day monotony. This time in the House had given him a taste of life filled with uncertainty and thrills. As Jimmie would say, it is a matter of perspective, live in the present, for that is all there is.

Matt's days comprised going on errands as an observer only, whenever he could. At first, Matt naively assumed he knew what that meant. He learned quickly when he and the Team ran an errand, it could mean several things. It could mean accompanying Fowler to a meeting, going and visiting the subsidiaries and making sure that the business agreements were being followed, enforcing the proper protocol and ensuring it was being adhered to, monitoring, indiscreetly, the competition, making sure a perpetrator knew who was in charge, and visiting unsuspecting new start-ups that were trying to establish themselves in the same type of work DMF specialized in.

Matt was grateful he was doing the on-the-job training to certain types of visits. He found he didn't have the true Henchman instinct to just react physically with no hesitation. Or did he? His first response would have been to talk, not these guys. It got violent so quickly; it made Matt question if that was always the best way. He didn't think he was the right person to make suggestions on the current business practices. Matt could only hope one day his opinion would mean something and they would take him seriously. He knew without a doubt he could change the way they conducted business.

During his brief time as a Henchman, Matt couldn't help but to notice gaps in the business model of their role. He did after all have a business degree. He had to write many research papers on business efficiency and deficiency back in college. He wasn't able to leave all of his past behind, his education taught him what to look for in successful business models. If he would write business plans that were successful for both The Basement and Tailgaters, then why not DMF? From what Matt could piece together about DMF, he knew it could be so much more with just a few changes here and there.

Even referring to the training videos, the Henchmen depicted in them were all the same. Their mistakes were not addressed, and there were no consequences for poor judgement and reactivity, except for their demise, which was the ultimate consequence. Times were changing. As with most professions, there was a movement to make it fit better in today's world. Matt decided he would keep quiet and not ruffle any feathers. Better to know his place in the company and stay in the Team's good graces. Matt acknowledged he was finally in a better place with the rest of the Team, and he didn't want to push his agenda. They could see that as another way of showing off his degree again or Matt trying to distance himself from the rest of the Team and show that he was better than them.

He and Liz had been hanging out more in the House. Matt was flattered when Liz had asked him to work some jobs together. He felt like he had made it to the big league. Matt felt like they had noticed his silence, and he may be ready to work, and simply not observe.

They were walking out to the car the first time when Liz popped the question, "Sport, I think it is time you were offered a promotion. Are you ready and willing to be my number two? I have an errand to run. Nothing special, just checking on an order I placed."

"Shit yes I am ready! This is huge for me. I'm no longer the silent backseat intern, but number two," Matt said.

He was thrilled and felt his evolution from retired college jock to real-life Henchman was on the right track.

"Right, no longer a backseat intern. I did let Jimmie know I was going to promote you. He wanted an update on your progress and trusted me to give a full, complete, and honest report back." *Of course this was set up by Jimmie.*

"I hate to ask, but what did you say? Is it a pass-fail thing?" Matt asked.

"No, that's too rigid. We would all be out of a job under those terms. I told him you are working at about a 'C' level," Liz said.

"Nice, I am not going to lie, I am not too happy about it. I am used to As. But at least I am making progress."

"You have a way to go to get to an A+ status. Keep working and you will get there." Liz winked.

"I do have a question if you don't mind me asking," Matt said.

Liz nodded with an affirmative go ahead.

"Cool. So the thing is, I haven't heard an update on the safety and security of my family in a significant amount of time. I assume if there had been news, good or bad, they would let me know."

"What is the one thing you learned very early on here?"

His stomach flipped. "Never assume. Are you telling me something has happened to them?"

"No, Sport, relax. Do you think I would let something like that go? They are fine, all is normal with them. The OT hasn't made any attempts to bother them. Shows you that he really is not up to speed on the way things are done in our part of the world."

"Christ, well that is a relief. What is this guy's deal? Jimmie said that threat, the OT, had still not been contained, which was perplexing to all involved with the situation. No one could remember a grudge being held this long," Matt said.

"That's true, and by a faceless entity at that. I know that the Team is still hearing rumblings about there being a bounty for your delivery," Liz said.

Matt had had some communication with his family and friends. He needed to have a story to tell them about what his new job was. He asked around and most of the Team told people who asked that they did security type jobs. That made sense, Matt thought, since they weren't lying about that. Matt had a terrible poker face, which made telling a lie pretty tricky for him.

Matt came up with a canned response to him being a project manager of a security team. He liked to call himself a manager, who would ever know that he could not even do much more than breathe while on the job running an errand? He kept it pretty vague, but his make-believe responsibilities included things like managing accounts, working in the IT-cyber division, and making onsite visits to the customers. Matt repeated this cover story enough times he believed it as well. When asked specifics of his new job, he would say that it was a combination of various businesses with an emphasis on cyber security. He certainly never used DMF's actual name, using Twilight Security as a pseudonym.

Even if he couldn't be totally candid, being able to freely text and call his friends and family made things less stressful. In the beginning, when he wasn't allowed as much freedom to communicate, it led to Matt having worrisome thoughts almost constantly about them.

Generally, friends and family had been supportive of Matt and his recent choice of career, as secretive as it may be. His siblings joked in their group chat Matt must either have gotten a high-security clearance, top-secret government job, or he was doing something criminal. If only they knew the half of it.

As Matt continued on with his on-the-job training, he became more interested in what the actual businesses they visited were all about and how they fit into DMF as a whole. He was progressing with the role of Henchman, but that was not his true passion. His curiosity about the intricacies of the DMF portfolio were what he wanted to hear more about. This was a touchy subject to breach because Matt did not want to again appear as an educated snob, better than the rest of the

Team. If he were to let on that he was bored with being 'only a Henchman,' it could cause a ripple effect of bad vibes from the Team. Matt thought about how to navigate the conversation with Liz, so that she would take the lead on initiating a meeting with Fowler to discuss DMF Enterprises.

Fowler never had to answer to anyone about his where-abouts. His comings and goings were simply met with shoulder shrugs from the Team. When Fowler's office door was wide open, it signaled that he was in the country and available to chat. A half-open door indicated that he was here, but working on some new project, and not totally accessible. A slightly ajar door reflected you had better have a really fucking important reason to disturb him. A closed door, everyone knew, meant he was out of the office, indefinitely, don't bother knocking.

Except for Liz and Jimmie, Matt didn't think anyone knew his agenda or itinerary while he was gone. Historically, Liz had never missed an overseas trip with him. Matt's original thought was Jimmie would be the next logical travel partner. It was pointed out to him that neither Jimmie or Fowler *ever* traveled together, and very rarely to the same destination at the same time, similar to the President and Vice President type of deal.

Who would be trusted enough to travel with Fowler? Any of them would have been on the approved-to-travel list. David H. was not skilled enough to take on that type of work, and Matt couldn't come up with any other suitable Henchman to provide the level of security Fowler demanded. This became even more of a mystery for Matt to solve. Pinky's was as good a place as any to nudge Liz into a conversation about DMF, and the fact that on Fowler's last trip, he had been MIA for longer than usual.

Liz seemed preoccupied on their way to Pinky's. Matt noticed her checking her phone more than usual and seemed extra fidgety. "What's bugging you today?" Matt asked.

"Nothing. Why do you ask?"

"You seem more stressed than usual, just an observation. Is it about your dad being gone for so long?" Matt said.

"Ugh. He was supposed to be back a few days ago. Those stupid Italian Henchmen can't be trusted, and they are soft. I should have insisted I go with him . . . " Liz trailed off.

"Italian Henchmen? How does that work?

"I don't know how it works, that is what's fucking with my head. He went to *develop a relationship* with this fancy-pants Italian, Rossi. In an effort to show his good intentions, Rossi offered to let my dad use his Henchmen to show off their skills. My dad agreed, saying he thought it would be seen as disrespectful if he declined," Liz said.

"Ouch. Have you been in contact with him?" Matt asked.

"Yeah, it all seems fine. It is just very, very different than how we work," Liz said.

"Sure is. But change can be a good thing, right?" Matt said.

Liz rolled her eyes. "Fuck off, Sport. I'm not good with change."

CHAPTER 20
DOUBLE DIPPING

THE NEXT PHASE of on-the-job training was something Matt was looking forward to, thinking it would be easier for him to fit in on the CM Team than the M&M Team. Getting the go-ahead from Jackson took longer than Matt wanted it to. Harry explained that if you needed something approved by Jackson, you better make sure he was in the right mood, meaning when he wasn't face-to-face with a couple of screens. Matt was just about ready to take matters into his own hands and get this visit to the CM team rolling when at breakfast, a groggy, disheveled, smelly man walked up to Matt.

"Dude, why don't you lay off my Team? If you wanted to come see what we do, why didn't you just ask? My guys are not people-pleasing people. Harry about lost his mind trying to ask me a favor for you," Jackson said in disgust.

"You must be joking. I asked maybe a couple of times. I was trying to follow protocol, not skipping the chain of command," Matt replied.

"What fucking protocol are you referring to? I can see why you don't fit in here. Leave my guys alone. If you need something, come to me. It's cool for you to stop by tomorrow. But don't harass anyone. You get to look don't touch. Gamers aren't coders, got it?"

"Yeah, sure, I got it. Thanks for the invite," Matt said. What he said and what he wanted to say were two very different things. What he wanted to say was, *Go take a shower you smelly, homeless-looking freak.*

———

The next morning, they met in the CM Team room behind the kitchen. Jackson didn't greet him when Matt walked in, just a quick nod, then he looked back to his computer. Matt noted that he was in the same stinky clothes he was in the day before, and he clearly had not seen a razor for weeks. He wasn't the physical size of the M&M Henchmen, certainly not as polished. Matt wondered when the last time was that Jackson has seen the light of day or taken a breath of fresh air.

Matt awkwardly stood behind Jackson while he checked his emails. Matt decided to try to make some small talk. "It's cool both you and your dad are with DMF and that you've known Fowler for so long. You must have plenty of good stories to tell about Fowler from when you were growing up. Did you know Liz too?" Matt asked.

Not making eye contact Jackson sighed. "How the fuck did you know that my dad works here too? Oh, that's right, the second you got here, you made friends with the boss's daughter, convenient. I knew Liz, yes, we would see each other here and there. I knew more about them from hearing stories from my dad than from actually spending time with them."

Ignoring the boss's daughter comment, Matt continued, "Your dad must be a badass at this. Did he get you into this, or did you naturally lean towards this as a career? I just find it curious how people get into this type of business," Matt added.

"Yeah, my dad knows his shit and knows his way around the cyber security world, and he can take one look at someone and know whether or not they are full of shit. He has a sixth sense about people and situations that few people have. He introduced me to this job, which is cool. I like it," Jackson replied, not leaving room for Matt to continue the conversation.

Matt finally pulled up a chair when he realized an hour in that Jackson was not planning on moving from his spot in front of the computer, still not talking to Matt. From what Matt could tell watching Jackson write code, Jackson's job was to continue to develop innovative ways to broaden DMF's presence in the cyber-crime network. Though he was a smart guy, Jackson had the same level of social skills as the rest of the millennial Henchman Matt had worked with, barely speaking to Matt.

Matt regretted asking for an entire week of CM training.

The next morning, Matt showed up at nine, the usual start-time, he had assumed, but Jackson did not come to work for another hour. Harry explained that Jackson worked odd hours; no one ever knew from day to day when Jackson would start work, as it depended on when he felt like it.

When Jackson finally showed up, Matt decided to actually try to learn something this day.

"So, what are you working on?" Matt asked.

"I'm coding a way to forge NFTs," Jackson said dully.

"Is that the next big DMF project?" Matt asked.

Jackson nodded. "Our next endeavor is going to involve the forgery of NFTs. The only super fucked up thing is that I was recently informed that it would be a 'collaborative' project with those assholes from Italy. I know you are close with the super-powers at DMF, so I won't talk too much shit, but let me say this, no one here on the CM Team is ok with it," Jackson fumed.

"I only heard about that in a roundabout way. I don't think it is common knowledge for the rest of the Team. Sounds like you are pretty pissed about that. Is this the first time you were asked to collaborate?" Matt asked.

"It's complete bullshit. That's all I'm going to say on that subject."

"Got it, bullshit. What have you worked on in the past?" Matt asked.

Jackson finally turned away from the screens and began to engage in a semi-thoughtful commentary on what he has created so far.

"I think I've proved my loyalty and worth with what I've produced. Let me give you a roadmap as to what I created here. It is the framework of one of DMF's largest revenue sources, codename *Cherry on Top*," Jackson said.

"Sure, I would love to hear the great work you have done," Matt said, thinking a little ass kissing was a good idea.

"You're fucking right it's great work! Our DMF cyber-Team hacks into a company's, or sometimes city government's, data and files, for example a medical office, a city's court documents, anything like that, and lock the data and files up."

"What do you mean lock the data up? You are talking holding it for ransom?" Matt asked.

"Yup that is it, we hold the files and information for ransom. When we first brought the concept to Fowler, he thought we were joking. After he stopped laughing, Fowler said that paying ransom back in the day was for a person, someone's child, or even a pet, not data. This has been brilliant, like hitting the jackpot. People don't realize the entire world ran on data, which is just sitting out there waiting to be breached. It's where the big, easy, relatively quick money is now. I transitioned DMF over to this a few months ago when the experts I communicate with on the dark web told me they were certain that this was the future of cyber criminals. I hate to use that word, criminal, but what else would you call it? Cyber thieves?"

"That sounds complex," Matt said.

"It is a more advanced and complex dimension," Jackson agreed. "However, it is profitable."

Jackson laid out in detail the whole flow of his project. The payouts were not always guaranteed, some targets wouldn't or couldn't pay the ransom. This was the one flaw that the Team could determine. They would need researchers to pick targets based on the criteria they created so as to ensure the ransom would be paid. Once the list of approved targets was verified, net worth, data to be collected, long-term effects, then the cyber experts would get to work on locking the targets out of their own systems. Once the targets figured out that it locked them out and had breached private information, then the cyber team would make the ransom request. Fairly straightforward, just like kidnappings used to be.

The twist in all this was that DMF, under another name, also offered a cyber insurance policy for anyone to buy. Whoever bought this cyber specific insurance policy would pay a monthly premium along with a sizable deductible if they were ever to have their data be ransomed. The brilliance of this was that after companies paid their ransom, it would bombard them with ads for this new cyber insurance. Not only would DMF be paid ransom, in most cases, they would then present themselves as a savior, saving them from this ever happening again.

"The insurance policies are marketed world-wide. Once a company purchases the policy, we run an algorithm to determine the perfect time to hack into their system, that we are protecting," Jackson said.

"Nice, I guess. I mean, I get the concept, but I had no idea how fucked people can be," Matt said.

Jackson continued, "The policies come with varied pricing of deductibles. Similar to any insurance, the lower the deductible, the higher the policy premium, and the higher the deductible, the lower the policy premium. Most of the policies purchased are an afterthought for the companies, never truly believing they would have to use them. What's included with the higher priced packages is a ransom negotiator to help get their data/files back. Offering the negotiator was a perfect way to get people to trust them."

"I would imagine people thought it was a joke. A negotiator, it was a pretty exceptional idea," Matt commented.

The team had a great time creating this role, the script they would follow, and how they would ultimately make them look like heroes.

"Matt, I think it may be helpful for you to sit in on call with a negotiator. It's better to show rather than explain how this works," Jackson huffed.

"Yes, that would be awesome, I would like that," Matt said.

"Alright, then follow me," Jackson said, going into a room Matt hadn't been in.

The room was set in the back of the House, where there would be less noise while the calls were being answered. There were cubicles surrounded by sound proofing cushioned walls with comfortable gaming chairs behind each desk. The lighting was dim in the windowless room.

"Come sit over here." Jackson showed Matt to a seat in cube number three. "Sit here with Caleb, he's a veteran with this shit."

Caleb gave Matt a quick nod as he put on this headset. Matt grabbed the second headset that was on the desk. Within seconds, Caleb answered the incoming call blinking on his screen. Matt recognized Caleb as being on the M&M Team, not who he assumed would be working in the mock call center.

"Do any of the Henchman Teams work here?" Matt asked.

"Yes, they both do. There is some cross training, but mostly the M&M Team comes here since it is pretty straightforward. They have a script to read from."

"I guess that makes sense. The CM Team probably has other projects to work on. How many calls a day come in?"

"I haven't ever tracked that data. Guess maybe I should. I am thinking on average maybe eight to ten," Jackson said.

Matt nodded and went back to listening to Caleb answer.

"Good morning, thank you for calling the Stratford Company, how may I help you?"

"I need your help! I came into the office today to find that my network was locked! All I could see was a message on the screen that said all of my files, everything has been taken. I can't have that! I am the office manager of a medical practice; I can't have that! We simply can't have a data breach with people's medical information! I need your help," shouted the panicked caller.

"Ok, ma'am, can you tell me where you are calling from, and if you have the policy number with you?" Caleb questioned in a monotone voice that in no way matched the hysteria of the caller.

"Yes, um, I am from Logistics Medical. I have the policy number here, it is 25-831257. You have got to help. I don't understand how this happened. We backup our information every night," the caller noted.

As Caleb heard the policy number on the second monitor, he scrolled through a script to follow, holding his finger on the correct line of the script, making sure he didn't skip ahead a line. "I see you have the addendum on your policy that includes a ransom negotiator, so the good news is that we can help with that. Can you read me exactly what the ransom note said, please," Caleb read.

"Sure, it just says that they need $100,000 deposited into an account in seventy-two hours, otherwise the data will be destroyed, and it gives an account number, that's it, nothing else," the caller said. "Are you going to be able to recover my data?"

"Yes, ma'am, we are. I will take care of things on this end. You don't have to worry; we will make sure you get your data back. One last question before I get off the call. You have a $50,000 deductible which leaves us to take care of the other $50,000, unless our negotiator can get the ransom. How much of the $50,000 would you be able to pay today?" Caleb said in his monotone voice.

"What? I hadn't thought about that. I say we could go up to $30,000–$35,000 today. Will that be enough to secure having a negotiator get started on my claim? Anything lower than that would obviously be better. When should I expect to hear from you?" the caller asked.

"I see, $35,000 is your payment for today. Upon receipt of the money, we will send you the decryption keys to unlock your data. We will have this resolved within forty-eight hours. Once the negotiator is finished with your claim, we will let you know the balance due, if any. We will be in touch," Caleb said, hitting the end call tab.

"See how fucking easy that is? What did that take, a couple minutes? I just made $35,000," Caleb said, smiling.

"Jesus, this is something. What happens now?" Matt asked.

"Nothing; I don't know. I only answer the calls. I think someone else calls them back and says that everything was taken care of, and that they need to deposit the $35k into the account given to them, and the decryption keys will be sent," Caleb said, taking a long drink from a Mountain Dew bottle.

"Decryption keys? What is that?" Matt asked.

"When data is ransomed, it needs to be encrypted and stored. To send it back, it needs to be decrypted, and the customer is given instructions on how to retrieve their data," Jackson explained.

As time went on, it became clear that when the decryption keys were given to the companies that paid the ransom, most of the time, they were not cyber savvy enough, and could not figure out the new security keys to open up their returned data. The company then needed to be walked through the decryption process to call the same 800 number, and have the cyber thieves, AKA, the Stratford Company, walk them through getting their data and files back. As an added service for those who didn't want to call, there was a chat box option set up. They also answered these calls in the back room where Caleb was stationed.

With this setup, the DMF Cyber Team double dipped, they had the cyber insurance company, but were also the cyber criminals holding the data and files ransom in the first place. This process was typically easy, and it offered a nice payday almost every day. The actual breaking into many if not all the files hadn't been an obstacle, not with the quality of the guys on the team. Most companies thought they were safe since they did a system backup each night, however, what DMF found was that many times, the backup was on the same server, which was incredibly lazy and not safe at all.

The thing that was not clear in the beginning was how they were going to get paid. No one could have a suitable means of collecting their pay until cryptocurrency. With cryptocurrency such as Bitcoin, it just made their jobs easier. The CM team could be everywhere and nowhere at the same time. Cryptocurrency was not traceable, a perfect fit for their business model.

While Matt was observing Caleb answer calls, he noticed another cubicle that was getting a lot of attention. Harry was seated in a cubicle with an intense focus energy about him, as others looked on. Harry's fingers were working at a frantic pace.

"Hurry up, Harry! I think you got it, you are on the right track, keep going," Finn said with an encouraging pat on Harry's back.

"Whoa, shit that guy is good! I can't believe he's gotten this deep into our system," Albert said.

"They better catch this guy, he's quick and dangerous. I'm sick of always being on defense with this guy. I would like to be the one that goes after his ass one time," Harry said.

"Just so you know, those guys are not working ransomware claims, they're on the dark web cruising message boards to see who and what is on our tail. This time, it sounds like it is the OT," Jackson mumbled to Matt.

"The OT? They have made contact with him? Do Jimmie and Fowler know? That's the guy who's after me, and they're looking for him! This is good news, right?" Matt asked.

"They know all about it. It's not like they can just ping his IP address and show up at his door. The OT is on here all the time. Sometimes he fucks with us, sometimes he doesn't. Depends on what mood he's in. He just plays with us, and it's crazy how easy he makes it look, I mean how close he gets to hacking our system."

"That sounds exhausting for you guys. I know I'm sick of him, and I don't even have contact with him, but he sure has fucked up my life for the moment," Matt said.

"We are all doing our part to take this guy down. I am not usually a violent guy, I leave that stuff for you guys, the M&M team, but I would really like to kick this guy in the nuts when we take him down. I think all the guys on the team would say the same thing. One kick after another, it would give us all so much pleasure!" Jackson said.

"I think that could be arranged!" Matt smiled. "What is he spewing about when you guys communicate?"

"Half the time, it just doesn't make sense. He rants about you, saying you don't deserve to be here, and how he is always watching you. Which is complete bullshit. There is no way he could have hacked into the CCTV here."

"Jesus, that is really fucking creepy. CCTV? What is that?" Matt asked.

"CCTV, closed-circuit television. DMF installed it years ago after there was some concern that one of the Henchmen was a double agent so to speak. Fowler and Jimmie spent a good amount of time debating how to discover the truth about what was happening with this particular Henchman. They decided that installing a CCTV system in the House was the only way to go. It didn't take long to catch him making calls to the rival group and feeding them rather classified information. Since then, it has only been used when unusual circumstances arise. Things like when you show up with Fowler injured and bleeding."

"That explains a lot. I never figured out how everyone knew everything that went on here. Good to know. As for the OT, I trust you to keep him out of the network. Does he talk about DMF?"

"Yes, all the time. He says things like he would do things differently, and he could take us down with two strokes on the keyboard. That is the shit that pisses me off the most. He is so disrespectful, ugh, I just really want to kick him in the nuts, man," Jackson said.

CCTV in the House, spying on all of them, whenever they felt like it? The thought of the complete lack of privacy left Matt feeling uneasy. *Do they follow us into the bathrooms too?*

Matt wondered. Living in a world where there can be no secrets must keep people on their best behavior, or it could lead to people finding out ways to avoid detection. For now, Matt would consider the first option, knowing that his safety was almost assured.

CHAPTER 21
A DAY IN THE LIFE

Since Matt had spent the next week shadowing Jackson and the CM Team, he hadn't gone on a single errand. Though the errands had been infrequent before, now it had been almost two weeks since he had gone anywhere but Pinky's and he felt himself starting to go stir crazy. It was getting to be a joke each morning when Matt would come to the kitchen, hopeful that his name would show up on the errand board. As he was walking in, the Henchman leaving would be laughing, saying, "Maybe tomorrow, College Boy." He had been going out on an as-needed basis, only filling in when someone was ill or injured. Errands with Liz were rare and infrequent. Her time devoted to working with the Team in Italy. It was getting to where Matt wanted to just scream, *I got this already! Let me do some actual work and figure out my style of being a Henchman!* Matt had spent enough time with Jimmie to know that things happened in the right time, which left Matt with nothing but to be patient and live in the present. *Nothing wrong with hoping for more*, he reminded himself.

Every morning, Matt would hit the gym with Franco and David H. When Matt was at Pinky's, he felt a certain sense of freedom and familiarity. The soreness he felt after a morning lift was a welcome distraction. The casual routine the three had become used was interrupted in a most violent way. This sunny, crisp fall day, Matt, Franco, and David H. walked to their car.

"Do you have much to do today?" Matt asked.

"Nope, only have a few phone calls to make and just one errand to run," David H. said.

Feeling hopeful, Matt asked, "I don't suppose I could tag along?"

"Jesus, how long is Jimmie going to keep you on his leash? It seems like it has been forever. You must have really pissed him off," David H. replied.

"He just isn't ready yet, quit busting his balls, David," Franco laughed while jabbing Matt with his elbow as they approached the car.

"Hey, I deserve some credit here! I have been patiently waiting, and I haven't had any more fuck-ups, I must be doing something right!" Matt shot back as he threw the long strap of the gym bag across his chest and reached for his sunglasses.

Just as they arrived at the car, out of nowhere, three unknown men in suits and dark sunglasses appeared. Their presence caught Matt, Franco, and David H. completely off guard. Despite Franco and David H.'s usually quick reactions, the three unknown Suits jumped on them before they even knew what happened.

It was determined instantly that they wanted Matt, only him, and were willing to take any collateral damage required to accomplish their goal. The three were grabbed simultaneously. Matt was instantly put in a vicious choke hold by the largest of the three. Matt felt himself being dragged toward another vehicle parked next to theirs. Being thrown into their van was not an option if he could help it. Struggling to get out of the hold, Matt found it impossible; the grip was like a vice around his slowly closing windpipe. This obviously untrained Henchman left Matt's hands free and was dragging Matt by his throat in the most awkward fashion.

The other two were holding Franco and David H. in very painful, seemingly inescapable, classic Henchman holds with arms and necks put in positions where bones near the breaking point. Everything happened so fast, Matt was having flashbacks to the night at The Basement.

There was shouting and demands being made, pure commotion. Six men all shouting at once made for a no-win situation. "Get your fucking hands off me, you stupid piece of shit!" growled David H.

"Shut your fucking mouth, we just want this asshole over here, that's it. Fuck off and let us do our jobs!" shouted the smallest of the three Henchmen, only 6'5" weighing in about 270 lbs, who had Franco twisted up.

"Fellas, you know we can't let you do that; it isn't how we run things, you know better than that," Franco replied calmly, though he too was struggling to break free.

"Hey, fuck off, you know how things work. We do what we need to, that's it. We don't get to change the way things work; we're just here for this pile of shit," the Henchman who had Matt replied.

While the shouting continued, Matt was thinking of how to make his escape. The would-be kidnappers/Henchmen didn't know that there were guns in the workout bags, as they hadn't taken the bag from Matt's hand. *Classic dumb Henchman.*

The Henchman holding Matt started again to drag Matt toward the van. Matt knew he was going to be dead if they could get him into their vehicle, most likely his friends would be left dead in the parking lot as well. Matt still had the gym bag in his hand. *If I can just slide my free hand into the bag, I can grab the gun out before he knows what I am doing,* Matt

217

thought. Quickly dropping his hand into the gym bag, he realized he had found the butt of one of the guns. Matt's other hand was trying to pull the Henchman's hand off his throat. He couldn't breathe. Matt's main objective was to get the fucking gun out of the gym bag, he had to, that was their only way out as he saw.

He was glad he had spent some time learning how firearms work. The recent trip to the shooting range was perfect timing. After a few hours there, Matt had a much better working knowledge of guns. Just because Matt got lucky pointing and aiming a gun that saved both his and Fowler's lives and shot guns in video games did not make him a firearms expert.

As the Henchman holding Matt reached for the door handle for the van, he cursed. "The door's locked! Who has the keys?" he shouted.

The Henchman holding Franco yelled, "Dude, they're in your pocket! Hurry the fuck up!"

The Henchman loosened his grip on Matt's neck a bit as he dug around in his pants pockets for the car keys.

Taking full advantage of the shouting and commotion, Matt thought it would be an excellent distraction while he maneuvered himself into just the right angle to get to the gun. As difficult as it was to breathe, Matt knew he needed to have both his hands free. He quickly released his grip from the hand on his throat even though he knew he was seconds from passing out. Flawlessly, he pulled the gun out of the bag. He had taken the safety off; he was ready to go.

Acting like a true Henchman, without hesitation, he aimed at the guys holding Franco and David H. The two stupidly had them pressed up against their car with their backs facing Matt. This made it an easy kill, as they didn't see it coming. Neither did Franco and David H. The two Henchmen slid to the ground as both Franco and David H. spun around.

The kidnapper released the grip on Matt's throat, and in that split second of reaching for his own weapon, Matt took one step forward away from the Henchman, turned, and fired. He shot the last Henchman between the eyes at close range. Three kills in three seconds. Matt instinctively grabbed his throat and coughed. He was trying to take some deep breaths to get his oxygen level back to normal.

"Dude, what the fuck just happened here?" David H. shouted.

Matt, who was bent over still trying to gather his thoughts, simply looked over and said in a raspy voice, "Nothing much, but you sure as shit owe me."

"Holy shit, dude, what the fuck?" was all that Franco could summon. Matt just shrugged, looking down at his hand holding the gun like it was attached to someone else.

"We need to get these assholes in their van, like right fucking now," Franco spat out.

Matt reached into the Henchman's pants pocket to find the car key. *They go to kidnap someone, and they don't have the doors open?* Matt shook his head, not very smooth.

Franco went around to the driver's side of their car and unlocked the doors for Matt and David H. By this time, Pinky had come out to see what had gone on.

"Are you boys ok? What the hell went on here? Do you need anything from me?" Pinky asked, out of breath from running over to them.

"Thanks, Pinky, we're good. Matt was a cool cat, I'll give him that," David H. said.

Matt just looked up with a slight nod as he was dragging Henchman number two to the vehicle.

"Oh my God! I have seen these guys! I thought it was strange. They have been at the coffee shop this week. I knew there was something about them I didn't like," Pinky said.

"Well, Pinky, next time you see assholes like this, who obviously don't belong here, please say something!" Franco snapped.

"Oh boys, I am so sorry, I know better than that, I really do," Pinky said with guilt apparent across her wrinkled face.

Franco walked over to her, put his hands on her shoulders, and said, "You know what to do now, right Pinky? Tell me you know."

"Please don't tell Eddie about this? Please. And yes, of course I know. When the police arrive, I have seen nothing unusual, and my security cameras are on the fritz," Pinky said.

They loaded the three dead Henchmen up into their own vehicle. Franco let the others know he would make the call.

"Who are you calling?" Matt asked. "Shouldn't we get out of here first?"

Franco was already on the phone making the call when Matt asked the question. David H. turned around and said, "He's calling the CUC. Who the fuck else would it be, the police?"

"Dude, I don't know what the CUC is, I haven't heard that acronym before. I'm just asking so I know what the fuck is going on here," Matt replied.

David H. turned to the back seat, rolled his eyes, and said, "After that major league move, I forgot for a second that you still don't know shit. The CUC is short for the Clean-Up Crew."

"Well excuse me, but how the fuck would I know about that?" Matt said back, rather irritated with the tone David H. took with him.

By now, Franco was off the phone and interjected that DMF had one of the best, if not the best CUCs in the business. They did an amazing job every single time. The DMF-CUC were on standby 24/7 whenever and wherever they were needed.

"Believe me when I say that they make all of our lives better. We never, ever have to worry about a thing. Have you ever wondered why no cops have ever come to look for you? It's because the CUC does incredible work, that's why," Franco said.

"The only thing we do is move the damaged goods out of plain sight like we just did back there. The CUC takes care of all the details," David H. said.

"Oh, well, good to know, I guess. Do we all know how to contact them? Will that be something I'm told about when I move off of the C- squad?" Matt asked, referring to the lowest level of sports teams in high school.

Franco laughed, "The C- squad, I like that. Another sports metaphor from College Boy. I'm sure Jimmie or Liz will update you on the CUC procedures when the time is right. To be honest, I have no fucking clue who they are. All I know is that they are there when you need them."

Once the call was made and the CUC were on their way, all three men became silent for the ride home. They were in deep thought, processing the events of the last sixty minutes. The walk to the parking lot should have been just that, a walk to their car. Instead, it turned into a rookie mistake.

Franco was fuming on the drive back. He grunted loudly and began pounding on the steering wheel, snapping Matt out of his trance-like state, a state that was becoming more common as he zoned out when things got too much for him to process at once.

"Fuck, fuck, fuck! God damn it! Shit, that should have never happened! God damn it, that pisses me off. Those guys were fools, and they had us before we even saw them. That's just fucking embarrassing!" Franco shouted.

"Dude, I'm sorry, this one is on me, you know it's my job to look ahead wherever we walk. This is on me. I'll take the heat for this," David H. said.

"Fuck that, you know we both fucked this up. Those assholes weren't here for us, it was for him," Franco said, pointing in the backseat. "We were on the job for fuck's sake, and we didn't do our job. I appreciate you offering man, but this is on me. I'm the lead, and I let my Team down."

"I hear you man, but come on, don't be so hard on yourself. It all worked out in the end. Maybe look at it as a gift, as a reminder, to keep on your game from now on," David H. said.

"Holy shit, you sound like Jimmie now. A gift? Whatever man, I guess so," snorted Franco.

Matt had only been privy to the one debrief conversation with Fowler, never one with the Team. He found it heartwarming and bittersweet. The bottom line was that they were there for him, to protect him. He had been feeling like one of the guys, but after this, it reminded him that his protection was a job for them. Being with him was equal to them running an errand, Christ, his protection was an errand for the Team. It made Matt feel disconnected and back to being a total outsider, not part of the Team. He felt sick to his stomach, not for what just happened, but for the realization that he was still so far from fitting in.

The rest of the ride back to the House, there was no acknowledgment of what Matt did. Neither one of them turned to say, "Good move back there, way to go." Nothing. It was as if Matt wasn't in the car, or did they perceive him as a burden? Matt thought he had done pretty well for himself back there. He was looking forward to telling Liz about it, maybe she would be proud of him, and say something about the progress he had made, and his quick thinking. *This is actually bullshit, they are up there feeling sorry for themselves, and they can't even give me a thumbs up?*

Matt broke the silence in the car. "Man, I'm glad I was carrying the gym bag." Even his shameless attempt for some sort of pat on the back went unacknowledged. *Wow.* Franco pulled in past the gates and drove up the driveway to the back of the House, then parked. As they exited the car, Franco pulled Matt aside. It was the death stare. It confused Matt. Why would he be getting Franco's death stare?

To Matt's surprise, Franco sighed, looking defeated, "Hey man, I fucked up. We're supposed to be better than that. I promise it won't happen again. But dude, that was heads up back there. I shouldn't have to thank you, since I'm supposed to look out for you, but thanks man, we owe you one," Franco said, releasing the death stare.

Matt shuffled his feet and nodded to Franco. "It's all good man, no hard feelings."

"Dude, you kicked ass back there, for real," David H. said as he walked past, punching Matt in the arm.

Matt felt a little less like an outsider after being formally acknowledged by Franco and David H. Matt was going to take the death stare as a 'we will not talk about this anymore' kind of look. Time to move on and get back to the rest of the day. Matt was curious about the CUC and wanted to know more about that entire operation.

He was still feeling conflicted, not sure of his place. Most days when they returned from Pinky's they would sit and have breakfast together. But after this, he was not hungry, and didn't feel like being around any of them anyway. He decided he would just go straight to his room, shower, and go to his computer for the rest of the day.

For a brief moment, Matt had been looking forward to telling the Team the rest of the story. Certainly, this latest adventure would become a legend in the halls of the House, but somehow it felt out of place to want accolades for what he did. The story would only lead to everyone knowing how Franco and David H. had fucked up. From what Matt had gathered, Henchmen on this Team processed immediately afterwards and then let it go. They didn't hold on to their mistakes, that would only lead to more mistakes. They were accustomed to having a short debrief, shouting and swearing, and then, it was as if nothing had happened. They used this coping skill with outstanding success. Acknowledge it and let it go. The karmic universe was at play again, nothing bad or evil.

As Matt turned to go up the stairs to his room, Franco called him into the kitchen. Matt just wanted to be left alone, to process his latest homicide, and didn't want to see anyone.

In the kitchen, Matt was surprised to see a projector shining the security footage from Pinky's onto the wall. Liz, Jimmie, Fowler, Garrett, and a few other Henchmen were watching intently as Matt, Franco, and David H. were grabbed by the rival Henchmen.

"Rookies," one Henchmen scoffed.

"Shut the fuck up man," David H. spat. Franco put a hand on his shoulder to silence him.

Everyone watched silently as Matt got the gun from the gym bag and shot the three guys. Matt felt entirely disconnected from that guy on the screen. Who was that guy, shooting those three guys at close range like a professional? It looked to Matt like a replay of his character playing COD rather than him.

"Seemed like it was a lot longer than it actually was. Christ, the whole thing was done in a matter of seconds," Matt sighed.

No one said anything as the tape ended. Were they angry with him, or happy with his actions? He had no way of telling since they all had the emotionally dead look on their faces.

Adding to his stress was that he was almost killed, kidnapped, or whatever those guys were planning to do, and he had actually killed three men.

"Well done, Sport," Liz said, breaking the silence. She smiled at him. Matt noticed a few of the other guys sitting at the tables give an approving nod.

"How are you doing, Matt? That was an intense scene back there," Jimmie said with his kind Jimmie eye staring deeply.

"I'm ok, I guess. I'm not sure what to think right now, I feel like I need to lie down," Matt replied.

"I don't know what it is about you, but you seem to have a knack for being in the right place at the right time. Is having that sixth sense something you can teach all of us?" joked Fowler. "I again want to thank you. We could have lost two of our top Henchmen today."

"You're welcome. I guess I was lucky enough to be the one carrying the gym bag," Matt replied.

"Liz, can you make sure he gets up to his room? I think a little downtime would be appropriate right now," Jimmie said.

"Yes, of course. Come on, Sport, let's go get you upstairs," Liz said while gently directing Matt towards the stairs. "That was fucking awesome what you did today. I knew you had it in you."

CHAPTER 22
MOVING UP FROM THE C SQUAD

In the days following the incident outside of Pinky's, Matt's social status moved up. The M&M Team wasn't as hostile towards him. He still felt like the new kid, but there were a few more nods of acknowledgment now, which was cool. The guys on the CM Team had taken to him like he was one of them. Since he introduced himself to them in the kitchen, there were always a couple of them grabbing him to talk to in the halls, in the kitchen, wherever they could find him. Interactions with them were on a whole different level. This positive attention from both Teams gave him a renewed sense of confidence that he was going to one day be a true Henchman, not just the guy they brought on out of a sense of obligation.

Some of the guys other than the CM Team had started sitting by Matt at meals. They may not be the cool kids, but at least Matt didn't have the awkwardness of having to sit alone at meals.

"I hope you are cool with us sitting here with you," Harry asked one day. "I don't want you to think we are smothering you and like we are a little clingy."

"I don't feel like that, all the time. Just kidding. It is nice to have company. Finn and Albert tend to get very chatty. Sometimes, I can't turn around without one of them being right there. Like yesterday morning, I was fine sitting alone with my coffee, I was in a chill mood. The two of them came to sit with me and did not stop talking. They were so excited to tell me about a new game they found that my head began to spin. Then they literally follow me down the halls, sometimes I have to say, 'hey guys I am going to use the bathroom, got to go for now.'"

"They're like your little Fan Club. I think it's kind of *cute* that they follow you everywhere," Harry said.

"Cute, sure we can say that. I don't mind, and I hope you know that. It is nice to have company," Matt said.

Matt had a gnawing feeling after the parking lot debacle and wondered if he should worry about the CUC getting things taken care of at Pinky's. He had killed three men in broad daylight after all, and no one saw anything? He was grateful for the anonymity, but he found it unbelievable and too good to be true. He decided he needed to have his anxiety relieved and went to find Liz. He knew she would tell him what the deal was with the CUC. He didn't have to look long to find her. As Matt was coming down the stairs from his room, he spotted Liz leaving Fowler's office. *Perfect.*

"Hey," Matt called to Liz.

Liz spun around and greeted Matt with a smile. "What's up, Sport? You look like you need something."

"What makes you think that?"

Liz's quickly surveyed him. "Hands in your pockets, shoulders up, goofy look on your face, that's a recipe for Matt to ask a question."

Matt smiled back at her. "I'm just headed down to get something to eat, you hungry?"

Liz shrugged. "I could use a coffee."

As they headed to the kitchen, they passed a few guys from the Team who gave both Matt and Liz a nod.

"Looks like the guys aren't ignoring you anymore," Liz commented.

"Some of the guys other than the CM Team have even started sitting by me at meals," Matt said.

"They adore you," Liz laughed. "You're half CM, half M&M, so you're cool, but approachable to them."

They grabbed some coffee and sat at a table on the far side of the kitchen, the one table that was used for conversations that needed to be had, but not for everyone to hear. Your space was respected if you sat at that table, Matt was hoping the CM Team would also respect the boundary the table gave.

"So, how are you? I haven't seen you too much lately," Matt said.

"I'm well, but that's not what you wanted to talk to me about. Let's get down to it, Sport. What do you want to know? I have other places I need to be today," she said.

"Oh, ok, well, so, I um," Matt stammered, suddenly nervous to know the answer, clearing his throat. "I am filled with anxiety about the parking lot incident. What if I have a warrant out for my arrest and no one knows about it? I wanted to ask about the CUC."

"We know what we need to know about the persons the local law enforcement have their eyes on, not to worry Sport. The CUC? What do you want to know?" Liz asked, looking a tad irritated as she glanced at a notification on her phone.

"Well look, I know everyone says they are so good at what they do, blah blah blah, but I'm sitting here having killed three guys, and I just would like a little reassurance that things are cool, and I won't have to go to jail," Matt said.

Liz laughed. "Sport, you're fine. It's kind of cute that it worries you, still a new guy thing to do. I'm not going to tell you anything about the CUC, except that they know their shit. That's all you need to know. I can tell you how things got cleaned up on the surface, but that's all, and don't ask anyone else either."

"I'll take what I can get, I guess," Matt said in a dejected tone. "I would appreciate having a better idea of what took place after we left, so yes, please tell me the rest of the story."

"In a nutshell, it just so happened that the security cameras on Pinky's store front 'were out of order' at the time of the incident. Pinky apologized to the officer, assured him she would get them looked at. The Henchmen's vehicle was moved before law enforcement got there. The CUC makes magic happen."

Liz said that there had only been one witness who thought they heard an argument. The CUC convinced that person what they heard was nothing for them to concern themselves with. Liz winked when she noted they are very persuasive when they need to be. The case ended up being closed due to not having a crime or a victim.

"Huh, so that's that? You make it sound so simple," Matt said. He had been following her recounting of the situation with full attention. He hadn't even taken a sip of his coffee yet.

"It is, there's nothing to report. You think anyone came looking for those assholes? That isn't how it works. Henchmen come and go, no one misses them. Mostly, they aren't worth missing," Liz replied.

"Ok, well, thank you for the explanation."

"Are you good now? Your anxiety gone? Can you get back to life now, knowing you won't be going to jail? If you still need more reassurance, then you can always talk to Garrett," Liz laughed.

"Yes, I got it, I'm good. I feel like I owe the CUC a thank you or something."

"The CUC get enough thank yous with the fees they

command. You have no idea what they get paid. But they are worth every cent." Liz rose to her feet, about to leave.

"Before you go, can you give me an update on the status of the OT? Are you the person to ask about any updates?"

Distracted by her phone, Liz replied, "Any updates on the OT need to come from Jimmie or my dad, you will have to check with them. I'm outta here now. You take care, Sport."

"See ya," Matt said as he took a sip of the lukewarm coffee, spitting it back into the cup.

————

Though Matt felt better after his conversation with Liz, he still needed some clarity. Why was he still being targeted by some demented, unconventional criminal? Everyone Matt talked to was confused because typically this sort of thing didn't happen, and grudges were quickly squashed. No one was sure why the OT was still pursuing the vendetta. There was not an obvious connection to the non-stop threats that came via message boards on the dark web. He had seen Harry doing battle with the OT on the dark web, perhaps he would be a good person to ask his perspective on the jealousy and revenge the OT was living off of.

Liz did offer Fowler up to collect further information. Maybe he would take her up on that.

Matt had always wanted more details about who was after him, who he had pissed off this badly. This was not a conversation for Liz, or even Jimmie. Matt knew he had to ask Fowler himself about this. He headed to Fowler's office, not sure of the protocol for speaking to him, he knocked on the half-open door.

"Come in," Matt heard from inside. It was Fowler, that was a relief. he didn't want to explain to anyone why he was knocking on Fowler's door.

"Matt, this is unexpected." Fowler was sitting behind his desk that was covered in documents, two monitors on. "Have a seat, don't mind the mess, you caught me in between meetings. What can I do for you?"

"Thanks for seeing me. I wasn't sure how this worked," Matt said.

"How what worked?" Fowler asked.

"Well, how can I get an appointment or a meeting, or whatever, a time to talk to you," Matt replied.

"Most times, if my door is open, and I have the time, you can stop by. Most of the guys don't need to speak to me. Normally it's Jimmie or Liz, and, well, today you." Fowler smiled at Matt.

Matt felt embarrassed for just showing up, maybe he should excuse himself. If any of the guys saw him in there, they may get the wrong impression. He had worked so hard to be accepted; he didn't want it to appear that he was anything but a low-level Henchman on the Team, to be sitting here may give a terrible impression. The sun was shining in from the outside, just as the first day Matt had come into this office. He reflected on how his life had changed since he first got to the House and was offered a job as a Henchman.

"Maybe I should just go, I don't want to keep you from what you are working on," Matt said.

"Don't be silly. You're here, with something on your mind," Fowler prompted.

"Ok, if you're sure." Matt took a settling breath. "I was just wondering what, or should I say who, is still angry with me? I have been thinking about who I may have pissed off, and I just don't get it, I haven't met anyone who I can think of."

"Listen kid, this OT asshole is the one who is pissed at you, I'm not clear to be honest. What I do know is that he has been trying to get our attention for some time now. He is the threat who keeps getting close to infringing on my Cyber Team's business model. He has been on our radar, old Army term. I should say, he's been harassing us on the dark web."

"It sounds like this guy has been a real pain in the ass. Does anyone know why he's still pissed off at me?"

"Jimmie's looking into it. He said something about the OT being upset that you were brought in from the outside, and he hasn't been. He thinks you are getting treated better than him. He brought up some unwritten code that we broke by bringing you into DMF," Fowler said.

"I'm sure he knows the circumstances of why I am here. He caused it for fuck's sake. I think he needs to get a life already," Matt said.

Fowler said, "His attitude is unconventional at best. Most times, no one gives a shit about the inner workings of business on the inside. Neither Jimmie nor I have ever heard of someone holding a grudge about an employee, especially not this long. Let me assure you once again, we are working continually on reigning this guy in.

"I heard from Harry with the CM Team that he has an impressive reputation. All the information they had gathered was that he was a really smart guy who could do some actual damage to DMF," Matt said. "I am feeling a small sense of relief, I appreciate your time. I will just be patient and have faith that you, well, me too will be able to take this guy down sooner than later."

"You're welcome, you will be one of the first to know when the problem has been eliminated. But while you are here, can you fill me in on what you are liking about the job so far, or any observations from a business standpoint. I always like to hear what a fresh set of eyes has to say, especially eyes that are educated," Fowler said.

Matt had plenty to say but was hesitant to blurt it all out at once. "Things are going well. I just see a few things that could be tightened up, you know?"

Fowler's eyebrows raised at Matt's comment. "You keep those thoughts, I would like to hear more, to touch base more often, but right now, I have to hop on this call," Fowler said.

Matt could see he had already checked out and Fowler's attention had left, and he was onto his next meeting.

"Will do, good to touch base today," Matt said as he got up to leave the room.

As he left the room, he saw Jimmie sitting on the couch across from the office, the same one Matt sat on the first night in the House.

The two simply nodded to each other as Matt headed up to his room.

CHAPTER 23
TOO GOOD TO BE TRUE

Matt was enjoying his new status with the Team and with Fowler. He thought back to his one-on-one conversation with him, about how he was the only one from the Team that ever really took advantage of just knocking on the door and meeting with Fowler. Life had finally settled for Matt; he had outgrown being the newbie or the rookie any longer. His schedule was getting fuller by the day. His name was on the errand board regularly, so much so, he barely had time to hit Pinky's or to sit in front of his computer.

Even finding time to hop online to game with the guys from The Basement had been challenging. He did like the contact with his friends from his old life, however, he was over the constant ribbing and negative comments from his old friends. The *you suck, you abandon us, you think you are better than us* comments, though made in jest, somehow triggered Matt in ways that were more confusing for him to decipher than when he killed a man. *I wish I could just tell them the truth, relieve my guilt. The truth is, I miss them,* Matt thought.

On the rare occasion when Matt was left alone at the front desk at Pinky's he found solace in the mundane task of welcoming people into the gym. It was a safe place to be since

Pinky had a built-in radar detector and knew everything about everybody. Matt knew that whoever came in, she would know about, and if she didn't, give her a hot minute, and she would find out.

Matt was taking a gulp from his water bottle when Pinky appeared in front of him, clearly showing signs of distress, her breathing short and labored.

"Pinky, are you ok? You look like you need to sit down, can I get you some water?" Matt asked.

"Oh, aren't you a sweet boy? I don't mean to be that dramatic!" She held up her left hand, with a clearly visible broken pink nail on her middle finger.

"You broke a nail? Is that all, Pinky? Why don't you let me know what I can do to help?" Matt said with a slight smile.

Rambling on, Pinky said, "I have to get this repaired. It is a pet peeve of mine. I can't stand to look at it another second! I do apologize for the disruption in schedules. Would you be a doll and cover the desk for me while I run out? That would be fantastic."

"Take your time. You don't need to be in a hurry to get back. I have got things covered, and Liz is in the back office. It's slow, I got this," Matt assured her.

Pinky hugged Matt goodbye. "Thank you for taking care of my baby, this place. I feel like a mom leaving her newborn baby for the first time."

Not long after Pinky left, Matt casually looked up from his phone to see one of the most beautiful girls he had ever seen walking into the gym. He did a double take as she timidly made her way to the front desk. Matt could not take his eyes off of her, he stood looking at her as she waited silently at the desk. Elegantly, she cleared her throat, to shake Matt out of his stupor.

"Good afternoon, can I help you with something?" Matt

awkwardly asked.

"Hi, yes, I wanted to know more about the membership here. Would you be the right person to ask about that?" the beautiful redhead asked.

"Sure, I can help you with that," Matt said quickly, but realized that he had to clue about the pricing of the gym. "How about we start with a tour of the place?" Matt offered as he made his way out from behind the desk.

"This is just the perfect size gym. I didn't want anything too big or crowded, I mean no offense, there aren't very many people in here."

"None taken, we tend to have a steady stream of regulars coming in. We have pretty much everything the larger commercial gyms have as you can see," Matt fumbled.

"You said 'we.' Are you the owner of the place?"

"Me? No, I'm not the owner. I'm just helping out. In fact, you just missed meeting the owner, she stepped out," Matt said. Matt thought this girl had spent some time in the gym, she was in incredible shape. "I'm sorry, I didn't catch your name," Matt said as they strolled back to the front desk.

"You didn't catch it because you didn't ask me. My name is Amber," she replied.

"You're right, I didn't ask. My apologies. Amber, I'm Matt, pleased to meet you," Matt said, offering his hand to shake.

As they completed introductions, Matt noticed Liz had appeared from where she had been working in the back office. The two women gave each other the once over. Amber's auburn hair, hazel eyes, and fair skin contrasted significantly with Liz's caramel-colored skin and bouncy curls.

"Matt, when are you trying to get out of here?" Liz asked, ignoring Amber.

"Whenever Pinky gets back. I'm watching the desk for her. Liz, this is Amber."

Amber smiled shyly and Liz nodded curtly. "Excuse me, I need to make a call," Liz said as she returned to the back office. Matt could tell Liz didn't want to talk to Amber, and he wasn't sure why.

Amber's smile faltered as she watched Liz walk away. "So, is that your—"

"Friend, we're just friends," Matt quickly assured Amber. He noted her lips turned up a bit at that.

Pinky came bouncing in from her nail appointment, Matt was relieved to see her since he was quickly running out of small talk, and surely he was going to sound like a rambling fool soon. He could see that Amber had piqued Pinky's interest. Hoping Pinky would use her considerable charm to find out more about what Amber's story was, Matt excused himself to find Liz. Finding her in the back office, Matt was curious to see what she thought of the newest member of Pinky's. "Did you see her? Wow! She's amazing," Matt gushed.

"I'll give her that, she looks amazing. A little too good to be true. I don't like the vibe I get from her. Something isn't right," Liz said.

Matt felt deflated. "What do you mean? Let's not pass judgement until Pinky can work her magic and find out her story. I bet it's as simple as she just moved here, saw the place, and wanted a gym close to home, you know, normal stuff."

"Yeah, ok. Sport, if you believe that, then I won't argue. I already called Jimmie. He'll find out how 'normal' Little Miss Redhead is," Liz said, staring at her phone.

"Really, you already called Jimmie? I don't see why, she's just a pretty girl who came into the gym. I'm not as suspicious of everyone as you guys are. Things like this actually happen you know," Matt huffed.

"Yes, sure they do, Sport. But when I get that feeling like something is off, it usually is, and I go with it. That intuition has kept me safe too many times to remember at this point. You can be insulted all you want, but something isn't kosher with her."

"And you think Jimmie will agree? I can't wait for your little report to come back with nothing on it."

"I'll keep you posted."

Matt rolled his eyes and stomped toward the door.

"And Matt? I wouldn't hold my breath if I were you," Liz said.

From the back-office window, Matt could see Pinky motioning to Matt for him to be part of her conversation with Amber. Matt let the door slam as he left Liz and went back out to the front desk.

"There he is," Pinky cooed as Matt approached. She grabbed Matt tightly around the waist when he got close. "Matt here was such a sweetie to offer to help while I ran and got my nail fixed. You must know how that is, just can't go on another minute looking at something like that!" Pinky said.

Amber laughed. "Matt was helpful. He gave me a tour of your gym. I really like it."

"Glad to hear that. We can talk more about what brought you in today. I just like to hear how people end up here if my advertising is paying off." Pinky winked.

"I didn't know you advertised anywhere, Pinky," Matt commented.

"Oh, sure we do, at a couple of local places. Amber honey, where did you say you heard of my gym?" Pinky asked.

"I can't say your advertising dollars were well spent with me. I'm new in town and I just moved to a cute little apartment nearby. The first time I saw it, I knew I would have to come by and check it out because of the name. Pink is my favorite color," Amber replied.

"Oh, pink is my favorite too, if you couldn't tell," Pinky

laughed. "New in town? How do you like it so far, here for work?"

"Yes, I own a consulting business. We like it so far, thank you for asking," Amber said.

"We?" Matt asked.

"Silly me, yes, we. My cat, Mr. Big, and me," Amber explained.

Pinky processed her membership information, welcoming her to her 'family.'

"Pinky refers to her customers as her family," Matt said to Amber, with a hopeful look in his eye.

"It was a pleasure to meet all of you. I need to get back to work now," Amber said, turning to leave, "but, you'll be seeing me lots! I can't sit in the apartment all day, it drives me nuts." Matt couldn't stop smiling as she walked away, only for his dream-like trance to break with Liz's disapproving tone.

"What in the fuck was that?" Liz said, watching Amber walk out the door.

"I have no idea; did you call Jimmie? I have her info to share with him if you need it," Pinky said, not taking her eyes off Amber until her car left the parking lot.

"What's so wrong with her? You two are way too suspicious," Matt argued. "And what was that crap about asking what advertising she saw? You don't advertise, why would you ask her that?"

"I wanted to see if she would try and make something up, or what story she would come up with. She seemed pretty vanilla if you ask me," Pinky said.

"Pinky has every right to feel unsettled with the story Amber told. We could chalk it up to being in the business too long and always looking for something to be off kilter with someone or looking for their shadows, but this chick had way too many red flags to let it go. You just see her and think she is

239

too cute to be a threat, and that is dangerous, my friend," Liz said.

"I bet when Jimmie runs the background check out on Amber, you two will have to admit you were wrong," Matt replied.

"Really? I guess we'll see about that. Pinky, we'll keep you in the loop, you do the same," Liz said.

"Of course. I'm glad you were here too, Liz. I love solving puzzles," Pinky said, then she turned toward Matt. "Matt, I've been meaning to ask how you're doing after the parking lot situation. First time can be rough," Pinky said softly.

"Oh yeah, that was intense. The thing is, I never knew I had reflexes like that. I guess I have never been in a murder for hire plot before either. All I knew was that I wasn't going to get in the van with those assholes, and I was sure as shit not going to let Franco and David H. be hurt or killed."

"It was impressive what you did. You didn't hesitate, and took care of business like an old pro. Maybe you aren't as far away from being a full time Henchman as you think," Pinky said.

As for the feeling of any type of remorse or the guilt about shooting dead the three Henchmen in the parking lot, there just wasn't any. Matt surprised himself at the lack of empathy he felt towards the three men. He went with the kill-or-be-killed philosophy, and that seemed to work. He wondered if he would ever feel more than that. At some point, he wanted to ask the other guys what their thoughts were after they took someone's life. If Matt learned one thing, it was that long-term survival as a Henchman required quick actions and even quicker processing. Being a Henchman came with being able to let go of all emotional attachments to the errands they ran. Though Matt had to question, was it letting go, or stuffing down emotions?

CHAPTER 24
I GOT MY EYES ON YOU

As PART of his security protocol, Matt was instructed not to engage in conversations with Amber beyond pleasantries. Jimmie instructed that for a couple of days, he shouldn't talk about anything more than the weather, or what kind of coffee she drank. He was curious to know more about her but knew he couldn't press the subject until Jimmie said it was all clear. Matt tried not to think too much into it, but he still couldn't get Amber out of his mind. It felt childish, he hadn't had a crush like this since high school. As Matt anxiously waited for Jimmie to come back with Amber's background check, he was glad to see his name more frequently on the errand board, which was a welcome distraction.

Despite the frequency of Matt's name on the errand board, he was still relegated to the backseat when traveling. Where one sat in the car was determined by one's status; to move seats took time. To be promoted into the front seat was huge. With the exception of sometimes sitting in the front seat when he went with Liz, and it was just her and him, he was always in the third or fourth spot. Matt made his next big goal to be invited into the front seat. He wanted to gain more status with the Team; he was getting impatient with waiting for the next significant event to happen that would surely catapult him into the front seat status.

"Look at that shit, College Boy is trying to be a lawyer now," said Snoop as he read Matt's name on the errand board next to Garrett's for a 7:45 a.m. ride along.

"Dude, come on, I didn't ask to go with him. Didn't all of you have to go with him at some point?" Matt asked.

"Nope. I guess we weren't smart enough. Hope you don't fuck this up too, College Boy," the Snoop said, walking away.

"I will let you know!" Matt shouted, mumbling *what an asshole* under his breath. He was wondering what type of errand Garrett would be charged with. All the other Henchmen Matt was paired with typically ended the errand in some destruction of property, slapping someone around, lots of yelling of insults and threats, things one would come to expect from a Henchman. From the few interactions Matt had with Garrett, he found it hard to picture him behaving in such an un-classy manner; he presented as much too well-bred to act with such violence devoid of wit.

7:45 on the dot, Matt was suited up and met Garrett at the bottom of the stairs.

"Hey Mattster," Garrett greeted him, starting to head toward the door before Matt could reply. "I wasn't sure if you were free today, but I thought this would be a great opportunity for you to tag along with me today. I have a couple of quick meetings that I wanted you to attend with me." Matt followed Garrett to the parking space at the rear of the house. "Bingo! I grabbed the right set of keys, I love the 450SL, such a sweet ride."

"I love this car too, probably my favorite," Matt said, climbing into the passenger seat. "Thanks for the invite, but what are we doing, where are we going?"

"Probably should give a little heads up. I meet with the

DMF legal Team each quarter. I provide them with a report on the amount of money DMF has paid to people either to keep them 'intact,' medical bill payments, or end of contract payments," Garrett said.

"Keeping people intact? I have heard some of the other Henchmen use that term, what does that mean exactly?"

"It's sort of a code word used for when we need to keep people either silent or for them to keep their stories the same over time, you know, like if they are being investigated. Maybe you should write this shit down."

"I've been making notes on my phone, I just hate to always be asking what something means. I have learned that making an assumption about certain things is the wrong thing to do," Matt said.

Matt noticed Garrett did not have a suit coat on and was not carrying any sort of bag, briefcase, or attaché. Matt felt naked having no other trained Henchman with them, because they had not cleared him to carry a weapon yet, even after what happened in the parking lot the other day. Jimmie was making him wait longer to graduate to the next level on the Team. He wasn't sure the reason behind that, but he assumed it was to keep the training going until he had more OTJT complete. He wondered what would happen if they were ambushed like the day in Pinky's parking lot. Who would be there to defend them?

"Garrett, this is cool and all to go with you, but you know what happened in the parking lot at Pinky's, right? How can we just go with no protection or weapons? I'm still on that guy's shitlist. Is this cool to go alone?" Matt asked.

Garrett shook his head. "Dude, first, do you think I'm a total asshole? We aren't alone, you really need to up level your observation skills. Have you noticed the car behind us?"

Matt twirled his head around to see the familiar DMF

black suburban behind them, with Franco and David H. in the front. As soon as David H. saw Matt's head turn, he flipped Matt off, motioning him to turn the fuck around.

"Jesus, ok, I didn't even notice them. That's kind of embarrassing," Matt mumbled.

"You think? It's one thing to ask questions, but it's another to ask before surveying the situation at hand. Did you think to look at my pant leg, the ankle area to be precise?" Garrett pressed.

"No, why would I do that?" Matt asked just as Garrett pulled up his pant leg to reveal a loaded ankle holster. Matt sighed. It was clear he wouldn't be promoted to the front seat anytime soon with his poor observation skills. So far, Liz was the only one to give him front seat access.

Garrett did not speak the rest of the way until he parked the black 450SL into a space nearest the large glass doors of an all-glass, ten-story, ultra-modern office building. "We're here. Now, I don't want to sound like all the other guys you went on errands with, but don't fuck this up," Garrett said, walking towards the beautiful glass entry.

Matt's vision went red at the words, 'don't fuck this up.' "God, I'm so sick of hearing that. I can't wait for the day that shit stops," Matt said. "Do I need to know anything about what's going on? What's happening here?"

Garrett stopped and turned to face Matt, "Just sit back and listen, that's all you have to do here," Garrett replied, briefly glancing up at Matt.

As soon as they checked in with the security desk, they were whisked to an office boardroom. The impressive room included a twenty-seat conference room table with elegant black leather chairs. Matt and Garrett were the first to arrive. Matt flashed back to his first errand and wondered whether clearing off this conference table to make a point was an appropriate use of force. Thinking it better to wait and see who else attended this meeting, Matt took the lead from Garrett and did not assume that traditional Henchman tactics were suitable here. Garrett was busy logging in to the laptop that was open sitting on the conference table.

"Guess I don't need to throw anything around in here, this is first class," Matt observed.

Garrett simply shook his head, side to side with a stern look, "Do not touch anyone or anything."

As the room filled with who Matt assumed to be other attorneys, he did just as Garrett had instructed: stay quiet and observe. Garrett was welcomed by each of the attorneys with a handshake and small talk.

"Before we get started, I wanted to make an introduction. For those of you who don't already know who this is to my left, this is him. The guy from the night at The Basement, Matt Clemmons," Garrett said.

There was shuffling in seats, and all eyes on Matt. *Jesus, now what? Do I say anything?* Thinking this may be a tough crowd, he decided to go with a simple nod of the head.

"Now that is taken care of, let's get to the reason we are all here, budgeting report, potential legal issues, and any other problem areas that need attention," Garrett said.

As Garrett spoke, flipping through slides and sharing the last quarter's spend on what DMF has paid out, Matt wanted to scream, "Are you serious? This is an insane amount of money, outrageous at best." The data Garrett shared revealed that over six figures were paid out quarterly for things Matt found to be unnecessary from a business standpoint.

"I know this line item may seem high, but we know the value of paying the cost for people's stories to remain the same. This is not something I feel comfortable with a cut back," Garrett said.

There was nothing but nods in the affirmative with the figures Garrett shared with the group. It took all Matt's Henchman training to not want to stand up and tell them what a gigantic waste of money this all was. Why didn't they just get a group insurance policy? The amount of money DMF could save by investing in insurance policies for both medical and life would be a game changer. Matt decided that this meeting was not the time or the place to propose such a radical change. Instead, he would include this topic in conversation another time, with a different audience.

———

The next day, Matt, Franco, and David H. were paired to run an errand. Matt enjoyed working with them more than any other. Matt felt a true budding friendship with both Franco and David H. The errand they were scheduled for that day wasn't anything noteworthy, just a visit with a potential start-up that needed to be reminded to stay in their lane. Those types of visits were routine, and typically never varied in script.

Matt decided that to get a bump in status, today was the day he was going to take the lead. He was going to show off his skills and give Franco and David H. another legendary story to take back to the House.

Matt gave no warning to his partners, he wanted to show that he could lead this conversation and that he could earn his spot in the front seat. Matt walked in like he was an old pro and ready to roll, pushing open the door into the dark, small office and shouted, "Hey motherfucker, what are you doing here? Wasting time is what it looks like! Such bullshit going on here." His actions stunned Franco and David H., leaving them with an unscripted visit, trying to put the pieces back together.

"What are you talking about? I have things under control,

back off man," shouted the little man sitting at the desk. He looked nervous and he wasn't making eye contact with anyone.

"I really don't think you do," Matt said, using his trademark move of violently clearing off the top of his desk with one sweep of his arm. The little man got to his knees to clean up the mess.

Franco stepped forward, placing a heavy hand on Matt's shoulder. Franco gave Matt a small shake of the head. Matt backed up, surprised by Franco's disapproval.

"I don't need this kind of harassment from jerks like you. I have been debating whether I would stay with you guys. Believe me, I've had offers that are just as appealing as yours, that don't include this shit," the little man said.

"You know what would happen if you went to another organization," Franco threatened.

The small man rose to his feet, fists clenched. "You don't own me, big guy!" he yelled. Suddenly, he locked eyes with Matt. The way the little man was eyeing him, it was like he recognized him, but Matt was certain he had never met this man before. Before anyone could react, the whiney little man drew a gun from his desk drawer. Matt wished he had a gun to draw, but before he knew it, shots were fired, and Franco went down.

Matt, standing in shock, not able to move, wasn't sure what his next big-time move would be, rush to Franco, or subdue the shooter? The small man had been thrown on his backside as he pulled the trigger. Obviously, he had never shot a gun before. As David H. pounced on him and was wrestling the gun away from the little man, a Henchman who none of them had noticed jumped him from behind. David H. was taken by surprise by the attacker and lost his grip on the little man. The small man was able to run out the back door. In a matter of seconds, David H. got his bearings, broke out of

247

the headlock, and began to beat the random Henchman senseless.

David H. looked up from the unconscious Henchman and turned to Matt with a look of utter disbelief as he ran to Franco, "What in the fuck was that?"

"I don't know what happened. I wasn't expecting that," Matt said, also rushing to the fallen Franco. The bullet had hit Franco in the shoulder and the wound was bleeding heavily.

"I'm glad that the asshole had such poor aim, little fucker," Franco gasped.

"I'm so sorry, I don't know what happened," Matt stammered.

"Hey College Boy, can you at least do something right and call ahead to let them know we have a situation and need the medical room ready?" David H. asked while helping Franco to his feet.

"Can you make it out to the car like this, or do I need to carry you?" David H. asked Franco.

"I got this, let's just go. Who was that little shit, anyway?" Franco quizzed Matt and David H.

"I don't know exactly, but I think we both have an idea. Am I right?" David H. asked, raising his eyebrow.

Matt went out first, making sure there were no other threats awaiting them outside. With Franco's gun drawn, Matt was the recon part of what was left of the Team. David H. walked, almost dragged, Franco swiftly to the car with Franco's uninjured arm over his shoulder.

"What the fuck? What were you trying to do back there? Seriously, what the fuck?" yelled David H.

"I'm so sorry. I don't know, I just wanted to . . . I don't know what I wanted to do. Jesus, I'm sorry," Matt stuttered.

David H. wouldn't look at him as he turned the key in the

ignition. "Just shut the fuck up, don't fucking talk to me. I don't want to hear another excuse."

Matt was sitting in the backseat with Franco, keeping pressure on his wound. At this point, Franco was having trouble keeping his eyes open, much less his mouth, otherwise Matt was sure Franco would yell at him too. Matt was sick to his stomach. This latest mistake made him want to leave the House, forget all this, and leave it behind. He had fuck ups before, but they were not anything to get his friends injured. What was he thinking?

David H. drove quickly with intention to get Franco back to the house and the medical suite. "You made the call right? Tell me you didn't screw that up too," David H. huffed.

"Yes, yes, I made the call. The room is being prepped right now, they said it will be ready when we arrive," Matt said with a glazed-over look in his eye. Matt knew Franco would be well taken care of once he was in the medical suite at the House. Matt wasn't all too familiar with gunshot wounds but knowing that the bullet went straight through was a good sign. He hoped it hit nothing that would make Franco's recovery difficult.

"Who was that little asshole who pulled the trigger? Who the fuck was that?" David H. was yelling at no one in particular. Franco grunted in pain as David H. screeched the car to a halt.

Matt said to Franco, "Dude, I'm so sorry, I don't know what I was thinking. We're here back at the House, you're going to be taken care of. You're going to be ok."

David H. had opened the back door. "Shut the fuck up, College Boy. I've heard enough from you, fuck off. I got this," he grunted as he lifted Franco's body over his shoulder. "Go cry to the boss's daughter," he fumed as he carried Franco into the House.

Matt followed David H. as he rushed Franco into the med

suite. David H. quickly closed the door behind him, telling Matt he was not welcome. Matt sat on the same couch as he did all those months ago and felt more out of place and awkward than he had that first night. He didn't know it was possible to feel this bad. He knew Franco had a family, and his careless behavior put Franco and David H.'s lives in jeopardy. He didn't even see that little shit of a man reaching for the gun; he was too busy trying to show off for Franco and David H. He wasn't acting *that* much off script; the only thing was he was the one being mouthy and domineering. The most unusual thing was that Matt was delivering the verbal smackdown, and not Franco or David H. Why would that little shit pull a gun? Thank God he had terrible aim. Franco had become a friend, and Matt had let him down along with the rest of the Team. He was back to ground zero with the guys; he was sure of it.

Matt got up from the couch and paced around in small circles.

After a few minutes, Liz and Garrett came flying into the room. Liz almost ran right into Matt. He grabbed her before she tripped in front of him. She looked relieved to see him.

"Matt? What happened?" Liz shouted.

"You don't want to know," Matt said in a shallow tone.

"Yes, I do! What went down? Who did this?" Liz demanded.

"Was the CUC called?" Garrett asked.

"I don't—"

"Where are Franco and David H.? Are they ok?" Liz interrupted Matt.

David H. opened the door from the medical suite.

Liz again asked, "Who did this?"

"Some little shit stain from the newest start-up, that's who did this. That little fucker is on my shit list now," David H. grumbled.

Matt was expecting David H. to pounce on him and get an ass kicking of a lifetime. Instead, David H.'s anger seemed to be directed at the shooter. Matt breathed a sigh of relief, at least he didn't get his ass kicked in front of Liz, but he knew he still wasn't off the hook.

"Franco is going to be fine. It was an in and out, no damage to anything important."

"Why did he shoot?" Garrett asked.

David H. rolled his eyes. "Matt walked in like Billy bad ass. Unprovoked, he threw things around, pushing, shoving, wreaking havoc, throwing the five rules of being a Henchman right out the window," he said. Liz and Garrett exchanged a look. "This was only visit number two," David H. added. Liz groaned. Matt turned his head down.

Flipping the script was never a good idea, especially when there was no discussion of the possibility of it. These things worked because the players all knew their roles, certainly with visits like this. This particular visit went south real quick. Matt's behavior took Franco and David H. by surprise, as they weren't prepared for it. A typical visit, especially early on in the potential start up and DMF's relationship, was a more gradual indoctrination into visits from Henchmen. This visit was only the second time, which called for more tact and manners.

David H. sighed and turned to Matt. "He's going to be fine, dude, stop looking like a kicked puppy. You fucked up by changing the script on us, but what you did didn't cause this. I think the dumb little fucker was trying to hit you anyway."

"Why would you say that? Trying to hit Matt?" Liz questioned.

"Me? How do you figure?" Matt asked.

"Because he was staring at you. Plus, that asshole had obviously never fired a gun before, didn't you notice? He landed on his ass after he fired the weapon. He had no idea

251

what he was doing. There's no other reason for him to take out a piece, except because it was you he wanted. He was trying to be sly and catch us off guard by not having the Henchman do it."

Matt nodded. "Right, we would have expected him to do it. I didn't even notice the random Henchman there. I think he was asleep when we arrived. He was totally motionless."

"Exactly, that's why I think they meant it for you. The dumbass was asleep, must have been. That may be the guy we have been looking for all this time. That has to be him," David H. said.

"That was the great and powerful OT, that little man? You really think so? Not what I had pictured. Christ, I wish I knew, I would have reached across the desk and dragged him out myself," Matt shouted.

"David H., you really think that was him? It makes sense, right? Think about it, if he is a newer start up, he would have an inside access to some of the DMF intel, right? He would know how to get into the server and play those non-stop games with the CM Team," Liz said.

"The good news is that we know who he is now. We can give this information to Harry. They can get to work and do what they do, find the IP addresses, and whatever else they do," Garrett said.

"Good news? Fuck that. Go tell Franco your good news, you asshole," David H. said. He walked off to the kitchen, mumbling he needed a drink.

"He will cool off, give him a minute," Liz said. "But I have to agree with Garrett, this is good news. We are closer to getting that piece of shit off our backs."

Matt felt some relief when he heard Franco would be ok, but still felt awful, like it was all his fault. Where did he get off thinking he would take charge and not follow the rules that had been spelled out to him many times. He knew better but wanted to push things along faster than they should have been.

Matt sighed, sitting back down on the familiar couch. He sat back, putting his hands up in the 'I give up' gesture.

"Get over yourself, Sport. This isn't all on you. Shit like this happens on the job. It sucks, but this is what we do," Liz said. "Garrett, let's go, we need to debrief."

Garrett paused in front of Matt. "She's right, this is the type of stuff we are prepared for. Shit happens, that is my mantra around here," Garrett said before walking up the stairs with Liz.

Matt nodded. He was left alone with his own guilty thoughts again. Matt should not have gone in with his leader's agenda, big mistake.

———

After a few hours, Matt was allowed to go in and see Franco. He timidly walked into the medical suite. He wasn't sure what to expect. Franco looked good—he was alert, though a little out of it from the pain meds.

"I know you must think this is all on you, bro. It really isn't. We can talk more later, when I'm not so fucked up on these pain meds," Franco mumbled.

"Are you sure, dude? I feel like I owe you an apology for just going in there and acting like an ass," Matt said.

"Before I fall asleep, you gotta listen to me, not your fault," were Franco's last words before he fell into a long pain med induced slumber.

The doctor escorted Matt from the medical suite, closing the door behind him. Matt looked up and noticed Jimmie standing in the hallway. Matt knew Jimmie well enough to read his facial expressions. This time, Jimmie was emanating a look of displeasure with the turn of events, but not angry or mad. Liz wasn't around any longer, no buffer for Jimmie's gaze on Matt.

"Franco's in there. He just fell asleep, but he's going to be fine," Matt said, trying to look hopeful.

Jimmie stood in silence, staring directly at Matt. His stare made him want to crawl out of his own skin. It was more than the look Matt's mom used to give him when she was disappointed in him, it was more of an 'I'm disappointed in your soul being on this planet look.' It literally made Matt cringe.

To break the silence, Matt said, "I guess you can still go in there, you know they say even though people are asleep, they still know you are there, right?"

"Yes, I've heard that. Can you tell me where to find David H.?" Jimmie asked in a bitter tone.

"A while ago he said he was going to grab a drink and then shower and relax, he's probably in his room," Matt offered.

Jimmie acknowledged Matt's response with a slight nod and turned to leave. He only took a few steps before he turned back in Matt's direction, and said, "I'm glad you are unharmed. Despite this latest event, you are a valued member of the Team."

His kindness almost made Matt feel worse.

CHAPTER 25
TRIAL BY FIRE

MATT LAID low for the next few days. His name didn't appear on the job board, he also didn't feel comfortable asking David H. for a ride to go to Pinky's. It was as if time slid backward to when he was just getting started. Liz had been by to cheer him up, with not much success. She had gotten a full-blown report from David H. and Franco. They both said that it wasn't really Matt acting like an ass that caused the incident, it was more likely that the little jerk had an itchy trigger for Matt, which was not a surprise once it was confirmed the little jerk was the infamous OT. It made Garrett's report to the DMF legal team easier to write since the identity of the OT was now revealed. The CM Team had been working non-stop to not only find out more about him, but to see how they let their security lapse and let him become as close as they did, to being a potential subsidiary of DMF.

Franco was up and around on his own in a couple days, even joking about how bad of a shot the little shit was. Around the house, there had been many tales told of the incident, none of them being accurate. Doing damage control to Matt's tarnished reputation was put on the back burner for the moment. Containing the gossip would be a battle to fight another day.

Matt had been sneaking around the House, trying to avoid seeing anyone. He couldn't handle the shame he felt, he didn't want the other guys to make him feel worse about what he'd done to Franco. Matt went down to the kitchen at the tail end of the breakfast time, hoping to grab food while avoiding the guys. Unfortunately, the kitchen was still quite full. Luckily, Matt found a seat at the CM table. The CM guys gave him a small nod of acknowledgement before continuing their discussion about the latest COD release.

There was a simultaneous beep and vibrate as everyone's phone received a message in the Team group text. Matt's stomach dropped. The message was from Jimmie. There was to be a mandatory meeting that afternoon in the GCR, aka the Global Conference Room, to clear up the rumors. It was not an option not to show up.

Matt was literally sick to his stomach and terrified about what was going to happen to him at the meeting. He had been a bundle of nerves the last few days, despite no one being shitty to his face. Since being in the house, Matt had cultivated the art form of beating himself up, shaking his self-confidence to a level that he had never taken himself to.

"Great, now College Boy is making us waste time in meetings now," Snoop whined loudly.

"When's the last time we had to go to the GCR? Oh, that's right, it's been months! I can bet this is about College Boy throwing this House on its ass since he's been here," David H. said.

"Jesus, they are more pissed about having to sit in a meeting than what actually happened," Matt muttered to Harry.

"These aren't sitting-in-a-meeting types of guys, in case you didn't notice. Getting shot is more normal of them," Harry laughed.

He couldn't eat breakfast. Instead, he went to his room, possibly for the last time. Matt wondered if he should just pack his bag now.

As if she could read his mind, Liz texted, promising to walk into the meeting with him and to sit with him. Their friendship had grown to where Matt didn't even have to ask, she offered. With everything going on, Matt was incredibly grateful for Liz, for he would be lost without her.

Matt had no idea where the GCR was, he had never heard of it. Liz came to Matt's door to walk over to the meeting, Matt walking with trepidation, Liz with confidence.

"Are you ready to go, Sport? You better pull up your big boy pants and walk in with your head held high. These guys have a sixth sense for people's weaknesses. Let's get going, it is a bit of a walk to the GCR. Lord knows we don't want to walk in late and make a spectacle of ourselves," she said.

"Shit, yeah that is all I need, interrupting the meeting after it starts would not be cool. I know they have that sixth sense, it leads me to be more anxious. I know they're like sharks that just got a whiff of blood in the water. Do you think it's going to be more of a verbal ass kicking, or more of a public lynching situation?" Matt asked.

"The 'poor little me' routine is getting old, Sport. How about you get over your pity party and move on. You're being a little self-absorbed, this isn't the first Team meeting we have ever had, it's not all revolving around you," Liz snapped.

"Wow, ok. Let me know how you really feel," Matt replied with an eye roll. Then he sighed. "I'll shake it off, or try to, anyway. This is unfamiliar territory for me, on more than one level. I'm not sure how this sounds to you, but until now, there hasn't really been anything I wasn't good at. I was always at the top of whatever I did. That was my comfort zone. Fucking up, not knowing the rules, just wasn't something I ever had to deal with."

Liz nodded, her face softening a bit. "That's probably the most honest thing I have ever heard you say," she said.

Despite seeing several other Henchmen on the walk over, none of them gave Matt the head nod that he had been used to receiving. They were not looking in his direction, he felt invisible. This time it was worse than when he first arrived. He could expect that since he was new, but now that he had burrowed his way into the social structure of the Team, the ignoring hurt more than he expected it to.

As all the Henchmen on the Team arrived, the vibe was tense, even more so when Fowler showed up. Matt wasn't sure how he and Jimmie were going to play this, or if he would walk out of the room with all his teeth, and limbs. The room was dead silent as Fowler approached the front of the room. Matt and Liz had picked seats that were in the middle of the room, choosing the two seats at the end of the aisle. Matt wanted an easy escape route to be able to run out at any moment. He had his head down, but Liz nudged him to sit with some dignity.

"Sit up straight, don't act like a little boy who did something wrong. For the last time, get over yourself," Liz said through tight lips.

Despite wanting to vomit and run out of the room, Matt shifted in his seat, and sat up straighter, next to his only friend in the world right now. Matt was surprised to see Randy, the guy who's desk he cleared during his first errand with Aaron, setting the room up to be Zoom friendly. There were always some Team members that could not be physically present at the meetings. These few Henchmen would attend virtually, with no mention of where they actually were in the world.

Once the connections were established and they locked in

the virtual attendees, Fowler made his way to the front of the large GCR and began the meeting with a speech about how important each and every one of them were to the organization.

"I want to welcome you all here today. I know it is rare that we are all in the same place at the same time. Thanks to Randy for getting all the systems set up. This virtual stuff is incredible. I wanted to make sure you all know that you are integral to the success of DMF. I know that many of you have heard this in the past, but always remember that each of you are the gears that make this great Team and organization run," Fowler began.

Heading into this meeting, Matt was expecting there to be some Matt-bashing, especially from Fowler. He had not been able to get a clear read on just how pissed he was, or if he was going to let Matt's latest fuck up go unpunished. Even Fowler's introduction had not revealed any emotion. There was some shuffling around and mumbling amongst the Henchmen. Jimmie, who was sitting in the front row, stood up, walked to the far side of the row, and faced the crowd. Matt had seen that look enough to know what it meant, as did the rest of the Team, and they became silent for the rest of the talk Fowler gave.

Matt secretly hoped that Fowler would be pissed and not let his grave error go. His assumption was that in the long run, it would go over better with the Team if he was not babied but held accountable. Matt figured that would be the only way for his redemption.

"Now, you all know why we're here, and that is to address a situation that happened three days ago involving our newest Henchman," Fowler said, making eye contact with Matt. His green eyes bore into Matt's like laser beams. Everyone in the crowd seemed to shift forward in their seats with renewed attention. It took every muscle in Matt's body to keep sitting upright and not to slouch with the weight of the eyes on him.

"Matt failed at his job. He failed as a reliable member of the

Team. Having confidence in who has your back is vital to the inner workings of being on the Team. We have our five rules for a reason, and sometimes, tragically, we all receive a reminder of their importance." Fowler paced across the room. "Let us all remember that this wasn't the first time any of the Team has fucked up, let's be honest. Matt's lapse in judgement was significant and could have resulted in a much worse situation. A mistake is a mistake, but this was a fairly basic one. I don't think Matt's mistake was because of a lack of training this time, but perhaps a lack of leadership. He knew the rules full-well, but he disregarded them."

Matt could sense what was coming next. He had messed up so many times; he knew he was pretty much at the end of the line. Unless Matt could pull a rabbit out of the proverbial magic hat, then he would more than likely end up out on the street, a very dangerous street.

"Matt, come up here. I know I'm looking forward to what you have to say, please enlighten us," Fowler said, motioning for Matt to come to the front of the room. Matt felt like sinking into the floor. Liz punched his arm, snapping Matt into action. She flashed him a look of 'you got this,' but with a slight eyebrow raise. He clenched his fists as he stood to join Fowler in front of his fellow Henchmen, hoping the guys couldn't see his hands shaking.

He walked up to the front of the room slowly to have those few extra precious seconds to gather his thoughts. He tucked his hands in his pockets when he got to his spot in the front of the room. As Matt reached Fowler, he tightly gripped Matt's shoulder, as if to hold him in place. "The floor is yours, Matt."

All the eyes were on him. Matt did not know that he would be asked to speak in front of everyone, obviously he had nothing prepared to say. He knew he had to use words that did not make him sound like a victim or whiney.

Jimmie was now sitting in the back of the room with a curious look on his face. Fowler took the seat Matt had been sitting in next to Liz. Matt wanted to try and make eye contact with everyone in the room. Professor Crane, Matt's old public speaking professor from college, would be proud of him. Matt was thankful that he had gotten an A in that class. Who knew those skills would come in handy at this juncture of his life? Having to give a potentially career-saving, or lifesaving, speech with zero prep was definitely more pressure than giving a prepared speech to his entire class. The room was silent as Matt took one look around the room and then fixed his eyes on Franco. He was going to make this time as impactful as he could muster.

"Thank you, Mr. Fowler, for the opportunity to speak. I'm not going to try to explain things away like I used to," Matt joked. No one laughed. "In all seriousness, there is nothing to explain away here. The only thing I can offer is the sincerest apology, not only to Franco, but to the whole Team. As most of you know, I have been trying to learn and fit in and I stupidly thought I was ready to take the lead without consulting my Team. My insubordination was inexcusable. I just respect you guys a lot, and I want to fit in."

He could hear mumblings in the room and wanted to address them. He wanted nothing left unsaid. It was time to clear the air once and for all. The mumbling were things like, "it's about time he gets held accountable," "he's dangerous," "he's careless," among others.

"Ricky, I see you may have something to say. Would you be willing to share with the rest of the Team?" Matt asked. Asking the guys mumbling to say what they wanted to say out loud was what his professors did when the kids in class got a little ruffled by something they said.

261

The room continued to hum with whispers and questioning looks.

Ricky, glancing briefly in Jimmie's direction, stood up before he spoke. "None of the previous Team meetings have been interactive, no one has ever asked for our opinions or feedback. Having us speak is unprecedented. I may as well not let this chance go to waste. Here it goes, I said that I never thought you would make it here. I thought you were a mistake. But I'll admit that it takes some balls to stand up here and do what you are doing. And, I have seen some progress."

More whispers and rustling came from the room as Matt responded to Ricky's comment. "I appreciate you letting me know. And thank you for noticing some changes I've made so far."

"I agree with what Ricky said. I don't want to speak for everyone, but I think most of us feel the same way," Skippy said from his seat.

"Fuck that. Better you don't speak for me. I think the guy's an asshole. I don't like him, and I don't want him here. He's dangerous to everyone here. Luck can only get you so far in this job," William grunted.

The room erupted in conversation, with many of the Henchmen clearly at odds. Matt didn't realize how polarized he had made the group. He knew he needed to reunite them. He tried to talk, but his voice couldn't compete with the roar of everyone else's.

Liz stood up. "Everyone shut the hell up and let Matt speak," she shouted. Every voice was immediately silenced.

"You know, William actually has a point," Matt said, making proper eye contact with William to show he wasn't being defensive. William's question provided an opening for Matt to begin a discussion he'd been wanting to have. "Like Mr. Fowler said, I'm not the only one who has made a mistake, maybe we need to have more formal training for the job." This comment made everyone shift in their seats. Jimmie and Fowler not only shifted but sat forward to hear more.

Matt continued, "Listen, we all know that one of the biggest assets, or liabilities, I bring is the fact that I'm an outsider. Believe it or not, it can have an advantage. When you're right in the middle of something, it's hard to see from a unique perspective."

The whispers in the room had turned to a lot of "fuck off's," and "no fucking way dude."

"I know my job better than you ever could, College Boy," William sneered.

"Look, I know that bringing up my education is a sore spot with you guys. But let me put my College Boy hat on here for a minute, hear me out on this," Matt responded and was met with groans and eye rolls. Even Liz looked at him with a 'proceed with caution' look.

"Here is what I think is partly going on here, with me becoming part of the Team. Despite what you guys think of jocks like me, we tend to have a particular skill set. Just like you guys have on the Team here. Let me use football as an analogy. When I played football, I was a defensive end. I knew how to play that position well, quarterback, not so much. Same with you guys. For example, I know Ricky loves working with firearms, William loves making things go boom and loves fire. You all have things you enjoy doing and are better at than others. When you're a Team, individuals just aren't expected to be the expert in everything," Matt explained to the crowd.

This led to more rumbling in the room, which no one tried to quiet. Matt got positive vibes from the energy circulating in the room. He thought some discussion about what he said was good. He didn't hear any "fuck off's" which made him relieved.

He looked over at Liz to gauge her reaction. She was in deep conversation with Fowler.

Matt let the discussions go on for a moment without interruption. He wasn't exactly sure how far to take this, but he was going to push the agenda. "If you all would have me, and if Mr. Fowler and Jimmie want to further discuss a more formal structured onboarding and training process, I would be happy to put something together, for the good of the Team, hoping to reduce mistakes across the board.

"I would of course work in close collaboration with the Team to include what you feel needs to be included," Matt added. "I want you guys to know that I value your insights and expertise. I guess the last thing I wanted to say while I'm up here is that I appreciate your patience with me."

As Matt concluded, he noticed Franco was standing and trying to make his way to the front of the room. Matt stayed up front and welcomed Franco to speak. Once in the front of the room, Franco turned to face his Team.

"Can I say a couple of things before we all head out?" Franco asked the rustling crowd. The room became quiet as he stood in front of his team. Franco was a natural leader amongst the Henchmen, which commanded a certain level of unspoken respect. "Listen up everyone. We all know I'm the one who was most affected by College Boy's latest fuck up, and I have the biggest reason to be pissed at him," Franco said, gesturing to his arm in a sling. Matt prepared himself to be punched with Franco's good hand, but Franco actually reached out to shake Matt's hand.

That was when Matt knew he had made it.

"College Boy here is actually doing pretty fucking good considering that it could have been a lot worse if it hadn't been for David H.'s quick thinking," Franco said. David H. looked extremely proud to have been acknowledged in front of the whole Team. Matt noted these guys were not used to hearing anything positive about them. Maybe they should do more of it? Selecting a Henchman of the Month Maybe?

"We don't travel alone for a reason," Franco continued. "We always have backup. When mistakes happen, we have each other's backs, just like when I made a mistake and Matt had my back." Matt felt himself swell with pride. Had Franco just called him by his name?

"What Fowler said was true. Every one of us has had moments when we weren't sure what to do, or we acted purely off survival instinct. And honestly, how did that work out? Not always good, I think we can agree on that. Having that feeling of uncontrolled chaos has never sat well with me," Franco added.

Nods of agreement and "no fucking kidding comments" echoed through the Global Conference Room's walls. Franco continued, "Yes, I'm still kinda pissed at Matt, but I also acknowledge that I had a part in him not being trained well enough for him to understand the importance of the rules. The reason Matt wasn't trained was because I wasn't trained. This shit isn't really anyone's fault. You guys know that it just has always been done that way, but that doesn't mean it's the best way.

"If I were to ask any of you why something was done a certain way, and your reply was, 'because we have always done it that way,' then we have a problem. I think that's where we are at right now. There needs to be an understanding about why something is done a particular way." Franco paused. "How many of you guys ever had to train anyone?" More than half the room raised a hand. "And didn't you ever wish you had someone to ask questions to? Until now, all of us just came in and pretended we knew exactly what we were doing. But we really had no idea, it was the blind leading the blind. How many people were collateral damage because we didn't know any better? How many of you got hurt because of someone else reacting before thinking a situation through?"

One could hear a pin drop; the room was silent processing Franco's words.

In closing, Franco added, "It's easy to sit there and judge Matt's failure, but we need to be honest about where we too have failed." The room was buzzing with chatter as Franco walked back to his seat. Jimmie stood up from the back of the room and made his way to the front.

"Hang on a moment. Let me say thank you to everyone and the comments made. I think this led to an insightful and productive conversation. This is food for thought. Changes need to happen, and perhaps we have come to that place. We are all in this together," Jimmie said, dismissing the Team.

As the meeting adjourned, people went their separate ways, most having conversations with the person they were walking with. From what Matt could gather, the conversations were positive. No one looked at him with disdain as they had an hour before. Matt awkwardly stood in the room and waited until everyone left. He thought it best to not intrude on the conversations the guys were having, since they were mostly about him and what he just proposed.

Matt noticed Liz was staring intently at her father and uncle, not with a pleading look, but with a look that showed Matt she was on his side. Jimmie and Fowler left quickly, likely straight to Fowler's office to bounce ideas off of one another on what they heard and to determine the fate of Matt with DMF.

As the room emptied, Matt saw Garrett was there. He hadn't seen him during the meeting and wondered if he had been there the whole time.

Garrett came up to him as the last of the Henchmen left the Global Conference Room. "Dude, that was totally awesome what you said up there. That took some guts. That easily could have ended up as a public lynching. I have always thought there needed to be changes made, but I had no idea how to broach the subject," Garrett said.

"Thanks man, I'm glad to be walking out of here in one piece. I had no idea I was going to be called on to speak," Matt confessed.

"No shit? I thought that was all planned. You did that on the fly? Even more impressive, my friend," Garrett praised, punching Matt's shoulder lightly.

"Thanks, I guess. I'm not sure what I got myself into. I just want to help in some way. We'll see how it turns out," Matt said.

"Look, dude, this could really turn into something. Almost a 'Henchman Training Academy' of sorts," Garrett laughed. "If there's anything I can help with, all you have to do is ask," he said as he turned to leave.

"I'm sure there will be. Thank you, Garrett," Matt said. *A Henchman Training Academy? Now there's an interesting idea.*

MEANWHILE . . .

THEY THINK *they are so smart. Who's the smart guy now? The CCTV in their stupid special DMF house was set up by an idiot, probably the moron I always beat in our little coding wars, Harry. They have no clue that I know everything about them, every move they are planning, I know about. I'm always listening. All they do is speak in acronyms, CUC, M&M Team, CM Team, oh they are so cool. They even gave me an acronym, the OT. Not what I would have picked, but at least I have messed with them enough that I earned a nickname. Nothing in this world has made me as angry as watching the ridiculous meeting they just had in the GCR. They absolutely disgust me. They just ignore me, day after day, and yet again the Precious Prince of DMF was granted immunity, not thrown out of the house. What is it going to take for them to take action? I may be the right person to take him down.*

NOTE TO THE READER

Dear reader,

Thank you for taking the time to read my creation. It is my hope that others of any age take a leap of faith, and do whatever you are being called to do. Starting a new career in your mid-50s, why not?

If you are wondering about how Fowler and Jimmie met, or wanting to know more about Matt and Liz or even the OT, sign up for my monthly newsletter to receive more character backstories, and other adventures of the DMF Henchman Team. Visit LKUrbanAuthor.com to join the HTA.

It would mean a great deal if you could leave me a review on Amazon and Goodreads, and of course, spread the word.

Remember, listen to that quiet voice that is whispering to you. Follow it, see where it takes you, this is your truth, speaking to you. It is always there; we just don't hear it after a while.

Follow me @LKUrbanAuthor on Facebook, @LKUrbanAuthor on Instagram, and @LKUrban on TikTok for more content.

With love,
L.K.

ACKNOWLEDGMENTS

I would like to thank all of the beautiful souls who encouraged me to take this journey into being a true creative. I have yearned to write a book for as long as I can remember.

A special heart felt note of immense gratitude to my little brown eyed girl, Kailey. When I pitched the idea of this book to her, for her to author, she encouraged me to write. As my editor and publisher and biggest cheerleader, Kailey, you have made all the difference. You are simply amazing.

To Nick, I'm so proud of you. Life keeps coming, and you keep shining through. Your students are lucky to have you in their lives.

To Chris, my go to. My inspiration, keep reaching, your life is just starting, you make me dream big.

To Jenn, my soul sister. You are my guiding light, my warrior, my outsider. You show me how life can be lived with passion, purpose, and love.

To Rick, my travel buddy, my best keeper of secrets, your friendship means the world to me. Thank you for your love and support.

- L.K.

ABOUT THE AUTHOR

L.K. Urban is a dreamer, writer, and adventurer.

When she is not on the road traveling around the United States in her burgundy Mini Cooper (affectionately named Ron), L.K. lives in beautiful Colorado Springs, Colorado, close to her four wonderful children.

Upon becoming an empty nester and entering into the pandemic of 2020, L.K. became one of many quarantine writers. Thanks to COVID, her first series, *The Henchman Training Academy*, was born and fulfilled her lifelong dream of becoming a published author.

In addition to being a creative, L.K. also holds a license as a Marriage and Family Therapist and is a working practitioner.

You can find her at:

LKUrbanAuthor.com

Or find her on social media.

- facebook.com/LKUrbanAuthor
- instagram.com/LKUrbanAuthor
- tiktok.com/@LKUrban

CPSIA information can be obtained
at www.ICGtesting.com
Printed in the USA
LVHW091529280222
712155LV00009B/245